Also by Jim Patton

*Il Basket d'Italia: A Season in Italy with Great Food, Good
Friends and Some Very Tall Americans*

Rookie: When Michael Jordan Came to the Minor Leagues

THE SHAKE

A Novel of Crime

JIM PATTON

CARROLL & GRAF PUBLISHERS, INC.
NEW YORK

Forever Grateful to
Philip Spitzer, class act, for confirmation, pardon, and perpetuity,
Jim McIntyre, DA extraordinaire and the smarts of the outfit, for bringin' it,
Randy Gardner, most esteemed, for everything and more—JP

First Carroll & Graf edition 2000

Carroll & Graf Publishers, Inc.
A Division of Avalon Publishing Group
19 West 21st Street
New York, NY 10010-6805

Library of Congress Cataloging-in-Publication Data is available.
ISBN: 0-7867-0737-2

Manufactured in the United States of America

In her bed afterward, in candlelight, Max props on his elbow and gazes down into the amazing eyes. Smiling a little, remembering what people in the DA's office used to say—what they probably still say, except Max isn't there to hear it anymore.

Paige asks what's funny.

"Your eyes. No, I don't mean your eyes are funny, but . . . Have I ever told you what people in the office used to say?"

"Do I want to know?"

" 'Those fucking eyes,' Higgenbotham always said. 'Anything she can't tell a jury out loud, she tells 'em with those Prescott looks.' I gotta say, you used to piss me off too."

"You're over it now?"

"Getting there."

She glows. The girl who had tears in her eyes in the San Juans last month, telling Max she's so grateful for him . . . and so hopeful about them, after all the men who've disappointed her and all the ones she's disappointed.

He likes to believe she glows because she's never been so much in love, but in more humble moments he knows it's because she's never had anyone so enchanted with her. Which is almost as thrilling, really: knowing he brings out the soft side of someone who's never hooked up with a man for very long. Too insecure, too prickly, too gung-ho in defending dirtbags, too something. Never letting the good stuff show. Yet in the last three months he's seen such unexpectedly wonderful stuff, he's almost forgotten the hardnosed Miss Prescott, the bane of the Multnomah County District Attorney's office.

Almost. Suddenly, as he lies back and brings her head up on his shoulder—"So, how long's Tommy staying?"

He groans. "The moment's over, huh? The good part?"

No answer.

He says, "Haven't we had this conversation before?"

"We have. You said you didn't know how long he'd stay. Do you have any idea now?"

"An old friend of mine needs a place to stay while he gets his life together—what do you care?"

"You really believe he's trying to get his life together?"

Jesus. "Don't you have bigger things to worry about?" The best public defender in Portland getting ready to defend her latest dirtbag in an aggravated murder.

"I'm taking care of my business, don't worry about it."

The intimacy gone, Max bumps her head off his shoulder and moves away a little. "If you must know, I do think he's trying. He's eaten a lot of humble pie trying to get back together with his wife. His agent says some publisher still might buy his novel, but meanwhile he's writing for the *Rose City Review* again, that piece of crap. And he knows he's got to get a real job. When he does he'll get an apartment, if he's not back home by then. He doesn't plan on staying with me forever."

"So he's thinking about getting a job?"

"Right."

So strange. They're two people who want things their own way—two lawyers—but for three months they've been going out of their way to accommodate each other, trying to make this thing work. We'll eat wherever you want to eat. We can watch whatever movie you want to watch. The small stuff. But something that matters to her turns her into the snippy, self-righteous Miss Prescott who turned him off for seven years, him and everyone else in the DA's office. And undoubtedly a lot of other men. There has to be a reason she's still single at thirty-five, a woman so smart and accomplished and great-looking.

A woman who *would've* been great-looking, as Charlie Witty said years ago, if only she weren't Paige Prescott.

"I don't want to fight, Max—"

"Then let's don't."

"—but he seems like such a loser. Milking this starving-artist routine when he should grow up and get a job like everyone else."

He lets it pass. Lets it hang there, hoping she'll realize how she sounds.

"And you say I'm the one who falls for losers," is what she finally says.

Which frosts him, coming from a bleeding-heart PD whose latest psychopath ambushed three police officers with a semiautomatic weapon, wounding two and killing the third. "You're kidding, right?"—his voice rising—"comparing Tommy to garbage like Royer? Come on, wake up. This is a regular guy, a good guy. Smart, funny, talented—"

"Irresponsible, immature. . . ." And she starts in again about how Tommy doesn't seem to want to work, how he's been living off other people since he moved out on his wife and she wouldn't take him back.

Max tells her he can relate to someone whose marriage falls apart. "If he's anything like I was he's in a fog, lucky to put one foot in front of the other and stagger through a day at a time."

"Come on, Max. All you were doing was running the Violent Crimes Unit, trying murder cases. Your buddy is writing a couple of sports articles for peanuts, probably drinking too much—"

"What do you know about how much he drinks? Listen, I single-handedly kept the Quandary in business during my last divorce"— where they even named a drink after him, the Max Blaster—"so I'm not about to judge him for drinking a little too much at this point, if it *is* true. And I don't know it's true, and you sure as hell don't."

"Sorry." She's not, but she knows you look bad when you make claims you can't back up.

"Let's just drop it, all right?"

Or maybe she's sorry after all: she finds his hand under the covers, squeezes it. "I'll stop," she says.

"It's OK. I just don't think you understand."

Mistake. Her hand pulls away. *You don't understand because you've never been married,* is what she heard. He knows she's sensitive about it.

He tries to breeze past it. "Look, I like him, that's all. And I admire him for going after what he wants. He says being even a small-time writer is better than being a big-time anything else, and I like that, I can't help it."

"Even though he's so small-time he can't afford a studio apartment?"

Lord! "I'm sorry he's struggling, but I'm impressed that he *is* struggling. And it's not like he's delusional. How many writers ever have *one* novel published? How many ever get published in *Sports Illustrated*? Some guy in San Francisco included him in an article called 'The Hundred Best Writers You've Never Heard Of.' So he's not chopped liver, even if he *is* reduced to covering jocks again for a while. All I know is, I respect him more than the people who give up their dreams and go sell roofing supplies."

"They make a living," she says icily.

And Max sighs and rolls the other way, done with Miss Prescott for now.

Seven o'clock Friday morning, twelve hours before opening night in the league, power forward LaPrince Wheatley lies in bed channel-surfing with one hand and fondling his nuts with the other, looking for *Bugs Bunny* on TV and thinking about those two girls that made him miss the bus the other day. Wishing they were here, or that he was at the slinky one's apartment again. The apartment had a funky smell and the bed sagged so bad that all three slid to the middle and couldn't hardly do things. This is a classy crib on a long, curvy, tree-lined road near this Lewis & Clark College, a few miles from downtown Portland, belongs to the son of some Plunder vice president. The son used to work for the team too; now he's in New York working for the league but he's holding on to the house—furniture, satellite TV and all—and when the Plunder wrapped up training camp in Salem last week and came up here they offered it to LaPrince until he gets his own place. So Turner Boyd, his buddy, moved into the Residence Inn by himself. Just as well, Turner-man being so touchy lately.

LaPrince wonders about the girls from the other day, but more important right now (since there's always girls) is whether he should allow himself a blast or two off what's left of last night's fatty, which sits tantalizingly on the edge of the nightstand with the ash still hanging on the end. He's promised himself he'll lay off on game days this season—on the day of his first game with another new team, for sure—but he's got all this stress and the game ain't till tonight. Shootaround at noon, but he can get a fade on now and go back to sleep for a while, be fine by noon. Nap again afterward if he needs to. He'll be good by tonight.

Reaches for the roach, shakes off the ash and fires up.

Two minutes later . . . still no *Bugs,* but he feels a whole lot better. Stretches out his legs on top of the covers, flexes, and admires the thick ridges of muscle that pop up on his thighs. A *specimen,* La-Prince Wheatley is, ain't no doubt about it. Six-nine, 260 and pretty—a perfect specimen except for those gnarly feet, all bumps and calluses and black toenails from getting stepped on. But everybody in the league has gnarly feet. Jordan did, even.

And LaPrince Wheatley ain't just pretty. Run the floor with any big man in the league and most little ones. Jump out of the building. Shoot the rock, put it on the floor, dish it off—got moves so sweet they'll rot your teeth. Break your arm with his dunk if you're fool enough to challenge it. Smack your shot back in your mug if you wanna bring it inside, leave the SPALDING imprint on your forehead. Scatter your teeth with an elbow if you wanna challenge for a rebound.

He can do it all, and after three years it's time to bust out. He's *gonna* bust out. A few games, watch, everybody'll forget all this bullshit the last few days.

With the remote he flicks past old black-and-white war film, *Three Stooges,* weather, *Home Shopping,* country music, rock music, Barney Fife, an old movie, crazy Mork from Ork, soccer shit on ESPN, the Road Runner *meep-meep*ing. Stops on some cartoon he doesn't recognize, a rat with an attitude talking smack to a snake even as the snake says "I can swalla you up, you'll never be heard from again."

Flick. Flick. And suddenly it's one of the Portland channels switching from a helicopter view of the morning traffic to a wrinkly, uptight bitch talking about *him,* with his picture on the screen behind her: how tonight's the first game and everybody's waiting to see what he'll do, how Puckerman's on the spot for making the trade more than ever now that LaPrince skipped the last preseason game and then yesterday—

He zaps the wrinkly bitch before she gets into that punky thing yesterday. Nothing but punky, but they're making a big damn deal out of it.

Flicks past Lucy and Ricky, more news, smart little Columbo with the weird eye, old ladies cooking. Pauses on a fine lady talking about scattered showers today, then flicks past more old war film, boxing, sorry-ass rock video. Can't hardly get cartoons no more.

Flick, flick, flick, nothing but weak shit. He's about to give it up when—*whoa!*—someone yelled his name there, and he flicks back and hears "LaPrince!" again and spots Turner's head over the top of a crowd and realizes it's the scene yesterday. There he comes behind Turner-man—his Dodgers cap—trying to get through the peckerhead reporters and out to his car after practice. Turner getting eased out of the way and the reporters crowding in. He, LaPrince, is shaking his head and his lips are moving. "Ain't talking, ain't talking" is all he kept saying, but you can't hear him over all the peckerheads yelling questions at him.

Now, there! There's the two chumps bumping into each other, accidentally clearing a lane to spring him, and he's coming right at the camera, right at the little fat cameraman hanging back near the exit knowing he had to come that way. And there!—LaPrince's UNLV sweatshirt suddenly filling the screen, out of focus, and the blur of his forearm pushing out a little bit. Just trying to ease the fat boy back and get by, a little push, nothing, but you hear a grunt and a girly "Hey!" and now the picture goes every which way as the punk loses his balance and falls—walls and ceiling and finally a bunch of feet as he lies there with his camera still running. People yelling "Jesus Christ!" and "What happened?" like it's some big deal. The punk flopped is what happened, which this guy Laimbeer made famous and every pussy in the league picked up, trying to draw charging fouls by flopping every time you breathe on 'em.

That's all. "Rob Wolf is all right," a pasty guy in the studio says, "and his camera survived as well, but the LaPrince Wheatley saga continues to unfold. Plunder president Bob Puckerman, after seeing the footage you've just seen, apologized yesterday to cameraman Wolf and to Channel Two on behalf of the organization. Puckerman said he hadn't yet spoken to Wheatley, who continued on to his car and left the arena after the incident. Asked if Wheatley's recent misadventures violate the so-called good-citizen clause the Plunder included in Wheatley's contract to quiet the outcry against the trade that brought him here, Puckerman said it's in-house business at this point and any further public discussion would only detract from a great opening to the new season, with the Plunder hosting Utah tonight and Seattle tomorrow." The pasty guy gives a little smile and adds, "Channel Two and intrepid cameraman Rob Wolf will be there. Tune in here for the best in Plunder coverage."

Flick. Peckerheads.

*   *   *

He's zoned out on the funk-doctor when Turner calls. Clock by the bed says almost ten. Shootaround's at twelve but Turner-man asks if he wants to go early, before the peckerhead reporters show up— take a whirlpool, relax awhile. LaPrince is glad he's not mad about yesterday, about LaPrince giving him shit in the car when they finally got out of there. And going early's a good idea. He says yeah and Turner says he'll drive, swing by around eleven.

Sure enough: by eleven they're circling the arena in Turner's truck and there's nothing but a Channel 5 van in the peckerheads' lot. Nobody outside the locker room yet but the old security man at the door and the Channel 5 crew leaning against the wall talking, another ratty cameraman and the dykey lady LaPrince has seen on TV. "LaPrince!" the dyke yells, and the ratty dude scrambles for his camera, but Turner and LaPrince are already in the locker room, the old security guy shutting the door after them.

Coach Colabello and a couple of the assistants are in the office to the left. In the big locker area to the right the equipment man is setting basketballs on a table for the players to sign, while his two young assistants stand in front of the big-screen watching tapes of a Portland–Utah game from last season.

At his locker LaPrince kicks off his loafers, hangs up his Plunder windbreaker and Tupac T-shirt and jeans, removes the diamond stud from his left ear and the gold necklace with the star-shaped "LaP 54" pendant (same design as his tattoos), locks everything up. Finally wraps a towel around his middle, ready to go whirlpool, but Turner's sitting in front of his locker still dressed, reading the little newspaper one of the peckerheads held up in front of LaPrince yesterday with his picture on the front.

Fuck it. More junk, probably. "You coming, Turner-man?"

Turner looks up with a funny little smile. "I'm reading about you, man. And I'll tell you, you got a friend." *Fray-end,* the way the country boy talks. "Your man Tommy Mason."

"Straight up?"

"Ain't read it all yet, but so far, yeah. Says you're a nice guy. Let's see"—turning back a couple of pages, looking for something— "yeah: 'Immature, maybe, but who isn't at twenty-five?' "

"My boy said that? Get outta them clothes and bring it with you, Turner-man, we can look at it back here."

Through the shower room and down a short tiled hall, in a whirl-pool big enough for the whole team and more, Turner holds the paper up over the water and goes back to reading. Smiling, nodding, glancing up at LaPrince every so often.

"What else my boy say?"

Turner reads a little more, finishing up, then holds the paper out. "Says you're OK, just need a little understanding. Here."

"Read me it, the good part. My hands' wet."

"Here. Mine about to git wet."

"Just read me it, Turner-man." Turner fucking with him about his reading like he did sometimes when they were in LA. Maybe he's a little mad from yesterday, and maybe he's got a right, but just the same, sometimes LaPrince feels like fucking the country boy up.

"All right," Turner says, opening the paper again and looking for a certain part. "He says here you're 'undoubtedly pampered, but that's true of most professional athletes. They get used to it and then they expect it forevermore. We can't expect them to act like regular people unless and until we start treating them like we treat each other.' "

"Huh."

Turner turns the page, folds the paper in half and searches. "Here. 'Talk to Wheatley for a while and you sense a young man who wants to do the right things but doesn't always know what they are. But who *would* know, if they didn't have structure and guidance and role models when they were young?' Let's see. . . . Tells about your daddy, your brother. 'Most of us hear about that world—but at a comfortable remove, so we don't really have any idea. Somehow we expect people who grew up in these circumstances to be like ourselves: see the world the way we see it, behave the way we behave. We don't understand. Most of the time, we probably don't try very hard to understand.' "

"Sound good," LaPrince says.

"Here's the end. 'Give the man a chance. If it doesn't work out, at least the Plunder aren't out much: LA considered the trade addition-by-subtraction and gave Wheatley up for two benchwarmers and a draft choice. If it does work, if this manchild fulfills even a fair percentage of his immense potential, we've got an All-Star to start rebuilding this fading franchise around.' " Turner tosses the paper away. "Like I said, you got a fray-end."

Mason. Tommy Mason. Remember it, make the nigga feel good when you see him.

M ax felt bad for Tommy before—the poor guy's life falling apart—but he feels even worse for him now. This cover story on LaPrince Wheatley in the *Rose City Review* is going to haunt him.

What a week. On Monday, Tommy finally got the interview he needed after Wheatley stood him up twice. He was pleased with it, chiding Max for cynicism, citing himself as the only guy in town with enough compassion to give Wheatley a chance, enough insight to understand him and enough balls to stand up for him publicly. Tuesday he tightened up the story a little, then went downtown to transfer it to the *Review*'s computer system. But things changed that afternoon when Wheatley missed the bus taking the Plunder out to Medford for the last preseason game. When Tommy came downstairs Wednesday morning, Max was sitting in the breakfast nook drinking his second espresso and contemplating the blaring headline on the *Oregonian* sports page: WHERE'S WHEATLEY? with the subhead *Plunder Forward a No-Show for Exhibition.* Tommy took one look and groaned. Max said, "No details here. Maybe it'll turn out he had a reason. His granny died, he got food poisoning, something."

Not believing it, of course. Not convincing Tommy, either. That afternoon they watched the smirking *SportsCenter* anchor tell millions of people "It didn't take Portland Plunder forward LaPrince Wheatley long to show his new team his old form. The same form that got Wheatley, third pick in the draft just three years ago, shipped out of Sacramento and then Los Angeles. Wheatley apparently decided to skip the Plunder's final preseason game last night in Medford, Oregon. No details yet, although Plunder president Bob

Puckerman told ESPN he's talked to Wheatley and is satisfied that the former UNLV All-American, who's provided a heapin' helpin' of controversy in his short and thus far disappointing career, was simply confused as to the time the team bus was leaving the Rose Garden." Followed by the anchor's skeptical look and strained punchline: "A source tells ESPN that Wheatley had a hard time in school because the family dog repeatedly ate his homework."

Tommy groaning about how this is what he gets for trying to see some good in a bad egg. About what a laughingstock he'd be when the *Review* came out the next day. Max repeating, Well, maybe Wheatley had a reason—because what else could he say?

That last hope blew up Thursday morning, yesterday. When Max rolled out of bed and went in the kitchen Tommy was already there, sitting in the nook with a suicidal look. He'd already been out to pick up a hot-off-the-press *Review*, with his cover story: NEW BEGINNING FOR THE NEWEST PLUNDER. It was sitting on the table in front of him along with the Big O sports page, the O's headline a little different: NEW TEAM, SAME OLD STORY. Tommy groaning, "What's in this fool's *mind?*"

Max skimmed the *Oregonian* stuff, which explained that Wheatley had missed the team bus by five minutes and then nixed a cab driver's offer to overtake it before it got two miles out I-84—telling the cabbie it was only an exhabition game, meaningless, and he might as well go home and chill.

"Thought he'd go home and *cheeill*," Tommy muttered as Max finished the column. "I can just hear him. Shit. I might as well not show my face in this burg again."

Max knew there was no point in uttering any consoling words the moment his eyes turned to the *Review*. Big picture of a smiling Wheatley at the August press conference announcing the trade, the NEW BEGINNING headline and the start of Tommy's story:

> "It's a new start for me here in Portland and I'm grateful to the Plunder organization for having faith in me," LaPrince Wheatley said after Bob Puckerman introduced his newest player last summer. "I haven't always been perfect in the past but I've learned from my mistakes and I'm ready to represent this organization with all professionalism."

Tommy! Damn! Setting yourself up. Asking for it.

In the story Tommy made every possible excuse for the guy. Or simply let Wheatley explain—say, about the pot bust in LA last spring: "I was in the car with some people but I wasn't doing nothing. The cops busted me because I'm a name." Followed by the repentant, reformed Wheatley: "But I was there, hanging with the wrong kind of people, and I know I've got to be different now. I got no room for slipups, period. No ifs, ands or buts. No bad luck. No 'I was there but I didn't have nothing to do with it.' "

Tommy! "Hanging with the wrong kind of people"? Those dopers were undoubtedly his friends, his LA homeys. Didn't Wheatley's Lexus Gold Edition, the pimpmobile with all gold parts inside tip you off?

Tommy's story went on with Wheatley's version of his youth in LA. Growing up in the 'hood; not seeing his father until he was nine and someone pointed him out, nodding on a stoop a few blocks away; seeing his crack-addict brother dead in a pool of blood.

A quote from Turner Boyd, a new Plunder who played with Wheatley in LA the year before last: "LaPrince is a nice guy who wants to do right. I'll bet my life he does well here, and I wouldn't risk something I can't do without."

Quotes from others saying nice things about the stud.

Worst of all, Tommy's impassioned ending: well-written, well-meaning tripe, a plea to the fans to give the guy a chance, try to understand him, etc. Almost too sappy for Max to stomach. Then again, at least Tommy hadn't included Wheatley's press-conference quote about how he was "good with God now."

Max didn't know what to say.

Tommy said, "I'll be the joke of the city by noon."

Max shrugged, recalling the late-night conversations last week when Tommy went on and on about the "new" Wheatley, about how anyone can change. Max had said that one of the first things he learned as a DA was that the best indicator of future behavior is past behavior. Tommy kept saying, "But people can change, right? People can mature?"

Max admitted it's possible, but as he fell asleep later he realized the question had more to do with Tommy's own situation than with Wheatley. Because Tommy's trying to convince his wife that he can shape up if she'll take him back.

*   *   *

Now, Friday afternoon, Tommy comes home and invites Max to the first game of the season tonight, Plunder vs. Utah. "I know you swore you wouldn't spend a dime on 'em this year, after they signed LaPrince and Mark Mona—"

"On top of all the criminals they already had."

"—but you don't have to. I've got my press pass, and one of the flacks called earlier to compliment me on the story and tell me I can bring a guest tonight if I want, they've got a few extra seats in the upper-deck press section. Positive reinforcement, undoubtedly, for writing puff pieces about assholes."

Sure, Max will go. He and Paige eventually made up after the spat last night and are getting together tonight—sleeping at her place, then taking off for Mount Hood early in the morning—but first she wants to do some prepping for her big trial next week, so it won't be until ten or eleven. Utah's fun to watch, with the future Hall-of-Famers, and Max has been a fan of Coach Jerry Sloan since meeting him at the Quandary when the team was up here during the playoffs a few years ago. And it's free.

Mostly, he knows Tommy wants him to go, figuring the other media people won't razz him as much if he's with someone.

It's not awful. Tommy imagines people looking at him, imagines them telling one another "That's the dolt," but no one says anything.

Wheatley disappoints Max by coming up big, as the sportscasters say. You'd expect Karl Malone to school him, but Wheatley comes out like he's got something to prove. The crowd boos him when he's introduced, and the first time he touches the ball . . . but less and less, then, as he strokes jumpers in Mailman's face and snaps down rebounds and runs the court hard. Pretty soon they're cheering, doing the raise-the-roof thing. Wheatley feeds on it, even dives for a loose ball, and the Plunder runs up the score.

Tommy's relieved, even though Wheatley's 33 points and 14 rebounds can't wholly undo his embarrassment.

They stick around with about ten thousand others for the post-game show, the radio man interviewing Wheatley at midcourt. Afterward, Tommy asks if Max would mind waiting five–ten minutes so he can drop by the locker room and see what Wheatley thought of his story.

Max waits by the main exit, the crowd streaming out around him. Looking forward to hooking up with Paige in a little while, whenever the best public defender in Portland feels she's done enough for a Friday night.

Tommy comes back feeling good. "LaPrince says he and Yuban and a couple of others are going downtown and he wants to buy me a drink, say thanks for the profile. I told him I'm with a friend and he said to bring you along. I told him you're supposed to meet your honey and he said to bring her along too. It's up to you."

What do you say? It's no big deal to Max—he prosecuted enough of these guys over the years to get over the thrill—but clearly Tommy wants to go. Hell, call Paige, let her decide. She has no interest in ball or ballplayers, and doesn't like Tommy, but who knows?

He's surprised when she says sure, she'll meet them. ("But at the Swim? These guys actually go to the Swim?") Wanting to make up for last night, maybe, when they argued about Tommy again.

The place is on First, near the waterfront. Used to be a nice restaurant called Chuck's, but for a few years now it's been a meatmarket for the young brain-dead crowd: semidark, music blaring, booze flowing, bodies wall-to-wall. The name the Swim must have something to do with the floor-to-ceiling aquariums built into parts of two walls.

They're standing near the packed bar when Paige shows up, looking great, with the nighttime drizzle sparkling in her hair and the amazing blue eyes shining. Far too classy for this place, in black slacks and a black silk sweater. Understated, in a place where big belts and costume jewelry and scary-looking nails rule.

"You made it."

"I said I would."

"You didn't have to."

"For love," she says, and shines a Prescott smile on him.

He still feels the charge. After three-plus months he keeps expecting reality to set in, but they're both still feeling it.

4

She's been trying to learn to compromise. Give a little. Do things she might not feel like doing. Like coming downtown tonight when she was cozy at home and ready for Max to come over. Not only downtown, but to the Swim. To see not only Max but his freeloading buddy and some basketball players too.

Trying to make it work. She and Max have been testy with each other for the last two weeks, since she was named co-counsel for Donald Royer. Max knows perfectly well it wasn't her choice, simply a matter of her name coming up on the list, but it's as if she's guilty in some way. He knows good and well that everyone is entitled to a defense, but when it comes to cop-killers, the "prosecutor's prosecutor" doesn't want to hear it.

Anyway, they've been testy, and last night she made things worse by asking, again, how long Mason's going to be staying with him. Saying she doesn't even like going over there anymore, even though Max has the bigger house and the stunning view and the hot tub in the backyard under the apple tree. Max getting defensive, then angry, saying some things that hit home: that she's judgmental, controlling, not very sympathetic.

Lying in bed alone after he got up and went home, she realized she needs to give a little, and when he called tonight she could tell he wanted to come down here, wanted her to come, so she did.

The look in his eyes when he spotted her coming through the crowd was worth it: the excited, happy-to-see-her look that still surprises her.

But things quickly go downhill. The three of them are standing in the crowd near the bar, waiting for the players, when two of them come in. A black and a white, both huge. "LaPrince," Max says—

LaPrince Wheatley, the bad boy Mason wrote the profile on—"and Turner Boyd, I think." The crowd parts, people gawking at them as if they're kings or movie stars. Turner Boyd—a benchwarmer, Mason says, lucky to have made the team—has a short jock haircut and is wearing a red down jacket that might have come from Kmart. LaPrince, the so-called star (as Max and Mason call him), has a shiny shaved head and a diamond stud in his left earlobe; he's got a black floor-length fur coat draped over his shoulders, over a black, baggy pants, wide-lapel suit and a white shirt buttoned to the top, no tie. Trying to look like who? Harry Belafonte? Snoop Doggy Dogg? Looking like someone with a lot of money but without a clue, who only knows he's *not* going to look like the ghetto kid who probably wore ratty clothes and worn-out sneakers.

"There's Yuban," Max says a moment later, meaning the guy who fills the doorway after the first two are inside. Even Paige knows the name Yuban Taylor: the star of the Plunder, everyone's favorite. He's stylish, tasteful, and even though Paige doesn't care for shaved heads she can't deny he's handsome. Looking especially good, especially tasteful compared to the one right behind him, a white guy who belongs in a Metallica video with his stubbly shaved head and a black leather jacket with silver studs and chains all over it. Mark Mona, Max says—twenty-four years old, he says, with three kids in three league cities by three different groupies.

The bar manager springs out to meet them, and the players stand by while he goes and talks to the people at one of the big round tables in the middle of the place. A moment later he straightens up, scans the room and points to a booth in the far corner where three guys are getting ready to leave—and the seven people at the big table, apparently thrilled to accommodate the celebrities, collect their things and move off to jam into the booth: three on each side, on seats meant for two, and one man pulling up a chair at the end.

It's too much for Paige already. As Mason leads her and Max over to the ballplayers she feels countless eyes on them: some people thinking they're special, others undoubtedly thinking they're jerks.

Introductions. Yuban Taylor shakes her hand with a bullshit-courtly "Ma'am," checking her out as if there's no doubt in his mind that she'll drop Max like a hot rock if he says the word. And why wouldn't he think so, with every bimbo in the place staring? LaPrince scans her too, and Mark Mona, who's got bad teeth and a stutter along with the raggedy head. Turner Boyd stands back, quiet, looking as if he'd rather not be here at all. He's got some kind of accent, southern or backwoods or both.

At the big round table Paige grabs the chair between Max and Mason. A fawning waiter takes orders—drinks all around except for Turner Boyd, who asks for beer. Boyd does sound country, and he's got a nice way about him. What's he doing with these others?

They're joined by a bimbo in a tight black dress who didn't waste any time sidling up and letting Yuban Taylor know she'd like to get acquainted—as intimately acquainted as possible. More bimbos walk by making eyes at the players, saying things, and a few dweeby men ask for autographs on cocktail napkins.

Paige would rather be home, and Max already looks as if he'd rather be somewhere else too. Yet it's a scene, a study, and part of her wants to see how it develops. When Max gives her a look saying *We can leave whenever you want* she smiles and says no, she's fine, she'll have another drink.

Another airhead squeezes in between LaPrince and Mr. Metallica, basically sitting in LaPrince's lap, and there's no room left at the table when two more guys show up: a slender light-skinned black in a nice suit, clearly not a ballplayer, and a pretty-boy blond who's heartily welcomed by LaPrince and Yuban Taylor. The manager reappears and goes to clear six customers from the next table.

The black fellow, smooth and subdued, is a league liaison for Nike. The prettyboy—pleased with himself, jiving through a series of insider handshakes with the players—is a realtor. "Rod Yardley," he finally introduces himself to the nobodies, "a friend of some of the guys. My pleasure," he tells Paige in particular.

When the manager gets the next table cleared—this group staring at him in disbelief before stomping out of the Swim—the players and bimbos pick up and move over. There are a couple of extra chairs, but Mason, Max and Paige are nobodies and the two new arrivals aren't invited over, either. The Nike rep, sitting down on Max's left, doesn't seem to mind. The pretty boy wants to be with the players but doesn't push it. He takes the seat on Mason's right. Paige isn't crazy about Mason, but she's glad he's in between her and this Yardley. Something creepy about the guy. Watching her like he's got ideas.

Max, the prick, starts chatting with the Nike rep, leaving her with these two.

Out of nowhere, Mason leans in and says he'd appreciate some womanly advice about his screwed-up marriage. Unexpected, but she'd rather talk to him than Yardley, and besides, she feels a little guilty about trashing him again last night. And he's hurting—at least, Max is always saying so. Maybe he's just trying to flatter her ("advice from someone I respect"), but maybe he truly wants a female perspective.

Yardley, on the other side of him, keeps trying to get her attention. When Mason makes a bathroom run, the guy slides into the empty chair and yes, he's got ideas.

Paige just wants to keep it superficial until Mason gets back or until Max, dammit, rescues her. But when she compliments him on his tan (thinking, salon tan, the loser) he seizes the chance to let her know he's got it all year round, even in gloomy Portland, because he takes so many vacations. "Just back from Barbados. Third trip there; I'm running out of sunny places I haven't seen before. But I've got to keep taking vacations, time off work, because I make so much money when I do work that I get killed on taxes. And where do you go except someplace warm and sunny? Lie on a beach, play golf . . ."

Waiting for her to ask what he does to make so much money.

She doesn't, but he tells her anyway. "I sell real estate, is what I do. That's how I get to know these ballers. Sold Yuban a beautiful Tudor in Forest Park when the Plunder drafted him four–five years ago, and when they signed B. B. Brisbee the next year Yuban introduced us and I got B set up in Lake Oswego. One thing leads to another, and I stay friends with the guys afterward."

A friend of the stars!

"Ever done the Greek islands?" he asks, back to sunny vacations.

"No, I never have."

"The best. I'm going back next month, maybe staying through the holidays."

What do you say, "Enjoy it"? She looks around for Mason, of all people, ready to hear more about his screwed-up life. About anything.

No sign of him. At the other table the stars keep drinking, yukking it up, signing napkins for dweebs. Bimbos keep strutting by, batting their overdone eyelashes and switching their tails, making it plain they're available for the price of a drink. Heck, they'd buy their own drinks.

*   *   *

After pounding three or four drinks apiece the stars start getting witty—all except the country guy, Turner Boyd, who quietly sips his second or possibly third beer.

Yuban Taylor gets them started. Paige, ten feet away at the no-bodies' table, happens to be watching as he scopes out a frizzy-haired redhead on her way to the bathroom. As the girl passes, Portland's favorite Plunder makes sure everyone hears him over the music and noise: "Hey, baby, how'd you like me to tickle your belly button . . . from the inside?" The girl tries to smile but keeps moving, while the stars whoop and high-five.

It's catching. LaPrince is ready when a curvy strawberry-blonde shakes her booty past the table: "Onliest way I'ma let you outta bed, sweet thing, 'zif you wanna do it on the flo' instead!" This girl, cool, blows him a kiss and keeps walking, and LaPrince has to be content with guffaws from Mr. Metallica, who seems to have the IQ of a flea-beetle.

Which Metallica proves by grabbing the wrist of the next passing female, a witchy-looking beanpole, and stammering "Hey, m-m-momma, whyn't you s-sit on my l-l-lap and we talk a-b-b-bout the first thing p-pops up?" The girl yanks her hand away before he's finished and Metallica's embarrassed despite laughs from the others, as if he suspects they're laughing at him instead of with him.

The country guy, Turner Boyd, looks as if he'd rather be anywhere else.

Yuban Taylor's drunk. Starting off toward the men's room he leans down and says something to a sleek black girl at a nearby table, even though she's holding hands with the guy across from her. It startles her, and Yuban walks away laughing. Coming back a few minutes later he prances by them with one hand behind his head in some kind of pose, grinning, and yells "Baby, you b'lieve in love at first sight? You don't, I be happy to walk by again!"

LaPrince drapes a long arm around the slinky brunette who's wig-gled into the seat between him and Metallica. It's apparently more than she expected, or at least too much too soon, because she tries to slide away. (Paige wondering, What did she expect?) LaPrince counters the rejection with a forced laugh and a moronic line he must have liked when some other moron used it: "Tha's a bee-yoo-tee-ful dress you wearin', sugar—it'd look great on the floor by my bed." And as she stands up and spins away: "C'mon, you don't wanna party with LaPrince?"

Paige finally nudges Max and says she's had enough. She's about to stand up when she senses someone behind her and looks up into the handsome, idiotic face of Yuban Taylor. Idiotic but dead-serious, Max or no Max: "Dance, ma'am?" When she shakes her head no he leans down so close she smells the booze on his breath and says, "I got more money than you could ever spend, lady."

"I don't have much," she snaps back, "but what'll it take to make you go away?"

Straightening him right up. He starts to say something, then simply backs off, hands up in surrender.

And she's up too, pulling her coat off the back of the chair and starting through the crowd. Max right with her, smiling, telling her she's a ten, an absolute ten.

5

Tommy didn't need to come downtown: five minutes in the locker room with the players and the press brought it all back. The dimwit multimillionaires . . . so huge, their mere presence intimidating everyone. Combine their size and money with the Lilliputians' need for heroes and it's easy to see why these guys look at any outsider as part of a lesser species. Actually they don't look at you at all, they look through you. You can be a third-rate local hack or *Sports Illustrated,* it doesn't matter. When Tommy wrote the *SI* profiles a few years ago he'd be treated like a prince by the team's flacks, be envied and flattered by the media people—then go in the locker room after the game and get that same bored look from the kings of the jungle as they preened, as they got into their hundred-dollar socks and two-thousand-dollar suits and obscenely spendthrift jewelry. Get whatever quotes he could, then watch them walk out into the sea of babes, babes dressed to kill and ready to undress in seconds. It made him especially crazy after the guy in the *San Francisco Review of Books* called him "one of the best current writers you've probably never read." Did that mean he was maybe one of the hundred best in America? Two hundred? Even one of the four hundred best? Because if you're one of the four hundred best ballplayers you're one of these guys, you're in the league, you're a millionaire with guys worshiping you and babes ready to do anything you want. As a writer, you're anonymous and broke.

Five minutes in the locker room tonight brought it all back. He didn't need to come downtown to be reminded of his place. He should have told LaPrince thanks but no thanks, no need to buy him a drink. But he didn't, and now he's sitting here thinking *Idiots, jackasses,* feeling ridiculous for being back on the Plunder beat.

Finally it seems to be breaking up. While Yuban and Mark Mona are out on the dance floor with twin sisters wearing matching flowered dresses, maybe twenty years old, the realtor moves to the other table and huddles with LaPrince. LaPrince smiles and whispers into the ear of the nymph on his lap. She's agreeable to whatever it is, and when Yuban and Mona and the twins come back to the A table there's more discussion, more nods, and the realtor, suddenly in the middle of the action, scribbles on some napkins and hands them to the players and LaPrince's squeeze. Directions. Yuban asks the twins where they're parked and says he'll swing by there in his Maserati and they can follow him.

No one says anything to Tommy or the Nike man or a couple of plain Janes who've invited themselves to the B table.

Except Turner Boyd, who's been friendly to Tommy the last two weeks—not a *friend*, of course, but more like a human being than any other ballplayer he's met. He gives Tommy a look that seems to say yeah, they're being excluded, and Turner's sorry but it's not his call. When the waiter appears with the tab and everyone stands up and gets their coats on, he comes around the table with an apologetic shrug.

"No sweat," Tommy says. It's not like he's dying to keep partying with these guys—it would be nice to be asked, that's all. LaPrince, wanted to buy him a drink, hasn't said a word to him the whole time. And Yuban's taking care of the tab.

Turner, uncomfortable, takes things back to the player–writer plane. "Listen, we can talk anytime you want"—Tommy having mentioned last week that he'd like to do a column on Turner if he survived the final cuts. "I'll be apartment-huntin' soon's we get back from the road next week, but you can reach me at the Residence Inn for a while. I enjoyed talking to you th'other day, and you wrote a nice story 'bout Wheat. He 'preciated it, I know, even if he ain't said much. He's just fulla himself tonight, the game he had. Been feeling like everybody's on his case and he come out and showed 'em."

"Full of himself" is the understatement of the year. They look over and the star of the night is giving his dolly a wink and telling her "They call me Milk, honey, 'cause I do a body good." Dolly laughs and Tommy's pretty sure she'll do anything LaPrince wants tonight, hoping for a return engagement.

Now the star comes around the table to them. To Turner, that is, avoiding Tommy's eyes. "You ready to fly, Turner-man?"

"I guess. Just checking out with your man here."

At which point LaPrince can't ignore him anymore. "Dude, we cool?" he says. "You got some drinks, got to hang out a little—we cool, you and me?"

"Cool," Tommy says, chilly. "I appreciate it. An honor."

He ignores the sarcasm, if he was listening at all. He's used one more pathetic writer and now he's done with him. "Dude, I 'preciate your story you wrote. You gimme a chance, you fair, not like these other peckerheads. We off on the road after tomorra but you gonna party with us sometime when we back home, huh?"

I'll bet. "Any time. Let me know."

"We be seein' y'at the games, huh?"

"I'll be around."

"Cool. Well, you leaving? C'mon walk out with us."

A last crumb. The three of them walk outside together and up Morrison. Tommy's parked on Second or Third—can't quite remember.

LaPrince isn't sure where he parked, either. At Second he says, "Where we at, Turner-man? Didn' we come along here?"

"Two or three times we did."

"I mean, didn' we *park* on this one?"

"Maybe. Or up yonder, maybe."

Tommy says, "I'm up this way somewhere," he says. "I guess I'll see you guys some other time."

LaPrince pays no attention, too worried about his fur coat sliding off his shoulders. Who does he think he is, a duke or something? Where are the spats and the silver-tipped cane?

Turner says, "Be seeing ya, then," and Tommy heads off as they stand there trying to remember where LaPrince parked.

A few blocks up Second, with no sign of his own car, he turns up Madison toward Third. Replaying the last hour or so in his mind. Recalling the last time he was out with some Plunder, three years ago, the night that convinced him to give up the beat. Curtis Waters, the phee-nom, getting smashed and losing it as Tommy drove him home, crazily grabbing the wheel and nearly crashing them into the freeway median; getting out in front of his townhouse—Tommy just wanting him *out*—and getting down on his knees and fumbling

around under the seat for some coffee mugs and ashtrays he'd ripped
off from the Ringside. . . .

He's back down on Second a few minutes later, walking north
this time, when he notices a match being lit in a parked car a few
feet ahead. A Lexus? Gold Edition? Hard to make out the color
under the streetlight, but glancing in the passenger side as he approaches he sees a familiar face looking out—

Turner Boyd. And behind him, dipping his head to see what
Turner's looking at . . . it's the Man, LaPrince.

"Get on in here, dude," the star says, and Tommy hears the auto-
matic locks click to let him in the back.

He's laid off weed for three weeks, expecting a drug screen when
he goes job-hunting, and now the smell hits him like sweet perfume.
LaPrince, a bone pinched between thumb and pointer, says, "You
smoke, dude?"

Warning bells clanging in his head. He hears his wife telling him
he's got a substance-abuse problem. Pictures someone telling him to
pee in a cup, then coming back saying "We were going to hire you,
Mr. Mason, but with these results . . . Sorry."

But these guys will never trust him again if he doesn't join them,
they'll feel like he's got something on them.

Not that he cares about that, not much. He's whiffing the cloud
of smoke and looking at the blunt LaPrince is holding out to him,
LaPrince sputtering "Good boo, dude," choking it down. Next thing
he knows he's holding it, staring at it for a split-second, then sucking
down a world-class hit before passing it up front to Turner (straight-
arrow farm boy!), eager for it to come around again.

Turner hits it, then LaPrince, and it comes back.

What can it hurt? These two can't say anything. And one buzz,
one, shouldn't show up on a test.

The reefer makes one more circuit and things start getting blurry,
wonderfully blurry, the weed hitting extra-hard after the layoff.

*Christ! Sitting in a Lexus Gold in the middle of downtown on
Friday night getting blasted with two Plunder!*

Yeah, and it feels great!

LaPrince up front talking about how he *needs* boo right now, all
the shit coming down on him lately: bullshit in the paper, his half-
brother in town looking for a handout. . . .

But Turner Boyd, lucky to make the team as the last man on the bench—what's he doing here?

LaPrince muttering about his half-brother fucking with him, everybody fucking with him, he *need* some boo.

Tommy, through the haze, recalling LaPrince saying in their interview that he doesn't go near dope or drugs after what happened to his brother. All bullshit, but Tommy can hardly be judgmental now. Floating away. "Crippler," someone's saying, possibly himself.

"No shit," LaPrince is saying. "Bitch of it is, this here's the end of my stash and I ain't got no way to score up here. You know somebody? Me'n Turner-man don't know nobody here, and we can't be taking no chances asking around."

Turner knows it's going to blow up in his face. Knows.
He kept waking up all night, thinking about it, and woke up
for good before seven. It's only eight-thirty now, LaPrince probably
still asleep, but tough titty. Turner picks up the phone.

You sound like some little old lady is what LaPrince was saying
when Turner finally got out of the Lexus around two-thirty this
morning. Well, fuck him. You work your way back to the league,
you don't want to lose it on account of someone else's craziness.

LaPrince picks up after five or six rings: "Yeah?"

"Hey." Turner hesitant, not sure where they stand.

"Yo. Word up, Turner-man?"

"You awake?"

"Waitin' for *'Center* to show the highlights again. Wishin' I had
some funk-doctor. Nothing like gettin' a fade on and watchin' yourself light 'em up, you know what I'm sayin'?"

It's clear he hasn't given another thought to anything Turner said
last night. Why pay any attention to a scrub when you've got a fat
new contract and you just dropped 33 on Karl Malone?

Or maybe he doesn't remember any of it, as messed up as he was
after killbud on top of a few drinks.

"Listen," Turner says. "I keep thinking about last night. Bad
enough you wouldn't wait till we got outta downtown and the man
seen us doing it, but then to ask him to score you some . . . that was
bad, Wheat."

"Damn, Turner-man! Everything cool, awright? I knew the dude's
a doper, the way he talked in the interview when he asked me what
happened in LA. And you saw how he kept grabbin' that fatty. So

why not ask him can he score? He's already smokin' with us, who he gonna tell?"

"Just 'cause he did it with us, you think that means he can't tell?"

"Shee." Like Turner's a fool, a little old lady. "Ain't nothin' gonna happen, awright? So chill, brotha. Everything cool."

"Cool? Sending someone you hardly know to buy you some bud? A reporter?"

"Cool, yeah, what I said. Whassup wit' you, man? Ain't nothin' gonna happen. My boy be glad to get some free bud for his trouble"—LaPrince having promised Mason a quarter-ounce if he scores three bags—"and then how's he gonna say anything? I tell you, just chill. Now, I'll come by for you, what, five o'clock?"

"Naw, I'm taking the truck. I can pick you up or not, either way, but I'm driving myself, make sure I get to bed afterward. We gotta be at the airport at eight tomorrow mornin'."

"Aw, *shee,* Turner-man. Listen, we won't do nothing tonight, promise. Maybe one quick drink but that be it. Anyhow, we sleep on the jet tomorra, we need sleep. This Plunder One, Yuban say it's nicer'n a hotel."

He's trying to make up. Turner hesitates. "You'll remember what you just said? No partying tonight, just straight home? Maybe one drink?"

"I know what I said, Turner-man. So five o'clock, cool?"

If they hadn't had such a good time in LA the year before last, Turner might not have gotten released after the season and had to spend last year in Italy.

Resting on his bed, Turner remembers that first training camp. In the first scrimmage they were matched up against each other— LaPrince the All-American, Turner a free-agent with a prayer—and LaPrince had it all going, busting Turner every which way. But mouthing, too, which Turner wouldn't take from anyone. After one more dunk it was "Y'ain't got nothin' but a white-boy game!"— something like that, and Turner got up in his face telling him he'd be better off sandpapering a bobcat's ass than talking that stuff to Turner Boyd. Surprised him. LaPrince kind of laughed and headed back to the other end. Kept busting him, but no more smarting off. And he came up afterward saying he liked Turner's spunk. His *spunk*—Turner laughed at that. "Pussies don't last in this league," LaPrince said, "but stand up to people the way you do and you can make it, even if y'ain't much of a af-a-lete."

They went to a dark little Mexican restaurant later. When La-Prince tried to get him to drink margaritas Turner said no, he'd stick with beer, and wound up telling about his experience with hard stuff. Moonshine. Turner first tried it at Jimmy Ledbetter's house, out of a Mason jar Jimmy's daddy kept in an old refrigerator in the basement. He liked it, the way it made you shiver and shake and make faces as it went down, but he felt bad the next day, even though people always said the best thing about white liquor was that a man could get drunk as a boiled owl and still feel fine in the morning. Next time he tried it, and the last time, was at Uncle Siler's annual ramps feed the next spring—his junior year at Franklin High, Turner already the top high-school player in the Carolinas and Tennessee (LaPrince laughed at that) and a little full of himself. Before going inside he got a load on out in Stumpy Mashburn's truck, got so numb he barely tasted those ramps that were so hot they left people burning at both ends for three days. Never really knew what led to the trouble, only that he got into it with a big dumb boy from town named Bean, cleaned Bean's plow right quick and wound up outside with Gum as a result, his own daddy—stepdaddy—Gum lecturing and Turner not liking it, sassing Gum back and Gum not liking that, saying "I'll knock you down, son, you keep it up." Turner back-sassing, "That right?" and moving up on him a little, six-eight and 220 already and drunk. Gum said, "Boy, watch yourself," and gave him a little light slap—not much, but enough to make Turner want to pop him. Except that Turner was suddenly doubled over, upchucking ramps and country ham and potatoes and eggs and biscuits with a bunch of people watching. Gum took him home, cleaned him up, kissed him goodnight, and in the morning said "We don't need to ever talk about this no more, son, long as you think you learned something. For one, that ol' liquor don't much agree with you. It especially ain't much good for a boy hopin' to go places, which you can do if you do what you oughtta and don't do what you oughtn't. You leave that liquor to no-'counts like Bean and folks who need a little pickup after one more day workin' themself to the nub."

LaPrince, full of margaritas, got a big kick out of the story. It felt like they were going to be friends, and when LaPrince asked what he did for fun if he didn't drink, Turner said "Well...," and LaPrince waited, and Turner finally said, "Well, corn for white liquor ain't all that grows in them hills."

Hesitated then, thinking better of it, but he'd said enough to prompt LaPrince to tell his own story. How he'd been smoking chronic since grade school, no big deal. Nothing a big deal in the 'hood, he said, until crack came in, and then everyone who wasn't wasting away or getting locked up or killed over it was saying how great it was. Said he tried it when he was twelve or thirteen and still smoked with the gangbangers once in a while even after his brother Tyrell, hooked on it, got shot dead trying to scam a dealer with a phony twenty-dollar bill. Said he quit it the summer he turned sixteen: people all around him were dropping; meanwhile, he was playing ball with some pros and seeing he could make it to the league. Nothing but chronic for LaPrince, he decided, and maybe a little booze.

So they were *compadres,* LaPrince said that night. "You gave up that moonshine, I gave up rock—we just a coupla mellow fellas, smoke a little bud is all."

And they did, that season. And three days after the season ended, Turner was released. Last year in Italy he didn't smoke, didn't even see or hear of any weed, and he led the Spaghetti League in scoring and rebounds. Which got him the offer to play for Portland's summer-league team in Salt Lake City and then come to fall camp, try out, try to make his make-good contract kick in. It's for the minimum, but at least he'd be in the league.

He was in Salt Lake City when he heard Portland had traded for LaPrince—LaPrince having infuriated and disappointed LA—and he wondered what would happen when they got together again.

They got high a couple times during training camp in Salem, on LaPrince's stash, and Turner knew LaPrince was doing it on his own, too, like the two nights he blew off Tommy Mason.

A few days ago, with troubles starting to pile up, LaPrince said maybe they should lay off after they finished his last few morsels, make it a good season. But now Turner realizes the revealing words were the ones he added at the end: "Don't know where to get no more anyhow, up here."

Only three–four days ago? What a week for Turner. Moving into the Residence Inn last weekend after they wrapped up camp in Salem, waiting to see if he'd survive the final cuts. Pretty sure he wouldn't after he stunk it up in the last preseason game on Tuesday out in this little town of Medford, the day LaPrince missed the bus. Puckerman calling him in when they got back on Wednesday— Turner bracing, thinking about another year in the Spaghetti League, but then getting the great news.

Followed by Puckerman's conditions.

At the time they didn't seem like much. Puckerman knew he and LaPrince were friendly and said he wants Turner to let him know anytime LaPrince, the organization's big investment, seems headed for trouble. Well, LaPrince had been saying all the right things about getting his career on track up here. "No problem," Turner said, ecstatic about being back in the league.

Back at the Residence Inn he called home. Gum said he and Momma were finer'n frog hair split three ways, not much new, what's new out there? He was thrilled to hear Turner made it. Now he and Momma could watch him in Atlanta and Charlotte instead of just seeing his picture in those Italian magazines they couldn't read a word of. Turner said he'd be making the league minimum, about half what they paid him in Rome last year, but Gum understood it was worth it to be back in the league, back in the U.S.A.— "and what the heck, son, a quarter-million?" Gum makes twelve dollars an hour working maintenance at the rec park and three or four thousand a year, when all's said and done, off his prize steers. As they say back home, Too poor to paint, too proud to whitewash.

And Gum was too sharp to miss what Turner finally said about Puckerman hoping he'd be a good influence on LaPrince. "Yeah?" he said, and Turner knew it sounded like he'd been hired as a baby-sitter and a snitch.

Turner reassured him, repeating all the good things Puckerman had said about his game and his intangibles, but after they hung up he lay on his bed thinking about it—because even though he hadn't told the part about keeping Puckerman informed, Gum was skeptical.

"I'd like you to let me know," Puckerman had said, "if there's ever anything the organization should know about LaPrince. I'm talking about drinking, about drugs, about what we call unsavory people. You understand me, Turner? Because I'll be honest: we've got some concerns about LaPrince, and we've got a lot of money invested in him. You understand?"

Turner nodded. Not quite sure what he was getting into, except that he was getting back into the league.

Heading up to Mount Hood early Saturday morning, Max glances over at Paige and his eyes stick. She's still half-asleep, staring blankly out her window, but the flawless profile reminds him how great-looking she is—when you see her straight-on, when you see her from any angle. Even now: half-asleep, no makeup, wearing jeans and a sweatshirt.

A few minutes later she's awake and in a great mood, a carryover from last night. She hadn't really wanted to meet them at the Swim, but she was oddly fascinated once she got there and definitely jazzed after slicing and dicing Yuban Taylor. Exceedingly warm in bed later, telling Max he looked better than ever to her—compared to cocky realtors and buffoonish millionaire ballplayers, was what she meant. She didn't mention down-and-out writers who move in with old friends, another good sign.

Now she's talking about the players again. "Not very original, are they? The shaved heads, the earrings, the tacky jewelry, the stupid lines they probably steal from one another."

"No, you wouldn't call them original."

"I asked Tommy about it last night. He said none of them shaved their heads until Magic Jackson shaved his a few years ago, and then—"

"Magic *Johnson*. But he wasn't the one who started it, anyway. Jordan did."

"Until Magic Jordan did, then, and then a bunch of them—"

"*Michael* Jordan. The one who did all the commercials."

"Whoever. Tommy said they all started shaving their heads after this guy shaved his, and they started wearing earrings when he did. And they all wore X caps for a while after Spike Lee's Malcolm X movie came out, even though I doubt very many of those guys know anything about Malcolm X. Lately it's WWJD bracelets, Tommy said—What Would Jesus Do? As if they've got any idea."

"I'm sure those guys don't," Max says. "But to be fair, those were the nitwits that go to places like the Swim and get stewed and act crude. Those are the ones we see. David Robinson, guy plays for San Antone, goes home to his wife and kids, plays piano, gives away millions. A guy named Buck Williams, used to play here—solid citizen, as far as anyone knows. There are good guys in the league, but they're not the ones the public sees. They're not the ones I prosecute."

"What's with the tattoos?" she says. "Tommy said half the players have them, at least. The obnoxious white guy last night—geez, he looked like someone shaved his head with a lawnmower—did you see that snake on his neck? On his neck!"

"Superman logo, Mighty Mouse, gangsta rap, name it. Stuff that might seem just a little bit silly to 'em when they're forty. Then again, maybe not."

She's shaking her head, amazed and amused. "Anyway, last night was enlightening. Sickening, too, but I'm glad you called me."

An hour later they're in bed in the cedar-smelling bedroom in Jerry O'Leary's cabin on Mount Hood. Where it all started, that Saturday back in July. Max had blown the investigation of dirty cop Andy Pink and been demoted from head of Violent Crimes to Intake, normally a stopping-off place for a junior deputy. No clue, at that point, that he'd been sabotaged by the Multnomah County District Attorney, his old friend Dan Tower. O'Leary, the lead investigator in the office and Max's great friend, told him to go on up to the cabin for the weekend, get away, relax. Max was up here brooding, trying to figure it out, when he heard a car out front. . . .

"I think I love you," he tells her now, propped on an elbow looking down into the priceless face.

She smiles. "Think?"

"I do. More than ever after last night. You even talked to Tommy, advised him—"

"I listened, that was all. What do I know about marriage, much less his?"

"Still. Thanks."

... She showed up here that sunny Saturday afternoon in July telling him to buck up, she'd try to help him out of his trouble, but Tower fired him before she could. After she brought the big man down a few weeks later, vindicating Max, he wasn't ready to go right back to the office.

He's still not. It's been fourteen years without a break, the last seven in charge of the Violent Crimes Unit, handling nothing but rapes, assaults, murders, internal police investigations. Maximilian, the so-called million-dollar prosecutor—"Million," Tower always called him—doing great things for the DA's office as months and years passed in a blur, friendships fell by the wayside, two marriages fell apart, his health suffered, his *mental* health was sometimes questionable. Sure, he misses the crime scenes and the big trials and the office politics, misses the succulent guppies in the office falling in love with him (thinning hair or not, the VCU boss is the Man), even misses the intensity of dealing with victims and their families. Sure as hell misses the camaraderie.

But. Fourteen years without a break. Big trials, even if you enjoy parts of them—the spotlight, the three-dimensional chess match with a good defense attorney—are nothing but streetfights in nice clothes, battling shameless defense attorneys who'll do anything and everything in the name of "putting the State through its paces." Defense-oriented judges. Lying witnesses. Juries looking at you, sometimes, like you're talking Swahili.

The puffery from management as they dump more and more on you: *You're the man, Million, the only one we'd trust with this.* On and on.

No, it's nice to step back. It was a dreamy Indian summer—with the bright cool days, and the slanting orange light in the evenings, mindbending sunsets over the Willamette and the West Hills that he watched from his front porch. Paige took a few days off and they drove up to Anacortes and took the ferry out to Orcas Island for three nights, then spent two nights in a great old hotel on the water in Vancouver, B.C. Now rainy season is setting in—the moody fog and mist and drizzle, things he's barely noticed for years. Hot-tub season, with time to loll out there under the apple tree as often and as long as he likes.

Get out of bed when he wants to, even though he automatically wakes up at six-thirty. Read a few novels, rent a few movies, do some crossword puzzles without a pager vibrating on his hip or a cell phone ringing every two minutes. Have a few drinks and watch late-night *SportsCenter* with Tommy, talk about the jocks, especially with Tommy covering the Plunder again for the *Review*. Hell, nice to be up late at night doing anything besides processing a murder scene or cramming for another aggravated murder trial.

Nice to see Paige whenever she's got time, because he didn't have much time for anyone when he was Trial Warrior. Ask his exes, his stepdaughter.

No, he's not staying away *only* to pimp interim DA Mike Johns, who took such pleasure in his downfall but has been begging him to come back—mostly for PR reasons, Max believes—since Paige bailed him out of the mess. There's just no hurry to go back.

Wink's pissed. Outta the joint for ten days now and things look like shit.

Finished another thirty months in Lompoc a week ago last Wednesday. Met his new parole officer in LA Friday, lady saying she expects he learned something from two stretches and he can turn himself around if he wants, still only thirty, plenty of time to have a good upstanding life. Wink—LaMetrius Jefferson to her—promised her that's what he wants.

What's he gonna do? He'd already hooked up with Titan and talked to Red Johnny about going up to Portland. Been thinking about it since summer, when he heard LaPrince got traded again.

Left LA in Titan's Nissan last Saturday morning, a week ago, thinking he'd stay up in Portland if things broke right. If not, he'd be back in LA to check in with the PO bitch next month.

Ain't nothing breaking right here so far—here in Or-e-*gun,* Or-e-*gone,* whatever it is. Wink calls it the sticks. Nice drive up the coast highway last weekend, but Portland's a punk town. Wink left messages with the Plunder PR man all week but LaPrince never called, so they're still crashed in Turtle Eddie's front room with the windows boarded up where drive-bys shattered the glass. Trying to sleep at night while Turtle's hosing his crack whore in back, scrawny thing making noises like she's dying. Crips wannabes stopping by all day, all night, talking big to impress Turtle, talking how they gonna hurt this one Bloods O. G.

It's a joke, Turtle Eddie being the big man up here or anywhere. Wink remembers him as a punk hanging around the O. Gs down home the same way these punks hang around him now, Turtle maybe fourteen at the time. Only been up here a few years. It was ten–twelve years ago when Red Johnny and them decided there was no sense limiting business to LA, not with crackheads and potential crackheads in every city in the great U.S.A. Turtle's twin brother Everett came up first with a few other Harvey Street Bloods and got started—but he was dead within a year, taken out in a turf war with some of the first Bloods that came up. Turtle came later. Now he's the man, and before Wink and Titan left LA, Red Johnny said to tell him Johnny said to treat 'em right.

"This all *bullshit,* you know what I'm sayin'? Johnny say Turtle gonna take care'a us, like Turtle so large and in charge, but I don't see where Turtle's the shit or nothing. Rule this little Rolling Sixties set, maybe, but far as I can see there ain't nobody else give him the time'a day. He ain't gonna help us none."

Titan says, "Depend what you wanna do."

"Stay alive and outta the joint is what I want, and hanging with the Turtle ain't helping my chances, you know what I'm sayin'? I ain't sellin' no rock on no streetcorner to get Turtle fat, and I ain't gonna be no bodyguard for the nigga neither. He what, twenty-six now, twenty-eight? Lucky he lasted this long, and he ain't gonna last much longer he keep playin' shoot-'em-up. These niggas crazy up here, do more shootin' than we ever done at home, and if Turtle keep fucking with people he gonna go down. Only a matter'a when."

"We outta here pretty soon," the little big man says. "Your blood'll help us out or we just go home."

"Fuckin' LaPrince. Muhfuh never helped me before, and now we come up here and leave messages all week and he ain't called. Or you got some idea?" Some idea how to *make* him help. Titan made a few people change their mind over the years. Five-foot-five, come up to your elbow, but all rock—'bout five-five wide, too, tree-trunk arms, break you in half you look at him cross-eyed. Done some shit that people down home still talk about.

Titan just smiles. "Things gonna be fine, Winkadoo. LaPrince prob'ly just been busy, why he ain't called."

"Busy, shit. The team go on the road after this game tonight, so we better see him tonight or we be stuck here."

"Hey, we gonna work things out with him. Prob'ly tonight."

"We better work out gettin' outta this shitty crib one way or other, 'fore these Bloods fucks start thinking we Turtle's boys and smoke *us*. Turtle axin' for it, you know what I'm saying? You hear him talking 'bout kicking this one cat's ass, taking his clothes and sending him out with nothing on? This cat, right this minute, be talkin' to his homeys 'bout cuttin' Turtle's balls off, and anybody's balls that's hangin' 'round the fool. We too old for this shit, man. Waaaay too."

"We gonna be all right, Winkadoo."

"And this parole," Wink says. "I get in any shit, the cops check me out on the computer and that PO bitch have me back in the yard by dinnertime just for coming up here without telling her."

Titan gives him a little shrug, chillin' as ever. "So, we go see your bro at the game tonight, get it straight."

Turtle Eddie gonna take care of 'em, shit. Got one of his wannabes driving them to the Rose Garden, punk with KILLL shaved on the side of his head. Punk talking shit all the way, and not hardly *knowing* the way. Drops them off a few blocks early, it looks like: they can see the big wavy roof on the place but the punk says he don't know how to get them there, all the one-way streets, and he don't want to take a wrong turn and get stopped with a rock in his pocket and his 10-millimeter nickel-plated under the seat.

So they walk. It's dark outside, and raining of course. "Always pissin' up here," Wink mutters—Titan sailing along like it's nothing, but Wink without a jacket pissed off again. Running the tip of his finger down the scar on his neck that feels slick when it gets wet.

"So," Titan says, "you think LaPrince help us out?" Mr. Chill, but wondering about the future just like Wink.

"Who knows? Ain't seen him since before this last stretch. That was his first year in the league, in Sac'to, I went up and seen him. Chilled for three–four days, but then he didn't want me staying in his crib when he went on the road. Cold, I thought, since I didn't have a place, no money, and I wanted to stay outta LA for a while."

"So?"

"So I reminded him I'm his brother and I need some help and he's in the league, number-three pick in the draft, with so many millions. And the nigga got the gump to tell me we *half*-brothers, that's all, and I gotta look out for myself, be responsible. Muhfuh, we live together all his sorry life, I teach him ball, and now when he got a deal for six million I ax for a little help and he pull out his wallet, pull out a roll big as my fist and gimme I think it was two–three hundred."

"Three? For real?"

"Ain't that nothin'?" Wink getting steamed, remembering the fancy condo, the roll, the little speech about *responsibility*.

"Then what? And how 'bout now?" The little big man getting concerned now.

"Ain't talked to him since. Got sent back to the joint pretty soon after that, 'member?"

Still walking, the weird wavy Rose Garden roof still out there over top of some buildings in front of them.

"I don't blame him for me gettin' caught in a man's house, but maybe I wouldn'ta been there if he'da helped me out. For him to give me two–three hundred dollars when he wouldn't miss a grand, a few grand, that ain't right. That's cold. Muhfuh paid Sac'to thousands that year for missing practice, missing the bus, all kinda fucking up. Paid LA a bunch these last two years too, I heard, so I know the money don't bother him or he'd get a 'larm clock."

Titan nodding, stretching his stubby fingers back the way he does.

"Or hire a 'sistant," Wink says, "make sure he get to places on time. Save money, not paying all them fines."

The little big man looks over, must be reading his mind. "What you thinking, Winkadoo?"

"I'm thinking two 'sistants, maybe. Get him where he need to be on time, save him all this trouble and all this coin. Do whatever he need. Watch his crib when he go on the road. Maybe he want a bodyguard like some'a these studs have—we do that too, kick ass when fools start up with him so he don't bust 'em up and get sued. Remember about Barkley? People always starting up with him, then suin' his ass when he th'ow 'em th'u a window."

The little big man nods, sounds good to him. Then gives a quick look and says, "Yeah, but what if he say no, he don't need no assistants?"

"I ain't sure. Depend how he act about it, maybe. I ain't seen him in so long, I don't know."

Titan drops it but Wink is seriously brooding now, remembering. "All I know is that I ain't up here to get in with Turtle Eddie and no bullshit Crips set, sell rock on the corner and wait to get drive-by popped. Don't wanna be nowhere 'round no rock or no rock-heads."

Titan's quiet. Maybe he understands about Wink and rock, even though Wink has never explained.

Wink wants to explain now, with the memories coming to the surface. "You 'member our brother?"

Titan says yes. "I wasn't but fifteen, sixteen, didn't know none'a you then, but I heard."

Wink remembers, like yesterday. Tyrell hooked on the shit and fucking up every which way. Fighting with Moms till she threw him out, then crashing in rock houses or anywhere he could; Moms crying, riding around looking for him an hour after she threw him out, afraid he'd be dead, bringing him home until the next time he got too crazy; Tyrell, one day, ashamed of stealing from her pocketbook, trying to rob the market and almost getting his head blown off. Finally getting blown away for real when he tried to pay his man with a dollar bill with the corners from a twenty pasted on it.

"Dumbfuck lost his mind on the shit," he says.

Titan keeps walking, looking out ahead, the arena a little closer finally.

"But get this," Wink says. "Fucked-up as Tyrell was, LaPrince at least talk about him. We was all half-brothers—different fathers, all of us, and them two no closer'n me and LaPrince was—but LaPrince act like I never existed. Last year I seen a magazine where he talk about his worthless daddy, who never even lived with us, and all about Tyrell, but I wasn't never mentioned."

Titan still quiet, but he finally looks over like he realizes Wink wants him to say something. "I don't know, man. Never met neither of 'em. But come on—you mad 'cause LaPrince didn't talk about you in some magazine? You want him saying 'I got another brother—in the joint, been mostly doing time since I was little'? Maybe he being nice, don't wanna do you like that. I say forget about that, Winkster. You wanna get next to him now, don't be coming at him with no woody, asking why he didn't name you in some magazine."

And Wink knows he's right. Act smart. "You right, man. All right—I'm chillin', like you."

"We get tickets and get inside here in a minute"—the arena finally in front of them—"we talk to the man, things gonna work out."

A udrey's disgusted.

"What's the definition of *worthless*?" Her father, entertaining the other half-smashed grownups around the wet bar in his Rose Garden luxury suite. "A seven-foot black man with a small cock who can't play basketball!"

They all laugh, and Audrey despises him. She despises him anyway, and he keeps giving her reasons.

As usual, these people watched the first half in their own suites, having a few drinks, then came to the VanKirkmans' to watch the rest of the game and get blotto. Audrey usually leaves when they start showing up—watches the second half with their teenagers—but tonight she ordered some food during the second quarter and it was a long time coming and she's still eating.

Her father is Dr. Henry VanKirkman, the "media shrink," whose private practice and endless self-promotion led to a weekly Q-and-A column in the *Oregonian* a few years ago, which led to the call-in show *Dr. Henry Says* on KXL radio, which led to his getting the gig as Channel 2's so-called expert on matters from anorexia to divorce to the minds of serial killers.

Safe in his $90,000-a-year suite high above the Rose Garden floor, he amuses his friends. "You know how you stop five blacks from raping a white girl?" Pause (so polished in his delivery). "Throw 'em a basketball!"

These people actually laugh. The ones who don't . . . well, they don't object, either.

Audrey thinks, *Daddy, if you only knew.*

And thinks, Maybe it's not over between her and the Plunder after all.

Over the summer she decided it was. She'd pushed her luck far enough. Zip Henry and Sammy Dee hadn't used rubbers because she told them it was her safe time, but later she was scared about AIDS, knowing they've got girlfriends everywhere. Besides, she'll never actually let her dad know—God only knows what he'd do—so what's the point?

But after last night, why not go back to men? She skipped the first Plunder game of the season to go to the Wilson High home-coming with the quarterback, a big hero who turned out to be scared to death of a girl, and when she finally took the initiative down in the rec room he didn't even know how to kiss. He seemed shocked when she opened her mouth, so she closed it, and then he spent a half-hour grinding his mouth against hers until her lips hurt and she told him she had to get home. She'd lost all interest in getting laid.

But Plunder guys aren't scared, and they know what to do.

And they're black.

The grownups are still clustered around the bar, mixing more drinks and being entertained by the renowned mental-health expert. "Why did God create the orgasm?" They're laughing even before he delivers the punchline. "So blacks would know when to quit screwing!"

At least he said *blacks*. Must not be drunk enough yet to be himself.

She's got to get out. Take her quesadilla, find the other kids, see if Kay wants to do something later. Saturday night, her dad won't be looking for her. On weekends it's understood he's going to get crocked and she'll get home somehow or spend the night at Kay's or somewhere else.

He doesn't give two shits, basically.

After LaPrince's bust-out game last night, it's no surprise the fans give him the biggest ovation during tonight's introductions. But Turner knows tonight won't go well, LaPrince jangled by the unexpected pregame visit from this half-brother and his sawed-off weightlifter-looking partner. Sure enough, Vinny Baker uses and abuses him from the opening tip, he starts losing heart, and by the end of the first quarter the fans are hooting. "Make an effort, Wheatley!" "Get him out, Colabello, if he don't wanna play!"

Seattle's up by 18 at halftime, and the second half starts the same way. When LaPrince clangs two free throws the fans get on him again and he makes the mistake of gesturing like *OK, bring it on! Bring it!* They get louder, and Colabello pulls him at the next dead ball. Michailovic plays the rest of the third quarter and into the fourth at power forward, and with the game out of reach Turner gets seven minutes of garbage time: two buckets, three rebounds.

A quiet locker room. Reporters asking how a team can look so good one night and so bad the next; no one having much of an answer. LaPrince, after an extra-long shower, trying to ignore them, turning his back and taking his time getting into his three-piece cocoa-colored suit. The chubby PR man he calls Porky Pig stands by looking nervous—wanting him to cooperate, but afraid of getting chewed out.

Tommy Mason's around, although he doesn't have a notepad or tape recorder. The other day he told Turner he hardly ever came to the locker room—no need for postgame quotes like the rest of them, writing for a weekly paper—so Turner figures he dropped by to tell LaPrince whether he scored any weed yet. It looks like he's waiting for a chance, waiting for the reporters to get what they need and move on.

Turner gets into his blue jeans, buttondown and work boots, pulls on his lucky jacket from Italy and waits. When the reporters finally leave LaPrince alone, and Mason says something to him and leaves, Turner walks over. He's sitting in front of his locker looking at a stat sheet. "Wheat, y'all right?"

He looks up, wads up the paper and lofts it into a towel hamper. "Awright, Turner-man, but lookin' to do better. You ready to jam?"

Looking to do better. Meaning get a fade on, or have a few drinks if Mason hasn't scored yet, something.

Turner doesn't need this. Should have driven himself tonight, he knew it, so he could go back to the Residence Inn now, get to bed, be ready to go on the road in the morning.

But he fell for the Wheatley sweet-talk, and now they're pulling out in the Lexus behind Yuban's LOVEME license plates, LaPrince saying "We gon' stop for a pop at this place Yuban say got some kinda special Spanish drink. My boy Mason got the boo and gonna meet us there. We have one drink and get it from him and jam out. Cool?"

Too late now.

"I can use that funk-doctor," LaPrince adds, looking all bothered. "For real, with these niggas showin' up."

He says his half-brother was the regular-looking one. "Name LaMetrius, dude been callin' Porky Pig all week tryin' to get me." Turner remembers a long ugly scar down one side of his neck, but the guy was normal size and definitely regular-looking compared to the other one, the sawed-off, pumped-up weightlifter type with cold eyes in a little angel face, wearing a heavy coat over baggy cutoff jeans that went way below his knees, more like long pants than shorts. The two of them showing up under the basket before the game, LaPrince uneasy, his half-brother talking to him while the Plunder ran layup lines, the little one just watching with those cold eyes in the little head. LaPrince coming back to warmups rattled, Turner could tell.

"He just outta the joint again," LaPrince says. "Last time he got out, I was in Sacramento and he showed up there, asking could I help him out with some cash. Then pissed off I didn't give him enough. Pissed off I didn't want him stayin' at my place when we had a road trip. Sheeit. Few months later he back inside. Now he get out and come up here, bring this freak Titan with him. People in LA scared to death'a the dude, people that ain't scared'a nothing. Built like a tank—you seen him—and he never say a word, then just go *off*. Fight like a muhfucker. I heard'a two bangers went looking for him one time, gonna fuck him up. They show up, he grab a tire iron, they ready to turn around, go home. But the Titan *want* the fools. Toss 'em the iron and tell 'em, 'Come on, but you gonna need this here.' Fools drop that iron and scram."

They follow LOVEME across one of the bridges over the river, toward a million downtown lights. LaPrince quiet, fretting. Turner finally asks him what the two said tonight, what they wanted.

"Sheeit. Say they wanna help me. I don't know what they talkin' 'bout. Like I need somebody take out the trash? Clean up? Bodyguard me? *Shee*eit. LaMetrius mad 'cause I ain't called back when he left his number with Porky. I told him I been busy, I'll call him when I can. He say, 'We s'poseda sit around spankin' off till you can make one call? And ain't the team taking a trip now? We s'poseda wait another week?' The Titan standing there with his look, don't say two words. Prob'ly got a piece in that big coat, shoot me right there."

"He's done time too, the Titan?"

"Caved in some Blood punk's head with a pipe and somebody snitched him off, yeah."

Turner thinking, Lordy, and flashing back to childhood in Macon County, where the crime report in the *Franklin Press* consisted of someone running a red light and maybe someone throwing a rec-park garbage can into the Little Tennessee, behind the softball field.

"How about your brother, wha'd he do? And what's his name again, La-what?"

"*Half*-brother, man. La-*me*-trius. Wink, his boys call him. First time, he do two years for trying some dumb stickup in the mini-mart with a knife. Get out, show up in Sacramento. Then went back home, I guess, after I wouldn't set him up, start this same bullshit he used to do—creepin', they call it. Sneak in people's houses, rip 'em off. Creep right in the room when they sleepin' sometimes. Fool told me one time how he like to creep right up to 'em in the bed, and when they wake up they be so scared they be tellin' him 'Take this! this! that! And the money's in the drawer under the rubbers!' Nigga didn't just want their shit—he get off on freakin' 'em out."

They're downtown now, trailing Yuban slowly around the same crowded block a second time, looking for parking.

"Lucky he didn't get his shit blown away," LaPrince says, "when this one dude hear him and get a shotgun out. But that time put him back in the slam till now. Now he get out and show up here with his hand out again."

Finally they follow Yuban into a 24-hour parking lot. LaPrince kills the engine but doesn't move to get out.

"Fuckin' punk all he is, is why I don't say nothin' 'bout his sorry ass. Why I didn't tell Mason 'bout him for that story. Never tell no reporter 'bout him."

"But you told about what's-his-name, the other one—Tyrell?— about him getting killed over that crack cocaine."

"Tha's different. It's all about how people gonna look at you, think about you. You tell 'em you never saw your daddy till somebody say, 'There, noddin' out on that stoop,' people say 'Tha's awful. Sad.' You say you had a brother got off into the rock and got killed, the same: 'Too sad.' But you tell about a punk like this, fuckin' *creeper,* they think you nothing but a nigger, come up from bad people. So . . . I never hardly knew this chump, he never did shit for me, but now he always come around wantin' something—fuck him."

"But you told him you'll call?"

"Told him after the trip. A week."

"You gonna?"

"Don't know, man. What I'm gonna say, 'I don't need no helpers?' I don't wanna have nothing to do with the fool. He prob'ly on parole anyway, s'poseda stay home. They find him with me, I prob'ly go down for something like what-they-call-it, hidin' a foojitive or some shit."

Turner wishes he hadn't heard anything he just heard.

11

It's one in the morning, maybe one-thirty, when things get crazy at Rod Yardley's.

Who'd have expected this? All Yardley wanted after last night was a little fun, no hassles. Last night was a disaster: the jocks being jerks at the Swim; the dipshit writer, Mason, cutting him off every time he started getting somewhere with the dishy lawyer; Mark Mona sneezing a gram of coke off the desktop; LaPrince's chippie from the Swim hanging around till 2 A.M., LaPrince never showing up.

And worst of all, no sign of Little Bang, making Yardley think she might not be on the scene at all this season.

So this afternoon he talks to Yuban and they agree to meet at Huber's for a Spanish coffee after the game, then maybe come out to the house and do a line or two. But when Yuban walks into the bar he's got LaPrince with him, and the bumpkin Turner Boyd, and the dipshit writer, who seems to be getting a hell of a lot of mileage out of one suckup story.

At least LaPrince is quiet after his sorry game and doesn't start getting rude with women, which would get even a Plunder thrown out of Huber's. On the other hand, he ignores their warnings and sucks down two Spannies in a half-hour.

Yardley's wondering about Little Bang—will he ever see her again, the nimble little minx?—at the very moment his pager vibrates and flashes a number he can't identify. At a phone in the lobby he punches it in, expecting some client or maybe a referral, and he's thrilled and chilled when the youthful voice says "Hi, it's Daisy"—her cute little alias. "This is Rod," he says, and even though she asks how he's doing and makes nice he knows she's still not interested, never will be.

"You guys partying?" she asks after a minute of chitchat.

"We're at Huber's. Yuban's here"—who had her for a while—"and LaPrince Wheatley and Turner Boyd."

"LaPrince Wheatley's there?"

She waits for an answer, and he's got to confess. "Yeah, he is. Not very happy after the night he had, and he won't be upright for long if he keeps pounding Spanish coffees, but he's here." Hardly caring, suddenly, whether she comes down or not, if he'll have to watch LaPrince score the prize simply for being LaPrince. No, not even for being LaPrince—for being a player.

"Do you have plans afterward?"

"Nothing for sure. Have a drink or two, take it from there. You want to come down?"

"I don't drink, remember? And I can't stand the smoke in bars. Think you'll be partying at your house later?"

"Maybe. Probably." But he's visualizing her: the most mouthwatering thing he's ever seen. Wanting to lay eyes on her, even if he doesn't have a chance of laying his hands on her.

OK, she says, she'll call him a little later to see what's happening.

Back in the bar, the drinks are working on LaPrince. He's forgotten Vin Baker and his abysmal game; he wants to know if Yardley knows any of the Plunder Dancers. "Couple of 'em I saw tonight, I'd like to get me some'a that leg."

Yardley doesn't know any of them. They're not allowed to date the players anyway; they can get fired.

"Maybe I can make it worthwhile to 'em," LaPrince says with the beginning of a slur, "they make it worthwhile to LaPrince."

"Whatever, but I can't help you there." And then, inexplicably, "But I know a hot young thing who might like to meet you. Tonight."

LaPrince's glazed eyes come to life, or something like it. "Who you talkin' 'bout?"

"Calls herself Daisy, which I'm pretty sure is bullshit. Yuban knows her."

Yuban looks up. "Daisy? Shit. Little Bang. She coming down?"

"Not down here, but she wanted to know if we're going out to the house after."

"You get a chance, you wanna jump her," Yuban advises La-Prince. "She rock ya, little college girl with legs up to her ass and titties all there."

Yardley's sick, remembering how she rocked Yuban on the tape he's watched more than any other.

Now Yuban gets a call on his cell phone, the girl from last night at the Swim—who must have rocked him pretty good, too, to get his cell number, though Yardley hasn't watched the tape. Yuban tells her yeah, he thinks they're heading out to his man Rod's house again in a little while, does she remember how to get there? She does, apparently, and Yuban tells her they're having one more round and they'll be there by midnight.

One more round: a second Spanish for Yardley, a third for Yuban and the dipshit writer, a dangerous fourth for LaPrince. Another microbrew for the bumpkin, Turner Boyd.

Yardley doesn't want the dipshit Mason coming to the house, but what can he say? He's with LaPrince, and Yardley's hoping to sell LaPrince this place in Kings Heights, almost $2 million. How many times, how many goddamn times has he ended up with a houseful of unwanteds drinking his booze and doing his drugs and screwing all over the place?

It's the price you pay for being realtor to the stars.

Five years now since his first Plunder sale. Nine in all, $1.6 million average, making him Tri-County's top agent at age thirty-three. The jocks can be arrogant, petulant, inconsiderate, unrealistic—expecting you to give them LA in Portland, or the East Coast on the West Coast, or country life in the city—but then again, one player leads him to another, a nice easy pipeline. All he has to do is put up with getting blown off once in a while, swallow the occasional insult in front of pretty girls, pay the bar tab when the players decide he should, score them some herb or toot or poppers every so often, let them party at his house.

And none of that's so bad. You're out on the town with them. You get some girls—the leftovers, of course, who fuck the daylights out of you hoping you'll put in a good word. It could be worse.

They're out at the house, starting to get happy—the players, the writer, Yuban's tart from last night, Yardley's starfucker friend

Kathy Densen—when the doorbell rings. His heart's going pitter-pat on the way to open the door, and when he does, yes! it's her, along with the same heavy, shapeless friend who always came with her, called herself Suzie Q (as if anyone cared).

It's a jolt, seeing her. She's wearing tight faded jeans and the same oversized OSU letterman's jacket she always wore, probably a present from the star quarterback. Same thick blond hair parted in the middle. The dimples. The *mouth*. ("Little Bang, she got that little rabbity mouf," Sammy Dee raved last winter. "Suck on your thumb till you 'bout to cry, then give you a *nasty* knob job.") The big white teeth when she smiles. . . . Smiling now, almost as if she's glad to see him! ·

And the ass—Jesus God!—as he points them toward the library and follows.

"Missed you last night," he says, hoping his voice doesn't sound as trembly as he feels. "Thought you'd make the first game. Your family still have a luxury box?"

"Yeah, but I had things to do in Corvallis and couldn't come up till today."

"How's school?"

"Not bad."

"I forget what you said your major is." As if he cares. As if it matters, when you look like she does.

Thinking, Why don't you wise up and quit giving it away to dumb jocks and let me buy you everything you ever wanted and fuck fuck fuck fuck fuck you for the rest of our lives, or at least until you put on twenty pounds?

"You said LaPrince Wheatley was coming over?"

Ouch. It's like the night last season when too much booze or dope gave him the illusion that he might have a chance with her, and he put an arm around her down in the karaoke room—casual, sort of, as if they were all just having fun and feeling good about each other—and she gave him the astonished look and squirmed away saying "I don't *think* so," a swift kick in the nuts. He could have died and would have told her to get lost except that Fleet Mays, the luckiest man in the world at the time, might have flattened him.

But what can he do? "Everyone's in here," he says.

In the library, where they're snorting lines off a mirror on his big antique desk, she says hi to Kathy and to Yuban, her first Plunder lover, and Yardley introduces her to the rest. LaPrince realizes she's the one Yardley mentioned at Huber's and he's interested it's clear. Yardley's sick. Then, properly buzzed after two lines, she asks if he's added anything to "playland." Not since you were here last spring, he says, but she wants to go downstairs anyway. He feels like a dirty old man walking behind her, fantasizing. Glad her dull friend is with them, or he might try something stupid again.

Downstairs she pops her head in the various doors as if to make sure everything's still here: pool table, video games, videotape equipment, karaoke, sauna, electronic putting green. But doesn't want to do anything, probably too antsy from the toot to focus.

But upstairs, LaPrince and Mason are stepping out the kitchen door, and when they reappear two minutes later—Yardley mixing drinks at the counter—it's clear why LaPrince invited the guy. LaPrince has two fat bags of herbs in one hand, one in the other. Asking Yardley, "You got someplace I can leave this so I ain't gotta drive home with it all tonight, shape I'm gettin' in? How 'bout I take a little for the road trip and pick up the rest when we back?" Mason gives him a look and he adds, "Oh yeah, you got a extra Baggie? Wha'd I say," he asks Mason, "a quarter?" Finder's fee.

The gracious host fetches him a Baggie, then goes and gets some papers out of the hand-carved paraphernalia box in the library. Returning, he tells LaPrince yes, he'll hold the herb for him, and for now he puts it in the back of the refrigerator, behind some leftover takeout from Hung Fung.

When he looks up after getting the drinks poured, LaPrince is expelling a thick cloud of smoke and handing him a soft, misshapen joint. Yardley takes a hit, says that's plenty, hands it to Dipshit—things already getting blurry, after a cocaine Saturday and a couple of Spannies at Huber's.

Time for bed, past time, but he won't get there for a while yet. Kathy Densen realized she wasn't going to get lucky and went home, but Suzie Q's still here, and Yuban and his trampy thing have just come back downstairs, and LaPrince is upstairs with Little Bang, and Turner Boyd and Mason are around somewhere. Nothing to do but another line.

He's dicing it up on the desk when someone out in the hall yells.

"Ka-a-a-ay!"

Suzie Q—Kay?—looks toward the door, alarmed. Looks at Yardley. He shrugs. She looks at Yuban and his girlie, who have their eyes on the blow and seem not to have heard or not to care.

She starts for the door.

"Bring her in here," the gracious host says. "Tell her I've got one for her." And goes on laying them out.

Then hears the front door slam and looks up. Even Yuban looks up.

Yardley gets up and goes out into the hall, where he finds Turner Boyd and Mason looking at each other, baffled. Asks them what's going on, even though it's obvious they don't know. "Where's LaPrince?"

They follow him back into the library—even Turner Boyd, the straight-arrow who doesn't want to be around cocaine, according to LaPrince.

Well, what the hell. Yuban and his dolly are waiting for their nightcap. The host is ready too—maybe it will give him the energy to chase them all out, send them home. He'd rather not waste any more on Mason, but he's standing there.

And now LaPrince appears. Bleary, fucked up, wobbling in the doorway behind the desk in nothing but bright red Mickey Mouse boxers. Dumb.

Yardley asks him, "Where's your girl?"

"Bitch gone," he mutters. "Fuck 'n' run." Spotting the treats on the desk, says, "Some'a that for me?"

Oh well. "Yeah, step on up here."

He inhales a line through the worn hundred-dollar bill and sags into the leather chair in front of the bookshelves—"ahhhhhhhh"—and Yardley, as always, chases away thoughts of Len Bias, the mid-eighties Maryland star who keeled over dead with a coke-induced heart attack the night the Celtics drafted him Number One.

Yuban and his honey step up. Mason, the dink, is over by the bookshelves talking to LaPrince, something about "the girl." Who she was, how old she was. . . .

The host lays out a fat line for himself. It seems only right.

Suddenly LaPrince is upset, getting loud, and Yardley looks up and sees him on his feet. "The *fuck* you sayin', honky *bitch*? Nobody *ast* you!"

"I just wondered—"

"Well fuck you and your wonderin', *fuck* you! Y'ain't nothin' but a muhfuckin' nobody hangin' around wantin' somethin' like every other muhfucker! Just *hangin'* around!" Mason keeps quiet, LaPrince looming over him, but LaPrince can't stop. "What the *fuck* you doin' here anyway?"

"You invited me, remem—"

"What the fuck?" LaPrince bellows, then turns on Yardley: "What the fuck this bitch doin' here? The fuck you bring him here for?"

"Uhhhh—"

"He your friend?"

Jesus. "Mine? I never saw him before last night"—up out of his swivel chair now, backing off as LaPrince comes toward him—"and *I* think he's a flaming asshole. I didn't invite him."

Which points the raging LaPrince back at Mason, even as Yuban tries to step in. "Just another fuckin' punk *wantin'* somethin'!" he roars. "Want a story, wanna hang out, want some boo for nothin'. . . ."

Now Turner Boyd steps in with a thick forearm across LaPrince's chest, slowing him, but LaPrince's bloodshot eyes are still boring into Mason.

Mason's gawking at him, looking scared and amazed and pissed off all at once. "I? Want?" he says. "What the hell do I want from you? I give you a break, write you up saying you're not an asshole, and you invite me out for a drink and then ask me to get you some dope . . . and now you say *I* want something? What the fuck're you talking about?"

At which point LaPrince shoves Boyd's arm aside, and Mason's not backing up quite fast enough and a huge meaty backhand thumps him—*whomp*—in the middle of the chest.

Everything stops, everyone in the room astonished as Mason reels back against the bookshelves. When he regains his balance he stands there—gawking at LaPrince . . . at Yardley . . . back at LaPrince . . . at Yuban, and Yuban's doll with her mouth hanging open . . . at Turner Boyd—stopping finally on LaPrince again, in disbelief.

It's a still-life, except for Mason's head still moving slowly around.

He looks around once more, looking at one, then another—lingering on Yardley, it seems to Yardley—and finally nods his head as if to say yeah, OK, he's got something on them all now. And walks out.

A moment later the front door slams again, and they look at each other . . . Yardley wondering what happened to Little Bang, and why the Plunder's newest zillionaire is standing there in Mickey Mouse boxers looking fucked up, and how it came to this.

Tommy's up until four-thirty in the morning, lying around his upstairs "suite" at Max's house smoking the blessed weed (praise Wheatley for that) and channel-surfing as he replays the scene in his head. Replaying the whole night, everything he can remember, but going over and over the last moments in the jerkoff realtor's library. It's a good thing he's got the weed to settle him down a little, otherwise he might drive out and burn down the jerkoff's mansion and then call Bob Puckerman about Wheatley.

He finally conks out, drifting off thinking about Julie, wanting her back more than ever. Can't she see? Won't she? If she'll take him back he'll gladly give it all up, not only dope and drink but also this fantasy of making it as a writer, as anything more than a hack on a third-rate weekly rag in Chickentown. Give up the struggle, get a job and be content to make an adult life with a good woman. Can't she tell from his letters that he's seen the light?

Sunday afternoon he drives out to see his great friend Martell, who always manages to make him feel better—but today it only makes things worse, walking into the happy menagerie with Mary Grace baking, Iris coming in grass-stained from soccer, Anna Banana fingerpainting, the big dog and the little dog and the cat hanging around. Martell says the novel is gonna sell, your agent said it might take awhile, and in the meantime we'll have some quality sportswriting around here; and one of these days Julie will be ready to talk, and she'll see you're different and you'll be back home. Things are gonna be fine. They eat lunch, leftover pasta and salad out of the jam-packed refrigerator, and then Grace walks him out to see the gardens. . . .

He leaves feeling a wee bit better, but he's not even back to the Burlingame intersection before reality comes crashing down again. His novel will never see the light of day, he's reduced to covering jocks again for an embarrassing weekly rag he swore he'd never go back to, and Julie's silence is thunderous. He needs to get out of Max's house, but he needs a job before he can afford even a cheesy apartment and he's got no idea what to do; besides, everyone wants you to pee in a cup these days and he just sat up smoking dope all night after three weeks off it, just when he was probably clean.

He turns right on Taylor's Ferry, headed back to Max's, and sails down the hill toward Macadam. Which reminds him of last night—the caravan from Huber's to the estate in ritzy Dunthorpe—and he's pissed off all over again, recalling the prettyboy saying "He's no friend of mine. I didn't invite him over here. I think he's a fucking asshole."

He hits Macadam and continues on to what he believes is the right street, hangs a left and drops down into the ritzy neighborhood. Another left, a quick right, down a little way and yeah, there it is on the left, the brick wall and the gates and the big white house way back in the yard, the driveway circling around back. No sign of the creampuff's cream-colored Mercedes, but it's probably in back where they all parked last night.

What are you doing, for Christ's sake? What are you gonna say?

He pulls the old red Civic off to the right. Locks up, crosses the road and enters Yardley's spread through a wrought-iron door next to the big gates. Up the long driveway, then up a flagstone walk to the front porch. Rings the bell.

No answer. Rings again, hears the chimes inside, but no Yardley.

Walks around back, past the pool and barbecue pit and playground, but there's no sign of anyone. No Mercedes.

Opens the door to the screen porch where they went in last night. Past the cedar picnic table and the padded chairs to the kitchen door where they went into the house. Tries to see in through the filmy curtain on the other side of the glass. No light on, no sign of the guy.

So come back later. Better yet, get over it.

But he's suddenly thinking, crazily, about three bags of killer dope

in the refrigerator, three ounces minus his quarter and the little bit
Wheatley took for the road trip.

He touches the shiny brass doorknob. It turns.

He walks back out of the screen porch, back around front, and
rings again. Waits. Nothing.

He could sell two and three-quarter ounces for a thousand bucks
and be set for a while—or two for eight hundred and keep enough
for a while—and enjoy the thought of Wheatley breaking the jerkoff
in half. *Where my boo at, honky bitch?*

Walks around back again, on shaky legs. Looks around and realizes no one can see him, with the houses on either side so far away
and huge old trees blocking the view.

You're nuts!

But there's no one here, and even if the pansy shows up, what
can he do? Call the cops about a guy stealing the dope he's holding
for LaPrince Wheatley?

He turns the knob again and opens the door a few inches, peers
inside. Nothing. Opens it a little more.

And now he's inside, standing in Yardley's spacious snow-white
kitchen.

*If you get caught, you say you thought you left your jacket here
last night; you came by to find out; he wasn't here. He won't buy
it, but what's he gonna do?*

A few strides over to the big top-of-the-line refrigerator. . . .

It's not here! Nothing but some beer and mixers and Chinese
takeout cartons and a few jars on the door, mayo and mustard and
pickles. It's not in the vegetable drawer, not up in the freezer.

So get out!

But he flashes on something he read somewhere, about how most
people keep valuables as close as possible, usually in the bedroom.
And he finds himself on the buffed parquet floor out in the big front
hall: lithographs on the wall, a leaded-glass dragonfly lamp on an
antique-looking table. He skips up the winding staircase, looking
both ways when he gets to the top and deciding to go to the left,
more doors down there. Glances into each room: a bathroom, a
small undisturbed bedroom that can't be the master, a little TV
room with a door out to a big second-story deck, a bigger bathroom—and finally this open door at the end, yeah, which will be
the master bedroom.

It's vast. One end is a living-room setup with a long couch, a loveseat, a deep soft chair and a gleaming antique secretary all arranged around a Persian rug, vases and decorative shit everywhere. At the other end, facing a big-screen TV, is a king-size bed with a blue satin comforter and lots of pillows. Nightstand, dresser. Filmy curtains over a row of windows facing the backyard, a door out to the deck, a hot tub out there. This jerkoff living like a sheikh, for selling houses to jocks!

Where to start looking?

Nothing in the top dresser drawers but some change, nail clippers, Mentholatum, pocketknife, stamps, an empty wallet and a little stainless-steel coke spoon. Tommy whips through the rest of the drawers, sweeping his hands through socks and underwear, T-shirts and sweatshirts and jeans, sniffing for the telltale smell. Nothing.

Feels behind the TV. Checks the nightstand drawer and the cabinet underneath. Opens the door to a walk-in closet as big as any studio apartment he ever lived in, full of clothes and coats and shoes, and understands the futility of the search. The closet alone is too much to search in a half-hour—the stuff could be in any pocket, any shoe—let alone the bedroom, let alone the whole house. And he *is* nuts if he stays here two more minutes.

LaPrince probably took the stuff home after all. He was stupid enough to sit in his car on Second Avenue getting loaded on Friday night, why would he worry about driving home with a couple of bags Saturday night?

He hears something outside and freezes. Now a car door slams, to his horror, and he looks out through the gauzy curtains and sees the pretty-boy blond hair Yardley coming from the Mercedes toward the back door.

Do what? Hide in the closet in that guestroom back down the hall, try to slip out after he's asleep?

But he hears the kitchen door and now he doesn't dare step out into the hall. If the guy comes straight upstairs he'll be here in a matter of seconds.

Move!

This walk-in closet? You'll be trapped in there, then it's only a matter of time. Under the bed? Get serious.

He runs to daylight. The door out to the deck. Shaky legs carry him across deep-blue deep-pile carpeting and he turns the knob and suddenly he's out in the air, out of the trap. *Christ!* He'll get out after all and never do anything so stupid again. Find the stairs down from here.

His head swivels around and the panic rises again. The deck is enclosed, all the way around.

You can't just stand here—he might be on his way up! Go somewhere, anywhere!

It's too high to jump, which pretty much ends his panicky process of elimination. There's nothing to do but get out of plain sight: tiptoe to the farthest window and lie down underneath it with his back pressed against the wall, giving the guy the fewest possible angles to see him if he looks out.

If he *comes* out, it's over.

Driving back down the long dirt road to quaint little Mount Hood Market on Saturday afternoon like they did that Saturday back in July, buying chicken and salad fixings and wine like before. Getting back and cranking up a fire in the stone barbecue Max helped O'Leary put in four or five years ago. Going to bed again while the coals burned through.

A late-night walk down to the creek—no moon this time, but just as romantic with the wood-smoky air and the spray coming off the flat rock. A relaxing Sunday: screwing, reading, walking in the damp autumn woods, making Paige's "Frank Sinatra pasta" for dinner.

And Max's favorite moment of all, Monday morning: Paige bursting out laughing, out of nowhere, as they lay there afterward, laughing so hard she couldn't even say what was so damned hilarious, tears in her eyes. So hysterical that Max got caught up in it, the two of them howling like a couple of idiots. Paige trying to stop. "C-c-c—" Trying to say it, whatever it was, and finally blurting "*C-cows!*"—and Max understood, and he was happy she was happy, even though the joke was on him. Recalling the sunny afternoon on Orcas Island last month when they got off their bikes and got naked in that seemingly deserted pasture—a breakthrough for proper Miss Prescott—Paige suddenly going rigid beneath him, gawking over his shoulder, Max glancing back and seeing two goddamn cows who'd materialized from somewhere and watched him hump away for however long. "Ha-*haaa!* You jumped up like you thought they were going to charge or something! God! The sight of you standing there with this look on your face, with your thing sticking out, grabbing your clothes and saying 'Let's get outta here'—oh, Lord!"

*   *   *

But now she's the bitch again, the bane of even a former prosecutor. Driving down the mountain Monday afternoon she gets quiet and Max knows she's thinking about the motions she and her sleazy co-counsel will start making tomorrow on behalf of Donald Royer. Sure enough, she finally asks him what he thinks Judge Keys will say about their position that no evidence from inside Royer's house should be admitted at trial because the cops didn't have a warrant the first time they went in.

This case makes Max wish he'd gone back to work before the incident, because he'd probably be on it instead of Charlie Witty. He knows this bullshit comes from Lou Pennington, Paige's co-counsel, but at this point it's hard to separate the two of them. In court she's got to take up his arguments as if she believes them.

And it sounds like she's convinced herself. It's a shame we had to lose a good police officer over marijuana, she says, but—

Now she's got him started. "We lost a good cop," he snaps, "because of a sociopathic asshole protecting his grow operation with semiautomatic weapons. This wasn't a harmless old hippie in a time warp, as Pennington keeps telling the press, growing a plant or two for his personal use. I *know* some old hippies, and harmless old hippies don't have sixty plants and sophisticated countersurveillance equipment and that kind of weaponry. It's an insult to old hippies to compare Donald Royer to 'em, a pure killer who's lower than dirt."

"He's a human being, Max."

"No he's not. And we both know it's bullshit to blame this on the cops for using knock-and-talks"—going to the door where they suspect a grow operation instead of going straight to a judge for a search warrant—"so please don't spoil our nice weekend by getting on a misguided high-horse like all these moronic editorialists and ACLU breastbeaters who've been sounding off. Please. If you can make this moronic argument, how can you get mad when I say you're a used-car salesman like the rest of us?"

Guaranteed to get *her* hot. Max wondering, again, how this can ever work, the true-believer public defender and the (former) "prosecutor's prosecutor." He's been out of the office since they got together, and he's made a point of not talking about crime and punishment, but now a cop he worked with is dead and she's defending the murderer—the lines are drawn again.

"*You* might be a used-car salesman," she says coldly, "but speak for yourself."

"Come off it. You've admitted you are too, you just frame it a little more elegantly. Let's see, I think I've almost memorized it: 'My challenge as a defense attorney is to work with people everyone else defines by the crime they've allegedly committed. To get to know them and figure out how to make them human beings to people who don't want to see them as human beings.' Meaning jurors, right? Your customers? 'There's so much more to a person than any one thing, even a crime. There's a whole life behind that crime.' Isn't that it? Something like that?"

Nothing from her. He doesn't look over, but he knows the hard face is back, the one that made Witty say she *would've* been good-looking if only she weren't Paige Prescott.

He can't stop. "Trying to make a jury see this piece of garbage as anything other than a piece of garbage is the same as a used-car salesman trying to make someone see a lemon as something other than a lemon, right?"

Nothing . . . for a moment, and then: "Max?"

He looks over, thinking maybe he's finally getting through. Who could argue with that logic?

"Fuck you," she says.

And Max finds himself smiling, because he's been encouraging her to lose the prim edge she's maintained even through eight years of representing inhuman beings. "I'm right, then," he says, "if that's your best answer. The DA's trying to sell a case that probably has some holes in it, like every case does, and you're trying to sell an inhuman being like Royer as human. Which is like trying to sell a 'sixty-eight Chevy van with the transmission falling out."

Which is exactly what she tries to do. She won't go as far as a lot of defense attorneys, but it's the same thing. Which she knows damn well, deep down.

Doesn't she? He's still not absolutely sure she doesn't believe all that tripe about how she's just standing up for society's victims against the rigid, oppressive empire.

But now she's not talking.

Great. She's obviously thinking the worst of him, seeing him again as the guy she referred to, icily, as *Mr. Travis* all those years, not only in court or in chambers but even when they'd bump into each other on the street. He's certainly recalling the Miss Prescott he disliked, who defended the scum of the earth as if they were saints and stood by them even after juries told her no, they're scum and don't belong on the streets. The Miss Prescott who embraced Judge Brubaker's ridiculous Victims–Offenders Rehabilitation Program. *Would you like to make friends with Mr. So-and-so, the man who raped you at knifepoint?* The most preposterous thing in the world to a prosecutor who spent years dealing with people who'd been raped, shot, stabbed, beaten, whatever.

"Am I right?" he says. "You're a used-car salesman like the rest of us?" Fuck her, if she's going to get stupid on him.

Nothing.

"Talk to me, Paige." Refraining from calling her Miss Prescott, though it's on the tip of his tongue.

"I don't see any point."

Somebody said be careful what you wish for, you might get it. Well, Turner wished to get back in the league—and did, except LaPrince was part of the deal.

Turner didn't say a word to him on the ride back to the Residence Inn at 2 A.M. Sunday, after the crazy, scary end of the real-estate man's party. He'd been ticked off ever since LaPrince drove them out to the guy's house after promising he'd take Turner back to the hotel after one drink downtown.

He didn't like so many people knowing he'd been in a house where people, including teammates, were smoking bud and sniffing cocaine.

He didn't like thinking about what might have happened between LaPrince and that girl upstairs, to make her take off the way she did.

And the way it all ended. Everybody in the guy's office after the girl and her friend left—all but Turner sniffing cocaine—and La-Prince in his shorts, messed up and getting out of hand with Tommy Mason.

All Turner said when LaPrince dropped him off was "I'll get myself to the airport," talking about the 8 A.M. takeoff on Plunder One. He didn't want to pick LaPrince up and sure as shit wouldn't count on LaPrince coming for him on time, or at all.

LaPrince did make the plane, a minute before eight, wearing shades to hide his eyes but looking so wasted anyway that even Turner could feel his headache. He acted like he didn't see Turner, and he probably didn't. When Turner woke up from a nap halfway to Indianapolis and walked to the bathroom, he was sprawled on a couch with his mouth hanging open, dead to the world and even to the dogass rap music on his Walkman. Turner thinking, The dummy's going to blow his career, find himself back in the 'hood wondering what happened, he used to be slick as a ribbon.

LaPrince played fair Monday night in Indy—but only fair, and Indy soft as mush inside. In Cleveland Tuesday night he was less than fair, looking bored with Cleveland's slowdown game or maybe just sluggish from getting high. Turner didn't know what he was doing in his free time. They were barely talking, Portland to Indy to Cleveland to Detroit.

Puckerman shows up at shootaround in Detroit, not happy about three losses in a row since opening night. Back at the hotel afterward there's a message for Turner to call him. They meet in the coffee shop, and it's not Turner's 2.5 garbage-time scoring average the boss is concerned about; it's LaPrince's weak 11.5 (on 30-percent shooting), six rebounds, and lackluster defense in prime time.

Is LaPrince all right, as far as Turner knows? Meaning, *I expect you to tell me everything.*

"Far as I know."

"Getting his rest?" *You want to stay in this league?*

"Far as I know."

"Anything bothering him, that you know of?" *A long way to Italy, son, and an even longer way back to the league.*

"Nothing I know about, no sir."

"You spending much time with him, Turner?"

"Not much, no sir." Easy to be truthful on that one.

Puckerman doesn't press him, but Turner doesn't like any of it. He knows he needs to talk to LaPrince if he can figure out how because, like it or not, his immediate *and* long-term future is tied up with the goof.

They nearly bump into each other right then, two minutes after Puckerman finishes with him, LaPrince coming around the corner from the lobby as Turner comes out of the gift shop with *NASCAR Monthly*, ready to go upstairs and drift into a nap before the bus to the arena. Face-to-face after a few days of uneasy looks and flat-out ignoring each other.

But LaPrince feels loose or at least fakes it behind his shades, asking "Whassup, Turner-man?" Like everything's normal. Like he wants it to be normal, anyway. Or maybe he's just mellowed out

on his bud. Turner feels bad for him somehow, again, and asks if
he's doing anything and then says "Let's go upstairs, I gotta tell you
something."

In LaPrince's room he tells him about Puckerman asking questions: Anything bothering LaPrince? He getting his rest? What's he
up to? "You ain't up to nothing I know of, I told him, and he didn't
keep asking, but I thought you better know he's wondering about
your game being up and down and all." Pretty sure LaPrince will
appreciate knowing. Hoping it'll wake him up.

But he doesn't like it at all. "He askin' *you*, Turner-man?"

"I guess he knows we're friends. And that's why I'm telling you—
'cause we're friends, I thought."

"I couldn't tell it lately, the way y'ain't had nothing to say. We
compadres or not?"

"I guess. But, you know . . . like th'other night at that real-estate
man's house, I don't like being around that. You don't need to be
around it either, all that. That's way different from smoking a little
bud in private. And we were even gonna lay off the bud, we said."

"Sheeit." He grins a little, shaking his head like Turner's a punk
kid fretting about nothing. "*One* time I do a little nose candy. And
we safe in the man's house, not like we out in public."

"But one time with that stuff is all it takes."

"Sheeit. You talkin' 'bout me gettin' addicted? Where you been,
man? One time!"

"One time caught using it, is what I'm saying. If it shows up on
one of these random tests. It's on the list, a prohibited substance."

LaPrince still shaking his head, with the little smile of the slick
one being patient with the country boy. "They can make us piss for
'em anytime, right? Yeah. But you ever had to, Turner-man? You
ever *hear* anybody had to? It's a joke, man. They afraid they might
really catch somebody, have to do somethin'. 'Fraid who it might
be, choirboy like Duncan or somebody."

What can you say?

LaPrince says he'll never get into that shit noway, only do a line
when somebody puts it in front of him. "Be cool, now, Turner-man.
Now, that all you got to ax?"

A head like concrete. "Not all," Turner says. "Look, I don't know
why you gotta buy three bags of smoke all at once—"

"Sheeit. So I don't have to go back, man. Get set up, then don't
worry 'bout it for a while."

"But you get caught, 'specially with all these conditions in your contract, Puckerman might be hardball about it."

LaPrince still smiling. "Uh-huh, uh-huh," hurry up and get done. And Turner snaps, "Fuck that uh-huh, Wheat. I'm trying to help." The smirk disappears, hard-guy ghetto-boy look in its place. "Heyyy, farmboy"—a warning in the tone.

Turner ignores it. "I'm telling you it ain't too clever, giving people the rope to hang you with."

"You *tellin'* me, huh?" Getting up in Turner's face a little, his chest puffed out.

But he's never gone farther than throwing his chest out and woofing a little since the day Turner called his bluff back in the LA training camp. "I'm telling you that much," Turner says, standing his ground.

"Huh. Sound like somebody's momma."

"Maybe." Standing his ground.

And LaPrince backs off. That is, drops the smartass stuff. Looks off, rolls his eyes, smiles a little. And then, almost sweetly, says "You make me laugh, Turner-man, you know it? 'You gotta act right, LaPrince, if we gonna hang out.' Well, you know what? *Fuck* you, farmboy, if you don't wanna hang out. I ain't no coke fool, but when somebody put it in fronta me I might do it once in a while. Fuck it, ain't no big deal. You wanna talk about chronic—well, I'm gonna do my chronic. So. You don't wanna hang with me, go fuck yourself."

15

Richie "Bodacious" Bodie is just back from the gym when Tommy shows up at his house on Northwest Pettygrove on Thursday afternoon. Still a workout nut.

He still has the trademark ponytail, too, although there's a lot of gray in it now.

He's wearing a Levi jacket with a bright yellow banana painted on the back—not the same one as when they met years ago, but it might as well be. Tommy never knew whether it meant "top banana" or was some phallic reference or what, but he always called him "Banana" and Bodie always smiled. He liked "Bodacious," which he came up with himself, but who calls anyone Bodacious?

Tommy hasn't seen him for a while—only a few times since he, Tommy, got married four years ago and tried to be a little respectable. He called a few times when he couldn't find dope anywhere else, but they didn't hang out together.

Bodie was never one for hanging out, anyway. Always hyped, always moving. If he wasn't at Gold's Gym or the martial-arts place he was remodeling his house, water-skiing, snowboarding, gambling in Vegas, mastering the computer, something.

He didn't talk about most of what he did, and Tommy never really wanted to know. What he does know, or believes, is that Bodie bought this house with a lady friend's name on the deed, has never had a job, never had a Social Security number or filed a tax return or voted—doesn't exist, for the most part. Supported himself all these years by betting on sports, selling dope, and occasionally buying an old house (in someone else's name) to remodel and resell. At least, those are the ways Tommy knows about.

And Tommy knew, after considering his options for three days, that Bodie was the only person he could talk to about the videotape. He made up his mind to come by, and if Bodie wasn't in Vegas gambling or up on Mount Hood snowboarding or somewhere else living the life of the eternal adolescent and career scammer, they'd have the conversation. You couldn't trust him, but his touch of sociopathy would be useful: he wouldn't make judgments about burglary and theft, and he'd have ideas.

"Tell me everything," he says after they've run the tape in his living room. His eyes are gleaming.

Tommy can't help telling every gory detail. The most bizarre experience of his life, and he hasn't been able to breathe a word of it.

"I felt like a fucking idiot, lying out there on his deck praying he wouldn't come outside. Breaking-and-entering, burglary, I don't know what I'da been up for." He shudders, just remembering.

Bodie's smiling.

"Yeah, hilarious," Tommy says. "But OK, I'd probably laugh if it happened to someone else."

"You would. It's funny."

"A scream. Fuck you, Banana. Anyway, there's no way down, it's dark and I'm lying there, flat up against the wall underneath these windows. Praying. He finally comes upstairs around nine-thirty. The light comes on. Pretty soon I hear the TV come on. And he lights some candles; when I cranked my head around I could see those flickery shadows on the ceiling. Yeah, *candles*—to get him in the mood, I guess, the pervert. So he's settled in bed watching TV and it looks like he won't be coming outside tonight, at least. My shoulder's killing me after lying there on my side for five or six hours, and I finally figure OK, he's not coming out and probably not even coming to the window so it's probably safe to turn over on my back, even though I'd be sticking out a few inches farther from the side of the house. So I do, and at that angle I'm looking at part of the ceiling and the top part of the wall on the other side of the bed. The *shadows* on the ceiling and on that wall, from the candles. After a while I realize the shape on the wall is the silhouette of him lying there in bed. Of course, all I'm thinking at this point is that this is way too close for comfort—one sneeze and I'm toast. I'm wishing I could fall asleep till morning and then it'll be over one way or another, but there's no way I can fall asleep there . . . and if I did, what if I snored? Lemme tell you, pal, don't ever get trapped out on some-one's upstairs deck. Especially on a rainy November night."

Enjoying it immensely, Bodie says he'll make a note.

"Anyway, I'm lying there feeling like the world's biggest jackass, and he gets up. Naturally I'm panicked, thinking he's coming out for a late-night hot-tub and I'm screwed. But a minute later he gets back in bed. I know now he was putting this tape in the VCR, because I could tell by the shadows that he started playing with himself. I mean, going for it—must not've gotten laid in a year. I thought about standing up and applauding when he was done just to see the look on his face."

Bodie getting a huge kick out of it.

"A few minutes go by and he does it *again*. I'm thinking, Either he's one horny bastard or that's one dynamite video."

But he had a lot more to think about. When the TV went off and the candles went out he lay there, thankful it was only drizzling, worrying about Yardley coming out for a soak in the morning or even just locking this door before he went to work. But daylight came and time passed and at last, too good to be true, the screen door slammed shut down below, feet crunched across the gravel driveway, a car door opened and then slammed shut. The Mercedes purred and then pulled out over the gravel, on around the house, down the driveway, and finally it was quiet again. "I'm thinking, Lord, I'll never do anything so stupid again!"

Back in Yardley's bedroom he saw a thick vanilla column candle on the nightstand, along with the TV's remote, and a red jar candle on the floor beside the bed, the one that must have cast the shadows up high on the far wall. A wadded-up white towel on the floor nearby.

He wasn't going to fuck around looking for dope anymore—just get *gone!*—but he impulsively hit EJECT on the VCR to see what had gotten the punk so hot and bothered.

An unlabeled cassette, not a rental.

He couldn't resist. He turned things on, slapped the tape back in, hit REWIND and then PLAY.

Near-darkness on the screen, a little light from the left. Murmuring, and some shadowy movement on the left. Now a light comes on and you realize you're looking *down* at whatever's going on, from overhead. You're looking down at a blonde, and sud-denly—if you were Tommy Mason, Monday morning—you *knew,* from the sweater the striking girl was wearing Saturday night. Then the dark shiny head appeared, the familiar voice growled "Now, girl, you gonna get a *treat*, see some *meat*," and there was no doubt.

He didn't think twice about ejecting the tape at that point and taking it with him. Yardley wouldn't have a clue who took it unless he made something out of the old Civic parked across the road—a longshot—and even if he did, what was he gonna do, call the cops? *I'd like to report a guy stealing my secret videotape of LaPrince Wheatley humping a young white girl at my cocaine bash Saturday night.*

He got out of the house, down the long driveway and out the wrought-iron door by the gates, crossed the road, got in his car—a little surprised it hadn't been towed—and bolted out of there. Drove back to Max's, glad to know Max wouldn't be back from Mount Hood until that afternoon, and had a couple of bongs and sat down to watch the whole tape, see exactly what he had.

What he had was naughty, naughty. First, the part that probably got Yardley started pulling his pud the girl sitting astride LaPrince, arched backward and whimpering as he bounces her up and down. Then the most interesting part, where LaPrince goes too far and she tells him she's only sixteen and he could get busted for rape and she'll damn well go to the police if he doesn't cut that shit out right now, don't think she won't.

And more. Amazing.

What was he going to do? What *could* he do? Who could he tell? I've got this explosive videotape . . . which I acquired by breaking into this Yardley's house the day after he gave me a ration of shit at his Plunder coke party, which LaPrince Wheatley invited me to after I scored three bags of dope for him . . . .

After thinking about it for three days he knew it was Bodacious Bodie or no one.

"Yeah," Bodie says, "I can see why you don't like this Yardley, and you could probably squeeze some cash out of him for the tape. But forget that. For one thing, if he's buying all these properties—he said he owns five houses?—if he's buying all these properties his money's mostly tied up, he probably doesn't have a lot of cash. Wheatley's the one with real money, plus he's got a hell of a lot to lose if this video gets out. And he started the scene the other night where this Yardley gave you all that shit, right? And he thumped you? Yardley just mouthed off a little, it sounds like. Forget him. He'll get his, anyway, when Wheatley finds out about the video."

Tommy doesn't even ask what he's got in mind. Isn't sure he wants to know. Something's telling him he made a mistake, coming here.

Bodie's smiling, nodding to himself, the wheels turning. "This is beautiful," he says. "But *you* can't do anything. They know you. You've got to keep going to games like you don't know about this, keep writing articles, doing whatever you do. You're screwed if anyone thinks you've got anything to do with this thing disappearing."

Tommy sees it coming. But maybe he knew it would come to this; maybe it's why he came over. Why else?

"When are they back in town?" Bodie says. "When's the next home game?"

"They get back sometime today. Next game's tomorrow night."

"And after the games these morons go where?"

"We were at the Swim Friday night, Huber's Saturday. I don't know where else."

"I'll start there, then. Gonna have a chat with Mr. LaPrince. If they happen to invite you out tomorrow night—I mean, maybe LaPrince'll want to kiss and make up for the other night—or if you hear for sure where they're going, let me know. Page me."

Tommy thinks about it and finally nods. Uncertainly. Uneasily.

"Forget about it," Bodie says. "Let me handle it. Sounds like they've got no idea you're involved, and I'll keep it that way. And we'll split anything I can get."

What can you say?

You could say no, of course; could say, Let's forget I ever came over. But Tommy doesn't want to do that either.

Besides, buffed-up Bodie, who could break your jaw with one kick and undoubtedly kill you within seconds, would lop off his cherished ponytail before he'd let Tommy walk out with that tape.

Turner wonders where it's all heading.

LaPrince was so-so again in Detroit, after they had it out at the hotel. Had his moments, as usual—a picture-perfect turnaround J, a wraparound pass through traffic for a Yuban slam—along with too many forced shots, turnovers, defensive lapses. When Brisbee shot him a look for letting a loose ball roll out of bounds he acted like he was sure it was going to be Plunder's ball, no need to go after it. Brisbee just shook his head, and Turner could see Colabello biting his tongue. It was about the fiftieth time lately that Turner had remembered the quote from LA's general manager after the trade: "They'll find out, up in Portland."

LaPrince hardly seemed to care that Colabello pulled him for Michailovic early in the fourth quarter, with the game still up for grabs.

Turner saw Puckerman watching, not happy, from the front row near mid-court.

Michailovic scrapped and scratched, scored on a couple of putbacks, and the Plunder stayed in it until near the end. In the locker room afterward Turner glanced over at LaPrince a couple of times: LaPrince dressing quietly, Turner wondering what was in his head and feeling sorry for him again, poor dumb guy headed for trouble. Thinking (as LaPrince put the diamond stud in his ear), These guys always look ridiculous with the jewelry, but especially when they ain't playing worth a damn.

Plunder One gets them back to Portland just before midnight, Pacific time. Before the trip Coach said there'd be no shootaround Friday, even with Shaq in town tonight, but after four straight losses he's changed his mind: be there at noon. Turner's in his room at the Residence Inn, in bed, forty minutes after Plunder One touches down.

Reading the new *Rose City Review,* which was in his box at the front desk when he came in. Tommy Mason must have dropped it off, or one of the hotel staff heard Turner was in it and picked one up. Mason's story is called COLABELLO'S VICTORY CIGAR. He tells about the legendary Celtics coach Red Auerbach always lighting up a big cigar on the bench when he knew a game was won, and says Colabello must have considered the Utah game won, opening night, when he put twelfth man Turner Boyd in with a few minutes to go. Some might take it as insulting, but Turner *is* the twelfth man, after all. And Mason goes on to say the guys at the end of the bench are almost the only pros with any sense of how lucky they are to be pros at all, and what a nice guy Turner is, and how you've got to root for a guy who battled his way back from the Italian League. All in all, it's nice. Turner will thank him.

And apologize to him for the other night—for LaPrince—because he knows LaPrince won't. Turner's still not sure the guy won't write something about what happened, or tell someone, and he, Turner, will have his ass in a sling along with the others. Except that, being twelfth man, Turner will just be gone.

The phone wakes him up at 10 A.M.: LaPrince, subdued, asking if he wants a ride to shootaround. They haven't talked since La-Prince went off on him in Detroit.

"Uhhhhh"—Turner shaking himself awake, recalling that scene in LaPrince's hotel room—"uh, naw, I'll take my truck." LaPrince knows he was wrong, that's why he's subdued, but he won't say he's sorry. He expects Turner to forget what happened, or pretend to, just because Turner's a victory cigar and LaPrince is LaPrince. Well, cowpies. Gum would say LaPrince crapped in his flat-hat when he talked to a Boyd that way.

"Whassup, Turner-man? You gonna stay mad at me or what?"

"Listen here," Turner tells him, "I just got done being mad before you started up again. And I ain't even mad, but I ain't takin' that mouth either. I'll take my truck down. I'll see ya there."

He pauses before hanging up, but there's nothing to hear but LaPrince clicking off. The star doesn't know what to do when you won't fall for his sweet stuff.

But Turner starts feeling bad for him afterward, as usual. The

man's messed up to start with and now he's got the writers and TV
and the fans against him, and Brisbee and a few other teammates
grumbling, and Puckerman wondering about him, and he looks to
Turner for a friend. Gum would say "Nobody talks to a Boyd like
that," but he'd also say "If you call a man a friend, you help him
put his hay up when the storm comes."

So Turner Boyd, Gum Boyd's son, is a pushover by the time La-
Prince shows up for shootaround a few minutes early and comes
over to him asking, "You gonna keep fucking with me, Turner-
man?"

A pushover, but he can't help messing with him a little more before letting on. "Fucking with ya?"

"Yeah, you heard it." Starting to smile, relieved, seeing the trace
of a smile on Turner. "You fucking with me, country boy. You knew
when I called today I felt bad about what happened, but you cold
as a witch's titty."

"Said I'd drive myself down, is all."

"Y'ain't gonna ride with me no more 'cause I said somethin'?"

"That ain't it, Wheat. 'Cause you missed the bus last week, and
then didn't take me back to Residence Inn th'other night like you
promised."

"Ain't gonna trust me no more, huh?"

"I wanna get to where I need to get to, is all it is. And you saying
I'm cold . . . hey, the way you went off in Detroit when I was tryin'
to help you out, whatta you think? I should just forget all that?"

He makes a face, rolls his eyes. "I'm sorry 'bout it, awright? You
the Turner-man, my main man, I shouldn' be doggin' you that way.
I know you was trying to help."

Turner still not quite ready to let him off. "You start callin' people
all kinda stuff, you know it?"

"Aw, come on, man. You was lookn' out for me and I shouldna
dissed you, awright? We *compadres,* right? Cool?"

"What'd you call me, 'Goody Two-shoes'? Say I sound like somebody's momma?"

"You ain't that, Turner-man. C'mon, ease up."

"You remember what else?"

"Forget it," he says.

" 'Member?"

"Awright, *what*?" Getting ticked now. "I said y'ain't got no game, is why you gotta be a Goody Two-shoes?"

"What else?" Turner can't help it, one of the rare times he's ever had LaPrince backpedaling. "I better get some game or *what*?"

"Sheeit, I don't know. Look, why you wanna—?"

"I better get some game or I'll be back fucking cows on my daddy's farm, I b'lieve it was."

LaPrince is about to laugh, but he knows he'd better not. "I said that? Sheeit." Knowing damn well he did.

Turner waits. See what he does.

But then they both smile at once, and LaPrince says "Well? Ain't that what you people do back there?"

And Turner says, Yeah, fuck you, and LaPrince says, I always wished I could fuck myself, be the best I ever had, and Turner can't help laughing.

LaPrince thinks, Quit fucking off and play some ball. Onliest way to get people off his ass.

He wanted a blast when he woke up this morning—nothing like wake-and-bake—but he left it in the drawer. Thought about it after shootaround, too, but left it alone. Took a nap instead, stopped at the little café for pasta and then came down to the Plunderdome early, feeling good for Shaq-dog.

He hits the floor early to loosen up, nobody around but a couple of ballboys, the Plunder Dancers stretching at one end, a few fans drifting in, little-old-man ushers in their white shirts and black vests. With a little redheaded ballboy returning the ball to him he drifts around the perimeter, breaking a fine sweat as he sticks it in from everywhere. Remembering what he did to LA in preseason, 28 points and 15 boards and the thunderdunk on Shaq-daddy.

As the place starts filling up he works on his free throws, and he's got eight in a row when he spots Mason passing behind the press row, his red plastic media ID on a string around his neck and his little notebook in his hand.

"Yo, dude!"

Mason looks over, their eyes meet for a half-second, but he just shakes his head with a sour look and goes on. Making his point, just like Turner-man. Everybody making their point with him.

Cool, then. Fuck the dude. Pansy-ass writer.

Just play ball. Play good ball and everybody loves you, your troubles clear up, everything's cool.

*   *   *

One thing some humpin' ball won't take care of: the two of them showing up under the hoop a few minutes before gametime again, LaMetrius and the little tank, the Titan.

After shootaround today Porky Pig told him LaMetrius called again while they were off on the road, and LaPrince wondered if they'd show up tonight. But either way, it was only a matter of time. He thought about giving LaMetrius a thousand bucks whenever it happened and sending him on his way—shit, give the Titan some too. He doesn't need them coming around.

Right now he doesn't need them standing there looking badass. And he can see they're gonna stand there till he goes over; gonna start yapping and make a scene if an usher tells them to move along, or even if security cops come in. They don't give a shit.

As the team starts running layup lines he walks over. "Say. Word?"

The Titan just gives him the cool eye and stays quiet. LaMetrius, not smiling either, stretches up toward him and has to yell to be heard over the ugly rock-and-roll on the arena PA. "You back in town, huh?"

LaPrince leans down, toward one ear: "Couple days, then out again."

"We was gonna talk, you remember? You was gonna call when you got back."

The PA man cuts in on the music, talking about *defending Western Division champion Los Angeles*, and the fans boo, the place starting to rock. Fuck these two! "Can't talk now, man! Not here!" Shit, this is the *league*!

But LaMetrius doesn't care. He glances at his homeboy, and the little man puts a look on LaPrince. Not a word, just the eyes. Hands jammed down in the pockets of the same heavy coat as the other night, one hand probably gripping a piece.

"I gotta go, man," LaPrince hollers, jerking a thumb back toward the floor like *Can't you see I got a little something going on here?*

LaMetrius comes up on his tiptoes and says, "We come see you, then. Where you staying at?"

The Titan moving in a little closer, taking an interest.

LaMetrius: "Where you staying at, bro?"

LaPrince's eyes dart around, as if there's anyone who can help him. "I gotta fly, dudes! I call you tomorra, I got the number."

"You said that before. Nah, that ain't happenin'. We come to you. Now, where y'at?"

They're not about to go away and he can't stand here trying to bullshit his way out of it, which won't work anyway.

It's a big mistake but there's no choice: "Palatine Street, long curvy street out near this Lewis and Clark College. One-four-six-oh-six."

"Palatine," LaMetrius shouts back. "One-four-six . . . uh . . ."

"Oh-six." The Titan finishing for him.

He *was* ready to play, ready to kick some serious booty, but he's all scrambled now. Shaq-fu's bouncing people around, his posse's running and gunning, everything falling for 'em. Portland's outclassed. By early in the third quarter some of the fans are leaving and the rest are quiet.

And now a few start dogging LaPrince for trying to *do* something, make something happen. After he hits a J and then dunks off a sweet dish from Brisbee he tries to keep the roll going—and get the crowd back into it—with a jumper off a slick spin move. But it barely catches iron, and as LA fastbreaks the other way he hears some boos—maybe intended for the whole sorry team, but he hears his name and he can't help it: before he knows it his arms are spread, palms up, and he's telling the fools to *bring it,* yeah, like they did in the Seattle game. Such great fans they're supposed to be up here, sheeit. Made up their minds he was gonna be the Man, and now he's the whole trouble when the team gets their butt kicked.

And now a lot more of 'em chime in, and LaPrince can't stop telling 'em to bring it, bring it! He makes more money tonight than most of 'em make all year. Fuck y'all.

He never makes it to mid-court as LA finishes the fastbreak. The Plunder come back this way and Brisbee, jogging by to set up, yells "Cool it, man! Get your head in the game, play ball, they'll leave you alone!"

Fuck you too, Briz.

He sits out most of the fourth quarter as LA runs away and hides, the Russian goon and Turner finishing up at power forward. Fine.

Some fuck-doctor and maybe some drinks, soon as he can get outta here. Fuck it.

*   *   *

And he's better, yeah, an hour later. A few puffs on the way down-town, a couple of Lemon Drops at the Swim.

He's starting another one, sitting at the same big table as last time with Yuban and Mona and Terry Wall and two chickies, when somebody comes up behind him and squeals in his ear, "*No!*"

Some fool trying to sound like a girl or a queer. He turns around and he's looking into some white dude's face six inches away, dude leaning down close to be heard by LaPrince and nobody else. "No! not there!" he squeals in the same girly voice, and LaPrince suddenly gets a bad feeling.

He *knows* it's trouble when the dude leans even closer to his ear and says, same voice, "You know how old I am?" and then moves off between the packed tables to the bar. Black jeans, blue wind-breaker, a long ponytail mostly gray.

What the fuck? It's exactly what the little bitch said the other night when his finger went around back.

Who *is* this cocksucker?

LaPrince is shaken, and from the way Yuban's looking at him he knows it shows. He tries to put on a chillin' look, shakes his head like it's nothing, then gets up and follows the dude to the bar. Gets within a few feet in the crowd, reaches over a Mexican-looking guy and gives the ponytail a yank.

Dude looks around with a little smartass smile, mouths the words "I'm waiting" and takes an imaginary sip from an imaginary glass. Waiting to get a drink, he means, and he turns back to the bar. Too cool. LaPrince wanting to go upside his head.

But he waits. Finally the guy gets his drink, works his way out of the knot of people at the bar and goes looking for a table. LaPrince follows him.

No free tables. LaPrince closing in on him now as the guy stops over by one of the huge aquariums, the weird aquarium light shining on one side of his face. Long gray hair parted in the middle and pulled back tight, tied in the ponytail at the back.

LaPrince gets up close and glares down at him, shake him up. "The fuck you talkin' 'bout, man? Huh?"

"The fuck you think?" he says with the little smile.

"I know you, man?"

"I don't think so." Sips his drink, some pink crushed-ice thing.

"The fuck you talkin' 'bout, then?"

"You don't know?" Gives him a look. "What are you, brain-dead?"

"Somethin' 'bout how old somebody is, but I never seen you before, man, don't know what the—"

"How old *she* is," he says, "is what you didn't know. Am I right?"

"Who you mean, 'she'?"

The dude shakes his head, smiling, and sips his drink again. Messing with him. LaPrince feeling the sweat under his arms, feeling hot all over. The dude finally says, "We both know who I mean, don't we? And what we're talking about? You told her you had a treat for her, your big black meat, and she liked that fine, but she didn't like it when you diddled her in back. Told you to forget it, *not there!*"—the girly voice again—"and she explained statutory rape to you. What was it you said then? 'Let's go downstairs, do another line, you'll loosen up'? She said forget it, which you didn't like—"

"*Fuck* you, man."

"Not a chance, buddy. Just like she said." Sips the drink. Holds it up to the aquarium light like he's studying it.

What the hell? Who the hell? But he knows something, ain't no doubt.

"Bitch tell ya this? You her daddy or somethin'?"

"I saw the movie." Not even looking at him. Playing cool, studying his pink drink in the aquarium light.

LaPrince is lost.

"The videotape."

Still lost. Is he supposed to understand?

"Now *you* say something. It's called a conversation."

But say what? "You seen . . . the movie?"

"The videotape. Yeah, I've seen it. I've *got* it, and I thought maybe you'd like to have it so it doesn't fall in the wrong hands. That could be awkward for you."

LaPrince's eyes flick down to the kangaroo pocket on the dude's windbreaker, but there's no sign of any videotape.

"I didn't bring it here, genius. Anyway, you interested?"

"Who the fuck *are* you, man?" He doesn't know what else to say, his mind flashing to the blond bitch at that Yardley's house, pulling her clothes on and taking off downstairs. But this chump wasn't there. Never seen him before. What the fuck?

"Put it this way: I'm your most important priority right now. Names aren't really important, are they? Now, can I interest you in the videotape or not?"

"What you mean, interest me?"

Chump gives him the look again and LaPrince wants to bust him. "What do you think I mean, Einstein? I mean do you want it, for a small fee, or should I take it to the press or the Plunder or the league or the police? Think fast, I'm ready to blow outta here."

His mind races. He looks back over the sea of heads at Yuban and the others at the table with the girls, even more girls squeezed in since he got up.

"Forget it," the chump says, "if you're thinking you'll kick my ass or some shit. I've got a friend ready to take the tape to the cops if I'm not home safe and sound in time for Jay Leno, which is in about thirty minutes by my watch. It'll take me almost that long to get there if I leave right now, so any delay could seriously exacerbate your trouble."

What does he do?

The chump won't wait any longer. "Meet me right here after the game Monday," he says, "or take your chances." And takes off.

Bernie Herman is awakened by the call from a babbling LaPrince Wheatley at three in the morning Cleveland time, midnight out in Portland. Something about someone trying to shake him down over videotape of him in bed with an underage girl, and can Bernie bail him out somehow?

Bernie doesn't need this at all, especially with this hotshot interior decorator finally making time to come out this afternoon and talk about getting the new place set up. But what can he say, considering he wouldn't have the new place if not for Wheatley? He promises to fly out there on Sunday, once he realizes the meeting Wheatley wants him to handle isn't until Monday night.

He can't fall asleep again for a while. What's this numbskull doing? You knew all along he wasn't too bright, but hell . . . all the work convincing Puckerman he was worth trading for, all the kissing up and the promises and finally agreeing to the behavior clauses beyond the standard good-citizen stuff in every contract. What's he thinking?

He's not thinking, that's always the trouble.

But he can play, or at least has the potential, which is why Puckerman came across with $12 million in the end (standard 4 pefor Bernie, $160,000 over the three years). If he can turn potential into production, they stand to make a hell of a lot more on the next contract.

If he can stay out of jail and in the league.

An underage girl? When a million cracks who are at least eighteen are throwing themselves at these guys?

But get out there and straighten it out if you can. Otherwise your biggest moneymaker is screwed, meaning you're pretty much screwed too.

Bernie went through enough to sign the guy, to put himself on the map in the agent business. He knew Wheatley had shit for brains the first time they met, Wheatley a freshman at Vegas, but he had the body and the game, a pro game even then. All-conference, third-team All-American right away, nineteen years old. Bernie loaned him a grand that first time, rented a car for him, set him up with Silky—none of it OK with the NCAA, but who was going to tell?

By the end of that season, league people were projecting Wheatley as a lottery pick if he came out of school, and Bernie—getting cash advances on his credit cards and borrowing from his mother—had fronted him more than $30,000 against his first contract. They had an understanding. Wheatley could legally hire an agent once Vegas got knocked out of the tournament, and he heard from everyone who was anyone in the first twenty-four hours. He waited a week, for appearances, before signing with Bernie. Some of the others smelled a rat—a lottery prospect going with a nobody like . . . Bernie who?—but if they looked into it, they looked in the wrong places. No one turned up any violations.

The stud has given Bernie a ton of headaches in three years, but he's still the biggest talent and biggest moneymaker on his brief client list. So, get out there and see what this is about.

And careful, don't go using your line about fifteen-year-old Scotch and sixteen-year-old girls.

Sunday afternoon, he grabs a cab at the Portland airport and gives the driver the address in this suburb, Lake Oswego—Edelstein Jr.'s house. Twenty minutes later they pull into a driveway under a lot of old towering trees, behind a line of vehicles. He sees Wheatley has bought a black Lexus Gold Edition, Oregon vanity plates WHEAT 53, and a blue Humvee, 53 WHEAT. There's a black Nissan too, with regular California plates.

When Wheatley opens the front door, his red puffy eyes tell Bernie he's been smoking ganja. Great.

On second thought, if he's not doing anything more than ganja, maybe that's a victory.

"Herm," he says, clearly glad to see him. "Thanks for coming out here." Then quietly, before moving aside to let him in, "Coupla dudes here we gotta talk about."

Two brothers smoking a bowl in the living room: one skinny, with a nasty scar on his neck, the other short and massive with a cute, fine-featured face that doesn't match the rest of him. "This La-Metrius, my half-brother," Wheatley explains. "Call himself Wink. And the Titan. They up from LA."

Bernie wouldn't have liked the look of them even if Wheatley hadn't whispered at the door. They go back to their bowl as Wheatley picks up Bernie's suitcase and leads him down a hall to a guestroom.

Bernie shuts the door behind them. "What's going on? Who're those guys?"

"Givin' me trouble, is who. Show up here from LA week before last, calling the team leaving messages for me to call 'em. My half-brother just outta the joint in California, track me down like he do every time he get out."

Beautiful.

"He got together with the little man when he got out and they come up here. Asking for a job with me, sheeit, wanna be my body-guard or some shit. Want *money*, what they want, they just ain't quite ast for it yet."

He tells how they showed up at the Plunderdome when he didn't return the calls—came right down to the court! The second time, Friday night, they stood under the basket during warmups and wouldn't leave until he gave them this address. Next day, yesterday, they showed up at eight-thirty in the morning and the half-brother explained some of the ways they could help him if he put them on the payroll as personal assistants.

"Like I need personal 'sistants. After a while I said I had to go to practice, but I could see LaMetrius didn't plan on leaving. Said they'd wait here. I tell him it ain't my crib, I gotta lock up—which he didn't like, like I don't trust 'em. He go outside to their car, the Titan's Nissan out there, and when he come back he lemme see he got a strap. Tellin' me it ain't loaded, but *sheeit!* I call Coach sayin' I got a upset stomach, diarrhea, and I just stay home—we get a fade on and sit around all day. I got no idea what they really thinkin'."

"All right," Bernie says, "we'll get back to them. How about this guy you've never seen saying he wants money out of you for this videotape? Anything new since Friday night?"

"Nah, nothing else. Like I ain't got enough problems going on. I was thinking maybe these two would understand it and take off."

"You told them?"

Naturally, the halfwit. He says he was sitting here Saturday morning, shook up about the guy approaching him about the videotape the night before, when they showed up, and he had to talk. Says he started thinking about what they said about helping him out however they could—maybe they could *hurt* the ratty motherfucker or something, help out that way, since they obviously weren't planning on leaving.

"So they were here all yesterday, and stayed all night?"

"What could I do? They crazy, Herm. LaMetrius anyway, and he got this strap, I don't know what he gonna do."

He's got a desperate look.

Bernie hears something out in the hall, and a moment later the bedroom door swings open and the half-brother is looking from one of them to the other, asking whassup.

"We're just getting me settled in here, pal," Bernie says. "Say, any more of that smoke out there?" For now, at least, act like you're all on the same side.

"Little bit. Come on, we set y'up."

"Be right there."

The yardbird retreats down the hall. Bernie quietly shuts the door and asks Wheatley where the scar on the neck came from, wanting to know a little more about these two. The question is just out of his mouth when something else occurs to him. "He's just out of prison, you said? Free and clear, or on parole?"

Parole, Wheatley says. Good. Doesn't touch the blackmail problem, but it's nice to know he can get rid of one of these dinks, anyway, with a phone call.

Meanwhile, until Artie and Eddie fly in tomorrow, *use* them.

19

Yo, up there! Yo!"

It's Sunday evening when they show up, Yardley out in his upstairs hot tub watching Redskins–Cowboys on the portable. His gut instantly tightens with the dread that hasn't been far off since the video disappeared last Monday.

He knows he locked the gates out front and the wrought-iron door alongside, meaning they scaled the wall to get in, meaning they planned on coming in no matter what. A bad sign.

"Yo, up there, muhfucker!"

Jesus. Black. At least two of them.

They can't see him up here; they must have seen the steam rising off the water, or heard the TV.

"Muh-fuck-er!"

He's paralyzed. What in God's name does he do?

"Hey! God*damn*you!"—a grunt on *damn,* as if from a great effort, and an instant later—thud!—something heavy lands on his expensive cedar deck. One of the rocks, big as cantaloupes, that line the flower bed along the back of the house.

Voices muttering down there, then another grunt and—*shit!*—another rock thuds down on the other side of the tub. Even in the faint light from the TV he can see the dent it leaves in the cedar.

Thud! Splinters in the twelve-dollar-a-foot tongue-and-groove.

Panicked, he gets out of the water, quiet as he can. . . . Shit, as if they don't know he's up here! He wraps his towel around his waist and looks around wildly. Now what?

Crack! In the faint light he sees his Italian terra-cotta planter shatter and fall away from the soil inside, the planter-shaped hunk of soil crumbling and the *Viburnum davidii* dropping out of sight.

"Yardley, my man!" one of them shouts. "Come out where we can see yo' ass!"

Thud! Two feet away from him, another rock that could break a foot or give him a concussion. Pricks! He feels like slinging it back down at whoever it is.

But mostly he's scared, and suddenly he's at the rail looking down into the dark, saying "Don't throw anything," a quiver in his voice. Can't make out anything but two faces looking up, the whites of their eyes.

They're laughing. Fucking spades. "Hey, he ain't ignoring us no more," one says. "He decide to talk to us now. Hey you," he calls, "come on down here."

Paralyzed. "Who's there?"—a squeak. "What is this?"

More laughter. "You axin' questions, man? Now, I said get your sorry ass down here."

Petrified. Run in and call the police?

Their voices, indecipherable, and now the sound of the screen door, the creak followed by the banging shut. They're inside the porch now. Did he lock the kitchen door?

What does it matter? If they want to come in they'll come in, break a pane of glass if the door's locked.

He's in the bedroom, frantic, nowhere to go.

Out in the hall he hears them down below, jive-talk and laughter as they come to the stairs—coming for him! Scared to death, scared of pissing them off, he scurries down the hall and presents himself at the top of the stairs as if to say, Here I am, see how cooperative? Let's be friends!

They stop halfway up, two burrheads checking him out. The one in front is grinning, knowing the honky wimp is scared—one of those spades who gets a kick out of it. His partner is a stout little guy with a soul patch under his lip, just watching.

"Nice, what you wearing," the one in front says. The towel. "What you got in there, Casper?"

Oh, please.

"Let's see. Let's see what the white boy got."

Yardley's about to cry.

"I *said,* and I ain't gonna say it again, let's see yo' meat."

A long scar on his neck, which he probably didn't get in grad school. He makes a move up the steps and there's nothing to do but drop the towel, let him see.

Let him laugh, the thing all shriveled up. "Shit, no wonder the man make kinky movies to get off on! I bet you sure ain't gettin' none, man, *that* all you got to contribit!"

He stands there chuckling a moment longer, then says "All right, now cover up your pussy and come on down here."

And there's nothing to do but cover up and start down the stairs. Maybe he can talk sense to the odd-shaped guy with the soul patch, who doesn't look half-crazy. Scary in his own way but not crazy, which is scarier.

Yardley's coming off the bottom stair and hitting the floor when the little odd-shaped one, who hasn't said a word and even seemed a little disapproving of the crazy one's taunting, steps in his path and explodes a fist into his gut, doubling him over, and then brings a knee up into his face, and Yardley feels bones snapping and blood spurting and he's on the floor. . . .

When the lights come back on he's propped up on the long couch in the living room, naked, a bloody white towel on the carpet at his feet. Trying to find a position he can tolerate, because the sledge-hammer fists did a number on his ribs and insides. His head throbs too, his face—it's clear the split lip and the bloody, undoubtedly broken nose are only part of the damage. He wants to tell them he's got Percodan upstairs, but they'd probably clean everything out and not even give him a Perc.

"Yardley? You're disturbed, you know it? Videotaping people doing it?"

It's a different voice. White.

Yardley tells himself to just keep quiet. As if he could move his face to say something even if he wanted to.

"And you won't get away with it, of course." Giving his foot a kick, whoever it is.

"I didn't mean—"

"*Fuck* you, pal! Hush your fucking mouth or these two'll kick your teeth in for you."

He must have been outside before, must have come with the two spades. Thirtysomething, maybe forty, wearing a nice brown cashmere V-neck and light linen slacks and tassel loafers.

"Dickhead," he says. "You know, it looks like you hurt yourself. What happened, you fall down the stairs? Or did you throw yourself down, 'cause you know you don't have shit to live for except a lot of broken bones until we settle up?"

Wait for permission to talk.

The man swirls ice in a glass of something. "Oh, I found the booze," he says, "hope you don't mind. Nice selection. Nice to know you're a man of wealth and taste. It might help you get out from under this little problem you've created for yourself—the wealth, anyway."

The burrheads pull the wing chairs over and sit in front of the couch, one on each side, smirking at him.

"We might as well understand each other," the boss says. "I'm Bernie Herman, a representative of Mr. Wheatley, and like I said, we've got a problem here. I don't know the dollar value of it yet, I'm just here to ask you some questions. My friends here won't kill you if you give me wrong answers, because I might need you later, but you might be in traction for a while. Personally, I think all your answers will be truthful, because you're afraid of what will happen if I catch you in a lie."

No kidding.

"Now that we understand each other"—enjoying himself— "who's your hippie friend, and what made you dickheads believe you could pull this scam off? Go on, you can talk now."

Hippie friend?

"Cut the shit," he says. "Ponytail."

Ponytail? He doesn't know anyone with a ponytail. He's hardly seen a ponytail in years.

"No? You probably don't know anything about a videotape either, even one that was made right here in this house . . . of LaPrince Wheatley, without his permission. Well, dickhead?"

Yeah, yeah, he knows about the tape, but that's all.

"I'll bet. You rig this place up, catch a big name in the act and figure it's good for money." Drinks his drink, shakes his head. "In your dreams, maybe, but not in this life. Now I want to know, who's Ponytail?"

Don't know, I swear.

The loud, crazy spade threatens to feed him his muhfucking balls if he keeps whining.

OK, OK. He tells them he made the tape but it disappeared almost a week ago, last Monday, and he doesn't know who stole it but he's got an idea: Tommy Mason, this writer who did a story on Wheatley

for the *Rose City Review* and was over here after the Saturday-
night Seattle game. When he realized on Monday that someone had
broken in he asked around the neighborhood; they've got Neigh-
borwatch and everyone looks out for everyone—

"Rich *faggots* like you?"—and the man in the cashmere steps
closer, grabs a fistful of hair and snaps Yardley's head back, jerks
it around. The crazy spade giggles and the little one smiles, perched
in the other wing chair with his little feet dangling a few inches off
the floor.

Yardley tells them the surgeon's wife a couple of houses down said
her husband noticed an old red Honda Civic parked on the grass
across the road all night last Sunday, and that he, Yardley, called
DMV with the license number and a story about sideswiping a parked
car and wanting to contact the owner, and found out the '92 Civic be-
longed to Thomas Edward Mason, which had to be this writer
Tommy Mason who had a flareup with LaPrince here Saturday night
that ended with LaPrince sort of shoving him. Well, giving him a little
bit of a whack. And Mason left then, pissed off for sure. "He doesn't
have a ponytail, but he's gotta be the one that stole that tape."

The cashmere man sips his drink, thinking it over. Finally says
he'll look up this Mason. "And this teen queen on the tape? She in
on the scam?"

No, no one *in on it*—there's nothing to be in on. He made the
tape, OK, and this dipshit Mason copped it, that's all. He, Yardley,
barely knows the girl.

"Wheatley says you invited her over to meet him."

OK, she's been here before and he thought she might like Wheatley; she liked some players before.

"Well, what about her? Who is she?"

Yardley repeats he barely knows her. "She called herself Daisy,
probably bullshit, and said she goes to Oregon State. She liked to
come over here and meet players. Sometimes do a little cocaine, but
not always, and never very much."

Then it occurs to him through the haze, through the throbbing in
his face and ribs: What will they do to her if they even suspect she's
involved in whatever's going on?

He doesn't tell Cashmere her family has a luxury box at the Plunderdome and they might be able to find her that way.

*   *   *

In the end Cashmere asks the burrheads if they like it here, the setup, and the crazy one looks around smiling, saying it looks comfy, yeah, and the man tells Yardley the two are going to stick around for a while, baby-sit him—

Then abruptly drops the smile and the fake-friendly tone, as if something just snapped: slaps him, then towers over him ranting about sicko pervert slime, demanding to know what Yardley's got against LaPrince Wheatley that he makes a secret tape and goes into this blackmail scam with his sleazy post-hippie friend—"because maybe this Mason stole the tape like you say, maybe, but without you there wouldn't be a tape to begin with. *You're* the one who's going to pay the blackmail if any is paid, because you're the little asshole faggot pigfucking piece of garbage that started it all. You know that, you sorry fuck? Do you?"

Yeah.

"You scared, dickhead?"

Yeah.

"You should be." He turns to one of his assistants, then the other. "Call me if you need me, otherwise just look after him. Do whatever you want, just so you keep his sorry ass alive."

Tommy's got to get out of Max's house. Now. Someone knows he's involved in scamming Wheatley and knows, somehow, that he's living here. No way a *Sports Illustrated* associate editor just happens to be in town, sees his column on Turner Boyd and wants to meet him.

But that's what the message says when he comes in Monday afternoon. Max is gone somewhere, but it's jotted on a yellow Post-it inside the front door—four exclamations points at the end, Max excited for him.

Maybe it *is* from an SI editor, but he can't chance it. His gut tells him someone's on to him. They noticed the car and traced it through DMV and got every bit of information. . . .

Uh-oh. The address on his license is his house in Burlingame. Did they go looking for him there and hassle Julie? If they did, would she have told where he's staying? Doubtful, unless they got rough, which he can't even bear to think about. If she did tell, wouldn't she have called here to warn him? Yes, even as fed up as she is with him.

Unless they killed her to prevent it.

Get out of here.

But no—he's getting crazy. If they traced the car and got to Julie they would have showed up before this. He's watched too much TV. The message probably *was* from an SI editor. Tommy knows he's as good as anyone writing for them, and this guy comes to Portland for some reason and discovers him on a fluke. It's how things happen. Maybe he'd better show up at the Hilton bar at seven.

Sure, and never be heard from again.

Go pick up an SI and see if Peter Blythe is on the masthead.

Forget it! Get the hell out of here!

*   *   *

Thank God for an old girlfriend with a spare room. And Max doesn't know she exists—nothing he can tell anyone who comes looking for Tommy here.

He's upstairs packing when Max comes in. Almost six now, and he wants to get going in case they come looking for him when he doesn't show at the Hilton at seven.

Five minutes later Max comes up the stairs asking if he feels like having a drink. He's baffled when he sees the packing. "What's going on?"

"You're getting a break. You and your honey, who I know doesn't like me being here. I've got a place to go, so I'm going."

"Right now? Just like that?"

"Right now. It's no big deal, but I've been here too long and an old friend offered me her guestroom and I'm taking advantage. Giving you a break."

Max doesn't get it. "I don't need a break. It's no trouble, you being here. It's been fun, hasn't it?"

"Yeah, but it's time, that's all." Pulling his shirts out of the closet, throwing them in the suitcase. "I'm sure Paige would say past time. I'm sure she'll start coming over again." Pulling more stuff out of the closet. He'd rather not look at Max, whom he's betrayed and whom he's possibly leaving in some danger.

"Hey, forget Paige. Look, you've been doing me a favor, sort of, as far as me and Paige. You're right, she wasn't crazy about you at first, and she seemed to think I'd throw you out if she said to. Which would've set an unhealthy precedent in the relationship. Which is one reason I've wanted you to stay—so she gets the picture."

"But she does think I'm sleazy or something."

"It doesn't matter what she thinks, that's the point. How about a drink?"

"Can't do it. Told my friend I'd be there by seven." Snapping the suitcase shut.

Max shrugs. "Well, you gotta do what you gotta do." And adds, as Tommy looks around for odds and ends, "What do you think of her?"

"I barely know her, I probably shouldn't say."

"Screw it. You've got opinions, and you're pretty good on people."

Well, what the hell, even though she's the last thing on his mind right now. "What do I think? Well, I know she's pretty smart, so sometimes I can't help wondering if she's right, if I am sleazy. But most of the time—since you're asking—mostly I think it's her. That she's one of these upright, uptight high achievers who never did anything she couldn't tell her mom and dad about and who's uncomfortable around anyone who's not upright and high-achieving."

Max waits for more.

"More? Maybe I make her insecure because I pre-date her in your life. I don't know. I know she's smart, you say she's a hot lawyer, she's certainly a babe—all this good shit, but I think she needs to lighten up a little. Since you asked." He looks for Max's reaction, but there's not much. "How's that?"

"Probably not far off. There's a lot more to her, but that's probably about right as far as it goes."

"I'd probably like her if I knew her better. Maybe. I mean, I liked her at the Swim that night when I was telling her my sad story, which I wouldn't've done if she hadn't seemed at least a little interested. But then, the way that night turned out, she probably thought I *must* be lowlife—to be out with a bunch of dumb, crude jocks in the first place. Hell, I don't know. She's your honey, I'm sure she's great."

"Not bad, once you get to the good stuff—"

"And you've been great to have me here for so long, but I've been in the way long enough and I've got an offer and it's time to go. I gotta get moving."

Max looks at him (Tommy imagines) as if he doesn't believe he's heard the real reason. But finally shrugs and repeats, "Do what you gotta do."

"I might even get back with my wife soon, so I'd be leaving anyway."

A surprise to Max, obviously.

A surprise to Tommy, too, where that came from. Wishful thinking. But maybe it helps his case a little, if Max believes it.

Max doesn't take it on faith. "You've talked to her lately?"

"We've talked. Talked about getting together to talk about it up-close and personal."

He's not sure Max believes him, and he feels like a jerk for lying to him again.

Mostly, though, he's got to get the hell out of here. "I'll keep you posted," he says, reaching for the suitcase. "Right now I gotta rip."

Monday night, Bodie's ready.

Play hardball, that's all. Wheatley's not very bright, but he doesn't have to be a genius to realize this videotape could ruin him. Tell him anyone can give up a month's pay to save his ass.

He catches the fourth quarter and *Plunder Post-Game* on the radio, doing his laundry, and then puts on his top-banana jacket and walks downtown. He's meeting his boys at Frank Peters Inn, not going anywhere near the Swim tonight without his escorts.

Randy, Gayland, Russ, LaVern, Luis. Ought to be able to handle anything less than an army. At Peters Inn he waves them up to the bar and orders shots for everyone, pays the tab as they throw 'em down, slams his own Glenfiddich and they head out, down Morrison to the Swim.

Luis wants to know wha' thees ees about.

Just a small personal matter, Bodie tells the guy who has personally broken his nose twice and inflicted various and sundry injuries. Tells him he doesn't expect any trouble, he just wants backup in case this fellow has ideas. Doesn't say the fellow is LaPrince Wheatley.

"A girl?" Luis asks. "Ees about a girl? You fuck somebody's girl-friend?"

"No, not a girl. Would I fuck somebody's girlfriend?"

"Not mine, if you smart, but somebody else's I can't say."

Gracias, Luis. But Bodie thanks him for coming, thanks them all; tells them to order drinks at the Swim, whatever, just keep an eye on him, it shouldn't take long.

The place isn't too packed on a Monday night. Four buff tae kwon do black belts take a booth twenty feet from the main bar while the fifth, Bodie, grabs a barstool and orders another Glenfiddich. No sign of Wheatley yet, but if he's got an atom of sense he'll be here. A tossup, whether he's got that crucial atom.

Ten seconds after his drink arrives, someone tugs on his ponytail.

Not Wheatley. Some guy Bodie's never seen: snappy dressy, fleshy face, soft body. Slick as an apple but soft as an overripe pear.

Bodie gives him a smile. "Not a good idea to pull on Superman's cape, remember?"

He's not amused. "You're the douchebag, right?"

"Excuse me?"

"Guy with a ratty ponytail sitting at the bar, I figure you're the douchebag. You're waiting for Wheatley, am I right?"

"Sure not waiting for you, mister. I don't know you from a bucket of shit."

"So you *are* the douchebag. Well, I'm here for Wheatley, so let's talk." He glances around. "Maybe get a booth, get out of the way."

"Fine." Bodie drains the single-malt, lays a ten on the bar and follows him to a booth. No legbreakers in sight, but just in case, Bodie makes a little show of waving to his own supporting cast, Luis and the others fit and formidable and within spitting distance. "My friends," he tells the smooth apple. "Don't want 'em losing track of us."

"That right? You worried about something?"

"Not hardly, with my buddies from the dojo looking out for me. Nothing like buddies, huh? We train together. We all got our black belts together."

If the guy's impressed, he doesn't let on. "So," he says, sliding into the booth.

"So," Bodie says. "Let's start with who you are."

"Who are *you*, douchebag?"

"Now, now. That kind of talk won't get us anywhere. And it doesn't really matter who I am, does it? Besides, I asked you first."

"Doesn't really matter who I am either, does it? I know why Wheatley was supposed to meet you and I came instead, that's all."

Bodie can smell his cologne. A guy's not very classy when you can smell his cologne from three feet away.

"Come on," the guy says. "What's this scam you're trying to pull?"

"All right. . . . What's happening is this. I'm in possession of a unique videotape that's of some interest to your friend, client, whatever he is. I know that because he and I stood right over there and talked about it Friday night. And because you showed up tonight."

"And?"

"And I'm willing to let him have it for a fair price, and that'll be the end of it. What I'll do with it if he doesn't want it, or doesn't want it bad enough—your guess is as good as mine."

"And? This fair price you're talking about?"

A waiter appears and Bodie, feeling good, orders Glenlivet this time. Tells the smooth apple, when the waiter's gone, "I like the woody taste sometimes, you know?"

"Fuck off. Get to it."

Fine. Bodie tells him he's not one to be greedy, he's just not, so he's only asking Wheatley for a month's pay—*after* taxes, how's that? Four million a year is a million every three months, three hundred-odd thousand a month. Minus taxes, because Bodie's not greedy. "Two hundred grand, I'm happy. You bring me the cash, I bring you the video, we have a drink and call it good."

Smooth leans in and says, "You're kidding, right?"

"I am?"

"You must be. You're in way over your head, trying to pull something like this."

"I've wondered about that. The thing is, I don't see what you can do about it, you and your boy."

Smooth holds his Grand Marnier up to the light and swirls it in the snifter, with a faint smile like he knows something Bodie doesn't. Bullshit. He's stuck for an answer to the unanswerable.

"That's what I thought," Bodie says. "It's right there on tape, this sixteen-year-old telling your boy they'll hang him for statutory rape if she goes to the cops. She spells it right out when he . . . well, I won't tell you what he did. Keep you in suspense, give you something to look forward to."

Smooth tries to be cool, but he's stumped. Finally he says, "If you go to the cops maybe we go to 'em too, and maybe you're busted for blackmail."

"Nice try. I'll say I've never talked to either of you, I'm just a citizen reporting some wickedness that's come to my attention."

"And where'll you say you got this videotape?"

Bodie just smiles. "Look, I'll take my chances here. If you don't believe me, take a chance yourself. Walk outta here."

"Who're you in this with?" he asks next. "It's you and this piss-head realtor, am I right?"

"I'm not in anything with anyone. Independent contractor."

"But this Yardley made the tape, I know that. What'd you do, steal it? No, actually I know this loser Mason stole it. What, you two are the team?"

It stops Bodie for a split-second.

"So it's you two douchebags, huh?"

How does he know?

Not that it matters. "Mason?" As if he's never heard the name. Not that Smooth's buying it, but who cares? "Don't know any Mason. Aren't we off the point here? You were saying I could get busted for blackmail . . . or *attempted,* it would have to be, because you won't go to the cops if you've just paid to keep this whole thing quiet. Either way you're getting them into an investigation I don't think you really want to get them into. And what do you care what happens to me? If this comes out your boy is finished and you lose a cash cow. You're his agent, right? So you're screwed, plus you look like a fool when you start trying to bail him out." Smile at him. "That's gonna be like bailing water out of the *Titanic,* right? But hey, whatever you wanna do."

Smooth holds his snifter to the light again, which means he knows he's caught between a rock and a hard place. Bodie flags a waiter and orders a Glenburnie. Might as well try 'em all, since he's going to let Smooth pick up the tab.

Finally Smooth says, "If Wheatley pays you, how does he know you won't keep coming back for more? I'm sure you've made copies."

"No copies. A one-time score, no seconds. I figure I'd be pressing my luck to try again, get you guys seriously pissed."

Smooth gives him a look, surprisingly cocky under the circumstances. "Oh, you've already done that, buddy. Which you know damn well. Which is why you're holding on to at least one copy: you think the cops'll find it if anything unfortunate happens to you, and even some dumb cops would be able to figure out why something unfortunate happened to you."

"Like I said, the idea of something unfortunate happening is why I'd never try it again."

"You mean, supposing you survive this first try?"

"Yeah, supposing. I'll be set up for a while anyway, so who needs the stress?" He studies his Glenburnie against the light, since they're playing cool-guy routines with their fine spirits: swirls it, sniffs it, takes a leisurely swallow, savors it. Takes his sweet time getting back to Smooth. Finally says, "I guess you've got to trust me, that's what it comes down to."

Bringing only a weak smile.

"Otherwise I go public with this, and what's in that for your side?"

"What if Wheatley won't pay? What if he *can't*? How many of these lamebrains do you think have two hundred thousand dollars sitting around that they haven't blown on houses, cars, dope, chicks, parties? You ruin the guy's career, maybe, but what's in that for you? Kicks?"

Ignore. "It's up to you, Slick. Make up your mind—me and my buddies want to get out of here."

He's boxed in and he knows it.

"Let me help," Bodie says, "so we can all go home." A little cocky himself now, but hey, loving it! "We'll meet at noon Thursday in the lobby of the Benson. It's up on Broadway, best hotel in town— you're probably staying there, a classy guy like yourself. Thursday gives you plenty of time to get the cash together. We'll both be carrying Nordstrom shopping bags—the store's right there on Broadway, a block or two from the Benson. I'll have the cassette in my bag and you'll have a shoebox or some kind of box in yours, with two hundred grand in hundred-dollar bills in it. Simple?"

"And I just take your word that the cassette you're carrying is *the* cassette?"

"Somehow I don't think you will, so we'll do this. You get a room at the Benson for Thursday, we'll meet in the lobby and then my buddies and I'll come up and we'll watch the tape."

"No buddies."

"Just to check the closets for buddies of *yours,* before we watch the tape. If it's clear they can wait outside and I'll take my chances with you."

Boxed in, Smooth gives him hard eyes and says softly, trying to seem menacing, "You'd better plan on watching your back for as long as you live."

"I always watch my back."

"I'm sure you've got lots of reasons to."

Bodie smiles and looks past him, waves to Luis. The guys slide out of the booth and head this way. "I think we're done," Bodie tells Smooth, and stands up. "Take care of the bill, huh? I'll see you Thursday at noon. The Benson."

"Cause I was small, was why I got into it," Titan says. "Everybody in the 'hood bangin', what you gonna do? But most of all, to show people I was just as big as them. Maybe not tall, but it ain't about tall. You get a sumbitch shakin' like this one here"—meaning Candyass upstairs—"then he the punk and you the man, nothin' else matter. Ain't about how tall, ain't about money, nothin' else. Ain't about nothin' you *say,* is why I never say nothin' I don't have to. Let 'em wonder. They wet their pants sometimes just wonderin'. Get *sca-a-ared,* wonderin'. You just wait, then *do.* Do whatever you got to, *when* you got to."

Wink nods, expels a cloud of smoke and hands Titan the pipe. They're fat with chronic after finding Yardley's stash, three oh-zees almost, and they're blasting off at the big kitchen table after filling up on tuna sandwiches and beer for dinner. "You don't hardly *need* to talk no more, do you? Not down home. Everybody know what Titan's about, ain't nobody gonna fuck with you."

Unhurried as always, Titan fires up. Closes his eyes, tips his head back and holds it in.

When he finally lets it out he shivers and blinks his eyes hard, the monster blast hitting home. When he remembers where he is he says, "Yeah, homeys heard when I took care'a Blueberry. Muhfucker start throwin' them Crip signs, callin' me 'cuz,' he gonna go down. I didn't say nothing, didn't do nothing till I did it—got him in a head-lock and come upside his head with a big ol' rock, just about caved it in. This muhfucker's so black he almost blue, why they called him Blueberry, but he for sure bleed red. Muhfucker don't know his own name to this day."

But people down there know Titan.

"Least I wasn't small no more, and never again. Least not in the hood. What you do is let people know the risk in fucking with you ain't worth what they hoping to gain. Like your boy upstairs. *'Course* he wanna go pee in the toilet 'steada pissin' himself. *'Course* he wanna sleep in that bed 'steada sittin' up on that hard chair all night. But it ain't worth gettin' cracked."

He's right: Candyass sure ain't looking to get cracked again. Maybe they'll crack him, maybe not, but the deal they gave him after Bernie Herman left was that if he stays on that chair and shuts up they might not hurt him any more. He's upstairs in an extra room that looks like it's never used—all white, walls and carpeting and furniture, the bedcover, everything. Up there sitting on the hard-back chair they took in and told him to sit on while they thought about what to do with him. When they went back in the room he was sitting there so obedient, Titan said "How 'bout we just leave him right here? Man, you ain't gonna move, are you, if we tell you not to?" The candyass stared at him, eyes wide, and Titan said "Tell you what. You stay on that chair, don't move a'tall, and maybe we don't bust you up no more. Huh? But we come up here and see you moved, we fuck you up. We hear that toilet, or we come up here and see something in it, we fuck you up. You stay where y'at, don't even lift your skinny ass off that seat, and everything be fine." Candy about to cry, blubbering about how his nose is broken and his ribs and he needed to call the doctor.

But he ain't moved yet. Yesterday morning they found him right there where they left him, no sign he'd moved all night, a wee-wee spot in front of him on the fine white carpet. Not looking so good, with his nose swollen and blood caked inside it, one eye bloodshot and surrounded by purple and black and yellow. Wanted to talk about permission to dump a load—have a BM, was what he said. Wink just smiled, letting Titan handle it. "Do what you please," the little man said, but stood right in front of him with those scary pumped-up arms crossed. "You wanna have a BM, have it. But you best have it right where you sittin', 'less you want your ass kicked."

Candy looked like he might cry.

They brought him his portable phone and made him call his work and say he's taking a few days off, family emergency.

Wink asked if he was hungry.

"Why're you asking? You won't give me anything, will you?" Whining. "Why're you doing this to me?"

"You want, we bring you somethin'," Titan said. "But food only gonna make you shit, and you not wantin' to shit, right? Right there where you sittin'?"

When they went in this morning he still hadn't moved. One more wee-wee stain, but he still hadn't shit. Looked pussier than ever: pale, tired, ass gotta be sore, face turning all kinds of colors.

But ready to beg. "Bring me something to eat, *please?* Or let me go get something and come right back here?"

"Cool," Titan said, "if you don't mind shittin' yourself. Not much left in that refrigerator, but we fix you a cheese samwich or somethin'."

"Anything. A cheese sandwich would be great."

Wink went down and slapped cheese between two slices of brown bread and poured a glass of water. Back upstairs Titan handed it to Candyass, Candy as grateful as you felt when they brought you a plate of some kind of dog-doo in solitary. His mouth was open for the first bite when Titan suddenly made a fist and faked liked he was going to splatter his nose again, Titan stopping just short as Candy's hands flew up to cover and he dropped the sandwich and glass of water. Poor thing, sitting there sad-ass as they laughed and high-fived. As they left the room he was reaching down for the bread and cheese, trying to put his meal back together.

It's dark out when Mike Johns stops by Max's place on his evening run. As acting district attorney since Tower crashed and burned he's too busy to run at noon with the rest of the guys (a relief to the rest of the guys), so he gets out after work. Since he lives in Westmoreland, not a mile away, he just loops down Sellwood Boulevard when he wants to make another stab at convincing the wayward son to come home. This is the third time.

Max doesn't encourage it. Johns always kissed up to Tower (no other explanation for his rise to first assistant), always resented the fact that Max was the golden boy anyway, and didn't hide his glee when the Pink investigation fell apart and Max got demoted and then fired. Once Paige put things together and Tower fell and Max was vindicated, the weaselly little bastard wanted to make nice.

Weaselly little bastard at the front door huffing and puffing in his sweats, an elastic strap holding his nerdy black horn-rims on. Max steps out on the porch, not inclined to invite him in.

"What's up, Million?" The old bullshit, the puffery they used to dump on him along with one murder after another. "Whatcha up to? Bored yet? Want your office back?"

"Not really. I'm not ready to do anything yet, and I'm not sure what it'll be when the time comes. I've got people telling me I should try defense work."

Johns makes a face like there's a bad smell on the porch. "Come on. You're not after money and you're not a bleeding heart."

"Like Paige Prescott? I'm still seeing her, Mike—best not say too much about bleeding hearts."

"You know what I mean. You're a prosecutor, Max. The best."

"Thanks a lot. I also know everyone's entitled to a defense, and it'd be fun to go up against some of my old pals."

"Except that you've never done defense."

Which, they both know, is beside the point. Who knows more than a DA about how a defense attorney should attack a DA's case? Besides, even when you handle a murder or violent crime case as a DA, you spend half your time defending the victim (dead or alive) when the defense starts trashing him in order to prove the defendant had a good reason for bashing his skull in. Because there's usually some merit to the trashing. A lot of your victims are just as bad as the defendants: dopers, dealers, drunks, crazies who put themselves in a position to be victimized. You defend them.

They've both seen plenty of DAs move over to defense and do fine. Johns is just counting on Max being a prosecutor through and through, a true believer on the right side, a guy who's constitutionally incapable of going into the business of keeping bad guys out of prison.

Max is savoring the unhappy look on Johns's face when two sizable guys in suits come down the sidewalk looking up at the house numbers, find the one they want—his—and turn up the walk. Despite the suits, Max is pretty sure they haven't come from mass.

They stop at the short flight of steps up to the porch. "Max Travis?" the bigger one says. About six-five, 250, with a tree-stump neck straining his collar.

Johns sort of slides off to the side as Max sizes up the two, trying to recall if he ever prosecuted either one. Always his first thought when strangers approach him, knowing who he is.

"Well?"

"I don't think we've ever met, fellas. And I know you haven't introduced yourselves."

"We'll say you *are* Travis, then," the big one says. "And we're not interested in you anyhow. Where's Tommy Mason?"

"Mason? No Mason here, fellas."

"When'll he be back?"

Something to do with Tommy taking off that way. "He won't be, that I know of."

"Then you know who I'm talking about."

"Maybe. I've got a friend named Mason who stayed here for a while, but he's not here anymore."

The two look at each other, then Jumbo comes up the steps, his partner following. Jumbo moves up close to Max, glaring down, clearly accustomed to intimidating people.

Max is about to introduce them to the Multnomah County District Attorney, but decides to hold off and try to find out what it's all about.

With Jumbo busy terrorizing Max, his buddy takes over the talking. "What's the story, then, friend?"

"I think you should tell me. I'm clueless."

They look at each other as if he said something amusing. "Look, Travis," Jumbo's buddy says, "we don't wanna waste your time, and we'd appreciate it if you didn't waste ours. We'd like to have a few words with your friend, that's all."

"Like I said, he's not here anymore."

"We heard he lives here."

Max takes a step back from Jumbo looming over him, smelling of Altoids. "He stayed awhile, but he's gone. Moved."

"And when was that?"

"Couple days ago."

"Why?"

"Why'd he move? He thought he'd been here long enough. He thought my girlfriend didn't like him."

"And *where'd* he move, assuming any of this is true?"

"Couldn't tell you. To an old girlfriend's place, I think, but I've got no idea who. Now let me ask you fellas something."

"We'd rather ask the questions," Buddy says. "It's simpler and quicker that way. And the quicker we make this conversation the quicker we're outta your way, so it works for everyone." A speech he's obviously delivered before.

Max says, "Just tell me who you are and what you want so I can let him know if I see him. I don't know if I will, but just in case."

Buddy harrumphs. *Yeah, you bet.* "Listen, Travis. You seem OK and we don't wanna bother you. All we want is to talk to your pal."

"Like I keep saying, he moved. And I can't tell you where because I don't know. He said he'd get in touch, but now that I've met you two I'm not sure he will. What's it about, fellas?"

Buddy studies him. Max studies Buddy. Jumbo turns his attention to Johns, shriveled up in the shadows off to the side. Jumbo pulls him into the light with a thick arm around the famous pencil neck, Johns's beady eyes popping behind the horn-rims.

Now's the time. "Fellas," Max says, "we've been talking so much you haven't even met this man here. Let me introduce you to Michael D. Johns, the District Attorney of Multnomah County, the most powerful law-enforcement official in the state after the Attorney General."

It sounds absurd—scrawny Johns in his sweatshirt and running shorts, with his pencil neck and horn-rims on a strap—but they can't disregard it.

Buddy says, "Who the hell are *you*, then?"

"Travis. You know who I am, you called me by name when you walked up. I'm nobody."

"Senior prosecutor." Johns speaks! Heads turn. "Head of the Violent Crimes Unit."

Max gives the muscleheads a modest shrug. "Used to be, anyway"—taking a little shot at Johns.

The two have had an instant attitude adjustment. Buddy flicks his head toward the street, *Let's go*, and Jumbo follows him down the stairs and down the walk, giving Max a last bemused look over his shoulder.

Max can't resist. "You fellas enjoy walking in the rain?" he calls after them. "Or you just didn't want to drive up in a car that could be identified?"

They don't look back until they're halfway up the block, indistinct between two streetlights. Then Buddy turns, cups his hands and yells, "Tell Mason blackmail's a dangerous game!"

Wednesday night, Wink and Titan are smoking a bowl at the big round kitchen table after more tuna sandwiches and beer, Candy's icebox pretty much cleaned out by now except for some pickles and ketchup and margarine. Nothing left in the cabinets, either, except some shit in cans.

Titan thinking: Time to go, get back to LA. They thought they'd hear from this Bernie, or LaPrince, but Wink leaves messages on LaPrince's machine and they still don't call. They thought something would happen but no, nothing but this chipmunk upstairs making yellow spots and dropping little Tootsie Roll turds on his beautiful white carpet and crying when they come in the room, asking how long they gonna do this to him, saying he needs to see the doctor. Who needs this shit?

Wink blasts off, then takes a pinch out of the bag and reloads. Getting too fried, but Titan's glad to see him coming down from the last of Candy's cocaine. Two days talking shit about getting hold of that tape himself and getting some respect, show fucking LaPrince whassup and get set up ourself! Talkin' 'bout half a million, a million—shit, wanna hose his own brother!

He's about to crash now after two days tripping on coke and smoking chronic, but he'll be talking the same smack as long as he's upright. "We be dumb to leave now," he's saying. "We know somebody got somethin' bad enough on the nigga that he thinkin' 'bout payin'. So we get our hands on this thing he willing to pay for, whatever it is, and *we* get paid. See? We be *fat*, you know what I'm sayin'?"

Titan thinking no, no, no, even though it might work. *Might*. But maybe they end up back inside, too: eating dog-doo, watching TV, watching behind you for who might object to your tattoos and come after you.

But Wink's so crazy, and so trippin', he won't leave it alone.

Still talking the same shit when they hear a car pull up out back.

They look at each other. First time it's happened, they don't know what to do.

Gotta be a friend of Candy, somebody knew how to open the gates down by the road. Wink gets up and goes to the door, Titan behind him worrying he might do something crazy, even do something with his damn nickel-plated nine-millimeter he's so proud of. He pulls the little curtain back. Dark outside, but the light from the kitchen lets you see a white lady with a floppy hat get out of her car, head this way.

"Damn." Wink straightens up and slides off to one side, out of sight. *Damn* is right, Titan's thinking as he moves out of sight on the other side of the doorframe. They're a couple of stupid shits to still be in this house at all.

They hear the screen door bang, then her footsteps coming across the porch. "Be cool," Wink whispers, like he's cool as can be and only worried about Titan blowing it.

Door opens and she walks right in, then freezes when they step out behind her and block the door. Black hair hanging out of the floppy hat, red lipstick, some kind of black outfit with gold buttons and buckles. No movie star, but nothing wrong with her.

She's confused, seeing them, like maybe she came in the wrong house. "Rod . . . ?" she says. Yeah, she knows something's wrong. Looks over her shoulder like maybe she can run out that way.

Wink snags her arm hard, gives a yank to get her attention and slams the door, a few more bits of glass falling out of the pane he busted the other night to get them in. The lady makes a little squeak, scared, and looks to Titan like maybe he can save her. Shit. Too late for any of 'em now, too deep into it.

Wink says, "Sit down at the table there, momma. Everything cool."

She's frozen. "Rod . . . ?"

And suddenly it's fun for Titan. The buzz you get when somebody's scared stiff, their eyes flickering all around looking for help when there ain't no help. Besides, it's too late to bail now. "Rod?"

he says. "You mean Candy? That who you come to see? Oh yeah, *Rod.* Well, we his friends."

"F-friends?" Her voice shaking. She looks over at Wink with his crazy grin, then back at Titan's hard stare. "No you're *not* his friends! Where is he?"

Titan says, "Candy?"

Wink says, "You mean the candyass? Sickie makes movies of people jammin'?"

She makes another little scared sound and Titan can't resist grabbing her arm hard and saying "We his friends, momma, like I said."

Wink grabs the other arm. "Maybe you be our friend too, huh? What you think?"

But she ain't even thinking. *Praying* is what she's doing.

"Your boy upstairs," Wink tells her. "You want, we take y'up there." Running his hand up and down her arm now, feeling her.

Crazy. But things have already gone too far. She squeaks again, tries to pull loose from Wink, but he jerks her arm hard and slaps her face with his other hand. "*Bitch!*" With that tone like he can't believe she's gonna resist, like she better cut that shit right out.

And suddenly there's something in his eyes and Titan sees what's coming, even before Wink looks over and says he ain't had none since before his last stretch, thirty months.

Titan says, "I ain't had none since we come up here"—because it's gone too far already, why not? They can always make her disappear afterward. But probably don't even need to. This Bernie cat, LaPrince's agent, said Candyass can't tell the police nothing about nothing without getting his own ass in big trouble, and if this bitch is Candy's friend she won't say nothing either.

And maybe it's the bitch crying, or maybe just because he ain't had any lately, but she looks fine to Titan now. A little prissy maybe in her suit and jewelry, with nails manicured and painted, but she's *shaped,* yeah, just fine. Even got some titty on her, rare for a white girl that ain't fat. "Momma," he says, "you up for a charge?"

She squeaks once more and tries to shake loose again, but they've got her. Titan likes the fight and reaches up with his free hand and squeezes her chin so hard it looks like her eyeballs are about to pop out of her head and she quits struggling.

"You lookin' good, momma, you know it? Let's get ridda this here"—taking the floppy hat off her head and sailing it—"and go find a quiet place to take off the rest."

"Upstairs," Wink says. "Come on, we go see Candy."

Bernie's got Eddie in the kitchen making martinis. Artie's sprawled out on the couch in the living room, explaining about tiny hidden videocams.

They flew in from Cleveland this afternoon, an hour after Wheatley left for Phoenix with the Plunder—a great swap, from Bernie's point of view. Too bad it's a short trip for the team. He's booked a room at the Benson for tomorrow and gotten most of the money together, but even if he gets the tape he'll be out here a while longer trying to sort this thing out, and he doesn't much like being around Wheatley.

Artie. Bernie can see him aging. Only in his thirties but nearly three hundred pounds, pale yet always flushed, wheezes a lot, doesn't sound good. But he always seemed old, even in his twenties. He was all about taking care of business, always.

"Piece'a cake, what this Yardley probably did," he's saying. "The pinpoint lens, the part that sticks through a wall or ceiling, it's about a quarter-inch in diameter, about like the eraser on a pencil. He could wire it easy, power it through an extension cord to the regular outlet in the next room, cover up the cut marks with a little drywall patch. A nice little low-light camera and some high-quality audio pickups, he's set for a couple grand. He could pull it off pretty easy."

"He did pull it off."

"Yeah, well, some people just ain't got good sense."

So true. And so reassuring, Artie is. Artie's presence. He might drop dead next year, or next week, or right now right in front of you, but as long as he's around he's as reassuring as can be. Always gargantuan, and always Artie.

*   *   *

He lifts his prodigious carcass off the couch when headlights flash across the front windows and they hear a car in the driveway.

"Taxi," he reports, at the window. "Looks like two guys coming."

Bernie moves up behind him and looks for himself. Yes, two figures crossing the yard toward the house, coming into range of the porch light.

Yeah, the two loose cannons, La-what and the Giant. Giant? Something like that. The shorty powerhouse who looks sixteen and thirty-six at the same time.

"Eddie!"

Eddie materializes, martinis on hold for the moment. Ready. They've been expecting these clowns to show up, with Bernie not going back over to Yardley's place or returning La-what'sit's calls. Maybe they understand they're *out* and they're just coming to pick up their car and go get on with their lives, but most likely not.

Artie's pumped—ready for some exercise if necessary, and as a rule he's happy when someone makes it necessary. Eddie's got his gun tucked in the back of his pants. Cleveland guys.

"These idiots don't get in the door," Bernie reminds them.

"Not a chance," Artie says, and it's easy to believe a guy who'll fill the doorway all by himself.

Feet and voices outside. Bernie wondering what the imbeciles will say.

They don't bother knocking: one or the other tries the door as if they belong here, as if they're all in this together. It's locked, of course. They try again.

Finally Bernie gives Artie the nod: open it.

The half-brother's in front, La-what'sit, and startled to find himself face-to-face with the three of them. The little babyfaced apeman behind him. They probably expected Bernie to be alone.

"Yo, men," La-what says, as if they're all friends, all in it together. Wink, Bernie recalls, is what he goes by.

Bernie gives him the dead stare, the fisheye. "Yeah?" Artie and Ernie, on either side, wait.

Rattled already, Wink looks over his shoulder at the little apeman—Titan—but Titan gives him a blank look back as if to say, You handle it, I didn't want none'a this from the git.

Wink turns back to Bernie. "I guess we done with the punk over there. Come over here to see what you want next. Maybe we help you get this tape back, y'ain't got it already."

Not in this life, Sparky. Bernie gives him the fisheye again.

"So?"

"I think we've got things covered," Bernie says. "But before you go, how is Mr. Yardley?"

"Busted up so he prob'by do whatever to get out from under. Like you said."

"Well, I appreciate it. Your half-brother will appreciate it."

Desperation in the fool's eyes now, as he grasps the reality. Yet he's still trying to ignore the reality. "So, what now?"

Bernie's got nothing for him but a faint smile and the fisheye. "We'll take it from here."

There's a wild look in his eyes and a lot of things on the tip of his tongue, but he's smart enough to stifle himself. The sight of Artie stifles most people, even pinheads.

"I do appreciate your work," Bernie says, "and to prove it I've got a little something for each of you, send you on your way in style. But there isn't much more you can do here."

Wink's crushed. He expected a parade, maybe? But he musters up a last stab. "We was thinkin' we come crash here tonight. Got noplace else."

You were thinking shit. You weren't thinking at all, knucklehead. Bernie gives him more fisheye as Artie and Eddie stand there like two boulders, ready to close ranks and form a wall the dimwits can't see past, much less *get* past.

"One night?"

"Can't do it," Bernie says.

Desperation in his eyes, resignation in the apeman's. "We kick this faggot's ass for you, scare him so he gonna do what you tell him—now we can't sleep here one time?"

"Sorry. Take what I give you and go set up in the best hotel in town. But not here."

"Shoo', man. Why you doin' us like this?" Beaten, and he knows it. He turns and gives his buddy a sad look and an elaborate shrug—*Look like we're out of it*—and starts down the short flight of steps from the porch.

Nice try. Bernie pokes Eddie, who's already reaching for the gun in his waistband.

Which is what Wink sees—Eddie's gun leveled at him—when he hits the walk at the bottom of the steps and turns back, pulling a pistol out of his coat pocket. Too late.

He's not stupid enough to push it.

"Toss it out in the yard, pinhead."

Looking like he might cry, he meekly drops the gun on the grass— "There"—like a kid hoping to get points for cooperating when he doesn't have any choice but to cooperate.

Bernie says, "Thanks, men. We'll call you if we need you."

The little apeman's heading for their car, ready to clear out, but pathetic Wink stands there looking at the three of them in the doorway. Finally gathers the nerve to say, "How 'bout that present you said you had, for us takin' care'a that punk for you? So we can get a place to stay tonight."

Eddie laughs.

Artie says, "Run on, boy. And don't let me see you back here."

Bernie spells it out. "If I see you again I'll call the police about a cementhead who's probably violating his California parole by being up here in the first place. Two of 'em, in a black Nissan with California plate WHM 660. Let the authorities take it from there."

It's almost sad, watching him turn and head to the car.

Then again, it's only one minor problem solved, if it's solved. Still no sign Bernie can solve the big one, and tomorrow's the meet.

That Darveena, *damn,* probably make a dead man shoot a wad. For sure, the best LaPrince ever had.

For a few minutes, until he got hold of her little sister. Or maybe Rashunda's older, who knows? Who cares? All he knows is, if there's any more sisters, he wants to meet 'em.

It's about four-thirty Thursday afternoon, a few minutes until the bus to the arena, and he's lying on his bed in the Phoenix Ritz-Carlton trying to recover from getting fucked silly. It's also the day he might lose two hundred K, but until it happens it ain't real. All he can think about now is those sisters.

Last night on the plane Yuban told him about these sisters he always visits down here, always glad to see some studly players. So after shootaround today they took a cab to the high-rise apartment one of them lives in and they were both fine, pretty faces and long legs and jugs. They laid out some coke on a glass-top table, fine shit, and pretty soon they were all dancing, floating, tripping, the big living room weirdly dim with the drapes pulled against the glaring sun. Yuban and the one called Rashunda danced off somewhere, and pretty soon Darveena came up close to him and reached down and asked was he ready to party. Sheeit. And this girl knew how to party. Wore his ass *out.* They were lying there after, LaPrince wondering how he could play ball tonight, when they heard the other two giggling out in the hall and then a tap on the door and Rashunda's head poked in, Yuban behind her. "Mr. Everready here say we better be switching now," she said, "so he can have time to take his nap before tonight." And she came on in, another fine body naked as could be, and when Darveena got up and went with Yuban she took him in the shower and soaped him until his pecker felt like a telephone pole down there, and kissed him like she wanted to suck the tongue right out of his mouth, and he just wanted to get out of that shower and . . . But didn't get out for a while, not until she rocked his world right there.

There was plenty more in the bed, but back at the hotel LaPrince is still savoring that action in the shower. Doesn't want to answer the phone when it rings, but Bernie said he'd call about the meeting with the guy. Picks up. "Yeah. This LaPrince."

"Big man. Bernie here."

"Whassup?"

"It's done. I didn't have any choice but to pay him."

Damn. All this time he kept thinking Bernie and his boys from Cleveland would figure a way out of it. "All? Two hundred grand?"

"All of it. No choice. I called some people this morning and came up with the last part, but we'll sort that out later—I mean, if we don't get it all back from this shitbird some way. I just want you to not worry about it now. Play ball, things'll work out."

Easy for him to say. "What you gonna do, bro?"

"Something came up. I'm going back to Cleveland for a few days, but my guys are still here at the house and they're going to check out some things. Locate this writer, for one—Mason—see how he's involved, make him take us to the shitbird with the ponytail. Shitbird with your *money*. Locate the girl if we can, see what she knows. And we'll lean on this Yardley, the pussy. He's the asshole, just as much as Mason and Ponytail, and I told him *he* owes you that money if we don't find the shitbird and get it from him. He can sell his house, his other properties, his cars, antiques— all his fancy shit, I don't care. None of this ever happens if he doesn't make this tape."

LaPrince stares at the ceiling, wishing he could get his hands on the kissass. Hoping *somebody's* wearing him out. "Them two still over there kicking his ass?" he asks. Maybe LaMetrius doing something worthwhile for once, maybe earning something 'steada holding that hand out.

"Nope. They're gone, way gone. Couple of fools, no offense, trouble waiting to happen. They showed up here last night wanting to stay and we had to tell 'em we don't want to see 'em again. We told 'em and they're gone."

Sheeit. They're gone until they come back, he means. Ain't never that easy.

Bernie says now they'll work on getting their money back—LaPrince's, Bernie's, Bernie's friends'. The dudes from Cleveland will stay at the house for a while: take care of LaMetrius and the Titan if they're dumb enough to show up again, check up on Yardley, maybe locate Mason, the ponytail, the girl Little Bang. You, La-Prince, just play ball.

Nothin' to it, right? Shit. How's he supposed to concentrate on ball? He's already out two hundred grand and Bernie's saying it might not be over, somebody might have a copy and try to hold him up again.

"Two hundred grand," he mutters. The dude just walked off with it.

"I went in there thinking *maybe* we could pull something," Bernie says. "Maybe grab the shitbird after the switch or something. I had Artie and Eddie and three other meats outside the hotel, and a car, but there was no way. He showed up with the same crew he brought to the bar last week and a few more, I think eight in all, and they walked him out and got him into a van and out to the airport, straight onto someone's little twin-engine and right on out of there. My guys followed the van afterward but got lost somewhere. But I swear, we'll make this burnt-out hippie sorry he was ever born. Believe that."

Hard to believe.

He tells Bernie to hold on to the tape, lock it up: he wants to see this thing that cost him two hundred grand, *then* take Bernie's advice and destroy it. He barely remembers what happened that night but Bernie says he watched the tape and yeah, it would be trouble, there was no choice but to pay.

He wants to sleep, sleep, sleep—come down after the coke and the amazing sisters and some chronic and now this shit. Headache. Last thing he feels like is standing up, much less ride down to bang with Phoenix.

But Porky Pig gonna call any minute, say come get on the bus.

Turner doesn't need this. The man's crazier'n hell.

He stops by LaPrince's room to make sure he's ready to catch the bus to the arena, and the man's sprawled on the bed looking like he just got pulled through a keyhole by his hair, if he had any hair. Finally gets up and pulls on his wraparound shades like nobody'll notice, but when they get on the bus out front Turner sees a couple of assistant coaches looking and senses they're looking at him too, Turner, wondering if he's been doing whatever LaPrince has been doing.

No point trying to talk to him. Look what happened in Indy, in Detroit. He blows up, apologizes, then goes right back to doing what he's gonna do.

He's lethargic during warmups, plays awful, cusses Colabello when the coach says something about his effort, then doesn't talk to anyone on the plane to Houston. Wearing the wraparounds at midnight, and the headphones, disappearing into his boogie music.

Coach, disgusted with all of them after Phoenix, makes Friday's practice the toughest since preseason. Hollers them through a full-court kick-ass scrimmage. Pushes LaPrince as hard as anyone else for a change, meaning he's fed up. Runs Michailovic at him, then Turner, then Michailovic again, pushing him.

Now Turner again, and Colabello tells the scrub team to keep calling Turner's number, make LaPrince work. LaPrince is worn out and pissed by now, grabbing to keep up and throwing cheap elbows when he can, taking it out on Turner.

But hey, Turner likes seeing the coaches get on him a little, and Turner will bang if he wants to bang. He doesn't have a fraction of LaPrince's talent but he's just as big and prides himself on toughness. And he's as fed up with the man as Coach is. More fed up.

And cheap shots coming now. And some woofing, that huffy ghetto shit Turner started hearing when he got to college and started playing against a lot of black boys. Muh*fucker*. Honky *bitch*. Fuck you, fuck this, fuck that.

Another elbow, and when Turner shoves back it's "What the *fuck*, man?" like Turner started it.

Turner knows a blowup's coming when LaPrince bumps him at the water fountain during a break. "The *fuck's* this shit, boy?" He's not Turner-man anymore, just a boy. White boy, honky bitch. "Ain't got no game so you start playin' pussy? You lookin' for trouble, dude. Best back off and go get some game 'fore y'end up back in fuckin' Italy, or back fuckin' them cows on the farm."

Then the little smile as he heads back to the court, like he's only kidding.

Then the whacking starts right back up, a shove on a rebound so that Turner almost hits the floor. Only kidding.

People watching now, aware it's going on, and you've got to respond. At the other end Turner steps around him, setting up for a rebound, and when the shot drops through the hoop and he turns the other way he gives LaPrince a bump. A slightly late bump, unnecessary, and LaPrince's head snaps around. Mean eyes, no smile now. "You pushin' it, boy. . . ."

It escalates until Turner's had enough and gives him an obvious shove. LaPrince stumbles, nearly pratfalls, and scrambling back to his feet he's *coming*, forget basketball, coming for Turner, and Turner plants himself, ready.

"I'll whup you like a yard-dog, white boy!"

"Bring it on, Wheat! You be better off shittin' in your momma's—"

"*Fuck* you, boy!" Faking a punch, but that's all. "*Fuck* you!" again, almost like he's waiting for people to jump in and keep them apart.

Which they do: Yuban first, then Michailovic and others.

"Fuckin' *punk*," LaPrince snarls, badass again with a half-dozen players and coaches keeping them from each other. Yuban telling them be cool, be cool, with a hand in each of their chests.

Coach gives LaPrince a breather, Turner and Michailovic going at it the last few minutes. LaPrince, on the side, whooping when Michailovic scores.

"Nice to see a little spirit out here," Coach says with a smile before dismissing them. "But let's save a little for tonight."

When the mad wears off, Turner feels sorry for him more than anything.

LaPrince plays better tonight—didn't wear his shades to the arena, so maybe he wasn't high—and on Plunder One back to Portland he flops on a couch near Turner and tries to make nice. Apologizing without apologizing. Turner understands, but it's hard to warm up when this shit keeps happening.

And Turner's wondering what Puckerman will say about the scuffle at shootaround. *I keep you around because you're his friend, and now you two are fighting?*

Getting off the plane at Portland International at 2 A.M., LaPrince tells him he's not *really* a honky bitch. "That ain't me," he says, "talkin' to my man that way." As close as he'll come to an apology, but it's bullshit. That's what they all say after they fuck up: "That ain't me." But it is. Who else is it? *They* slapped somebody, *they* got the girl knocked up, *they* got arrested, *they* talked trash. But LaPrince says, "I got shit on my mind I can't even talk about. You know that ain't me, Turner-man, comin' at you that way."

Trouble is, LaPrince doesn't know who he is, what he is. Never knew his daddy, so he never had an example. Never had that man around to cool him off when he got het-up with himself. Gum whipped Turner's ass at Siler's ramps feed and made things as clear as a wart on a hog's back: Act right.

Not even "Mr. Basketball" of North Carolina was too big to cut wood, put up hay, string fence, dig a well, tend livestock—feed 'em, breed 'em, worm 'em, show the prize ones at the Macon County fair and the state fair in Raleigh.

Get your marks at school.

Stay out of people's business and out of trouble.

But so many of these guys . . . Turner remembers the day in LA two years back when the team visited LaPrince's elementary school. Remembers watching LaPrince that morning, picturing him in those same classrooms not so many years ago, one of those same kids. Kids with their crazy black names, third- and fourth-graders supposed to be showing off their reading to the players but couldn't read *Cat in the Hat*. Everyone applauding anyway, to be nice. LaPrince probably glad, Turner remembers thinking, that *he* wouldn't be called on to read.

Out in the hall that day the teacher told the PR man not to leave the gift T-shirts and basketball magazines unattended—"These kids're so poor, this'll look like Christmas." Yet it seemed like half of them were wearing $150 Jordans. How many of their families went hungry so they could have those shoes? Who was making those choices?

The parents didn't have time to help their children learn to read, but they could spend hours doing their hair in cornrows.

No wonder these guys grow up not knowing what's real.

Out in the hall that day they looked at the poor kids' "I wish" assignments taped to the wall. "I wish I lib in a house with stairs." "I wish I hab a house with two batrooms." Later LaPrince drove Turner through some scary neighborhoods and finally past a run-down place he said they lived in for a while when he was a kid. Sad, even before he said that was the *nice* place they lived in.

He was a little sad-ass black kid, like the ones at the school. So young they had no idea how bad they had it. Had no idea they *better* learn that reading, no idea school was for more than showing off your Jordans or the stupid hairstyle your momma thought up while she was cracked out.

No wonder they don't know who they are. No wonder they don't know how to be.

B odie was out of town for less than forty-eight hours after turning over the video and collecting the money from Smooth at the Benson. Luis and the guys escorted him to Randy's van around the corner after the swap and they sailed out to the airport, Smooth's gorillas following in a rental—more gorillas posted in the terminal, maybe, but Randy turned into the landing strip for private planes and pulled right up to Lonnie Shank's Baron. In a matter of seconds Bodie was inside the four-seater with Lonnie, and Lonnie got clearance from the tower and yelled "Anchors aweigh!"—the most fun he'd had with the plane, he said, since he quit smuggling dope—and they were gliding down the strip and then elevating, leaving the three or four gorillas in the rental car to sort it out with seven black belts if they thought they could.

They didn't try very hard, Bodie found out an hour later on the phone from Lonnie's cabin in Black Butte. They followed the van out of the airport and for a few minutes more, but either Rocky lost them at the I-84 interchange or they just gave up. What could they do, after all?

Bodie spent the rest of Thursday getting high, counting and re-counting the money, lolling in the nearby hot springs. It was Friday morning, yesterday, when he hatched the idea of going to the Plunder with one of his copies of the tape. Fuck 'em. They've got the richest owner in the league, and they're assholes.

Saturday afternoon, he's sitting in the office of Plunder honcho Bob Puckerman. "You can believe me or not," he says. "I've got the tape and I can take it to the press, or the police, or I can let you have it." Pretty sure the honcho doesn't want it getting out.

"Suppose we call your bluff? Suppose we decide we don't have a quarter-million dollars for a bottomfeeder like you?"

"Sticks and stones, Mr. Puckerman. Look, it's up to you. You call my bluff, I go to the cops—or to the press, and they go to the cops—and Wheatley's arrested and you're a putz for signing him. You almost have to get rid of him, arrest or not, after blowing so much smoke about this good-citizen clause you put in his contract."

A hard look from the honcho. "Why're you doing this?"

"What does it matter?"

Honcho ignores it. "Money, obviously, is why you're doing it. You wouldn't think twice about ruining someone's life, would you?"

"Neither would your boy. Neither would you. Don't start throwing stones, you're in no position. Let's cut to the chase."

He considers for a moment, more than a moment, and finally asks, "What do you want?"

Bodie smiles. "Well, I figure it's worth more than an autographed ball to you to make this go away. You want to keep your boy on the court, right? Not that's he's doing much. More important to you, you don't wanna look like the putz of the year for signing him."

Behind the big desk, Puckerman scans him up and down like he's inspecting a giant turd. Fine. Bodie doesn't claim to be a model citizen, but *he's* not a public figure representing an organization that's the biggest thing in town. If he was, he'd be different.

"Suppose you let me see it," Puckerman says. The video.

"Not now. Not yet. I didn't even bring it. Let's just talk about what it's worth to you, besides an autographed basketball."

"I asked you before, what do you want?"

"I just asked *you,* what's it worth to you?"

"I can't say, because I don't know what you've got. And frankly, I'm not so sure you'll do anything if I don't pay you."

"Ah. Wanna play chicken, huh?"

He ignores it. "You sure you'd go to the media? Or the cops?"

"Pretty sure. If you don't believe it, try me."

"Then you go to the press or the police—they both end up knowing, whoever you go to first—and you come out looking like a blackmailing piece of garbage. A *failure* of a blackmailer, didn't even get paid. So, what do you gain?"

He's bluffing, gotta be. Bodie turns his palms up like, Hey, OK, it's your call, and says, "It'll be interesting, anyway. It'll be big—ESPN, the networks, *Sports Illustrated,* the whole bit. Maybe I'll write a book."

Puckerman grunts. "Beautiful."

"Yeah. So, are you saying you're not interested? You'd rather play chicken?"

The honcho spins in his swivel chair, shows Bodie his back, contemplates his corner-office view of the river and the West Hills.

Bodie waits, knowing damn well who's holding the royal flush here.

It's at least a minute before Puckerman spins back around. Bodie wonders if he's come up with something. But all he says is, "How much do you want?"

"A quarter-million, I already said. Because I'm not greedy. Nice round number, pocket change for you guys."

Not a flicker in the flat expression as Puckerman studies him again, considers the number. "I don't think so," he says at last.

"What's fair, then?"

"How 'bout an autographed ball and I don't go to the police about blackmail?" He doesn't look like he's kidding.

Don't let him throw you. He's kidding or he's crazy, one. You've got the tape, you're in charge. "Seriously," Bodie says. "I don't have a lot of time."

"You don't have a lot of smarts, either. You actually think you're going to pull this off? You think I fell off a turnip truck or something?"

What's he thinking? Bodie searches for a clue in the blank slate of a face, the cold eyes. Mr. Personality. Bodie remembers seeing him at the Stones concert at the Plunderdome last summer, down in the front row with the owner and the owner's latest dog of a girlfriend—the place going wild, even the dorky owner, and Puckerman sitting there like he had a cob up his ass, like he just didn't *get* it, forcing himself to applaud every so often for appearance's sake.

But maybe he knows something. You don't get to the top by growing a ponytail and going crazy over rock-and-roll. You develop a steely look and play hardball.

"An autographed ball, asshole," he says, "or you just go ahead and do whatever you're gonna do. What I still don't understand is, what will you get out of blowing this up? Get interviewed on *Inside Edition,* show the world what a scumbag looks like?"

Saturday night, in Kay's parents' luxury suite high up in the Plunderdome, Audrey and Kay sit on barstools at the Plexiglass windows, looking down at the Plunder and Detroit, third quarter. As usual, the rearrangement happened at halftime: the adults from six or eight suites, half-crocked by then, drifted over to Dr. Van-Kirkman's to spend the second half getting completely hammered and listening to his racist jokes, while the kids got together elsewhere. Most of them are at the Brutons', a few at the Haydens'.

Audrey didn't feel like being with them and asked Kay not to go either.

It's different now, since that Saturday night two weeks ago.

This is when she always glued on the fake nails—third quarter, free of her father, end of the game an hour off. The guys love it when you scratch, they think they're driving you crazy, so she turned her chewed-down nubs into claws and raked their backs and moaned things like "I never felt such a big one! I don't know if I can take it!"

But that's over now. She's just watching the game, and without much interest. The games were boring before she started partying with the players, and they're boring again now.

"So," Kay says, "you don't want to do anything later?"

"Not if you mean . . . you know."

"Fine." Kay knows what she means. "Just making sure."

Audrey stares down at the court, remembering. Trying not to remember. She'd rather not come here at all anymore but her father will give her a hard time if she says so: it's his idea of a shared experience for them, even though he starts boozing as soon as they arrive and rarely sees her at all after halftime.

Kay, concerned, asks if she's still freaked.

"I don't know about that, but I sure don't want to be any closer to *him* than this"—the sight of LaPrince Wheatley down on the court bringing at all back. "Or any of them."

"You're freaked."

"It was scary. He was scary just fucking—something about him, even before he started messing with me." And she is shaken now, talking about it. She slides off the stool, wanders away from the window. "Can I have some of your dad's tequila and orange juice? And then we get out of here? Let's go over to your house, if your folks are going out after the game. Maybe I'll sleep over. My father won't care, if he even notices I'm not home."

Unable to shake the memory. He *was* scary. His finger back there, just the tip of it, it hurt. And he wanted to put that fat black monster in there, and he would've. . . .

What was she doing there at all?

She must be messed up. Think of what she did with those guys. She couldn't just blame her father.

It started two years ago, in a way, when he said she was out of control and sent her to his friend Lefkowitz. (Same thing he did to Mom: called her crazy.) "Out of control" because she smoked cigarettes, told a few lies and—last straw, such a crime!—got caught skinnydipping in Lake Oswego with some friends when she was supposed to be sleeping over at Candy Gilbert's house. The skinnydipping set him off because the police picked them up and the news could have gotten out that "media psychologist" Henry Van-Kirkman, who was making a fortune advising the people of Portland on everything from marital problems to drug addiction to the latest presidential peccadillo, couldn't keep his own daughter out of trouble. He was still holding his breath waiting for people to find out his wife had left him.

"Do you realize how I'd look?" he snarled on the way home from the police station that night. "You're going to see a guy I know."

His friend and colleague Howard Lefkowitz had an office in the same downtown building. By the third session Howie ("Call me Howie") was no longer sitting back stroking his beard and pondering her statements, talking about "adjustment reaction" and "borderline personality features," encouraging her to take her time growing up even though her intellect was ahead of schedule, he was sitting close to her, looking her over, touching her whenever he could and pretending it was casual. It was the fifth or sixth session when he lost it altogether. "You're not a borderline personality," he said. "Not psychotic, not manic. You're beyond diagnosis. There's no model for a fourteen-year-old who's so fully flowered. You're fourteen, yes, but you're not a child at all, not even what I'd call a young lady. You're a *woman,* a woman in a young lady's body— but no, even that's not right, because it's every bit a woman's body. You *are* a woman, that's all—all woman at a young lady's age, is the best I can say it. That's why you don't fit, why people don't understand you. And being misunderstood is what makes you act out a little bit. *Preternatural* is the word that keeps coming to me. You know it? It means extraordinary, even supernatural, and that's what comes to mind when I think about how sexy you are. It's as if, even at your age, you're crying out for physical love, with a full-blown appetite for love that you might not even be aware of. And an incredible talent for it, I can't help thinking."

Meaning he was horny. She was a virgin but she'd heard a lot, and had kissed and groped and been groped a fair amount, and she let him talk and then let it happen, right there on the couch in his office. How about this, Dad?

The next week Lefkowitz seemed nervous, guilty. But he got around to it. She liked it more that time, knowing what to expect.

Before she left that day he gave her two packages of birth-control pills, prescribed by a Dr. Krell for a Barbara Baxter.

She wanted to tell her father everything, throw it in his face, but that would ruin it. Lefkowitz might go to jail, and even if he didn't, it wouldn't happen anymore.

She watched some of the dirty movies her father hid in his closet and started gasping and squealing when Howie pumped away, telling him he was sooooo big, scratching his back. (That was when she started using the fake nails, because she couldn't stop gnawing hers down to nothing.) He went crazy every time, sweating and swearing, his thinning black hair falling in his face as he humped away.

A thrill, doing it and thinking about Daddy—right down the hall in his office, sometimes—but even a fourteen-year-old knew Howie Lefkowitz was a loser. Besides, he had skinny legs and bad breath and kinky black hair all over his shoulders and back, more of it there than on his head.

It was the year the Plunderdome opened. She didn't care about basketball but her father had the suite and made her go with him sometimes, usually the weekend games—partly for the appearance of father and daughter doing something together, mostly to keep her from running around. It was after a late-season game (after four or five hump-sessions with Howie) that her new friend Kay, two years older, took her down to join a crowd of fans and groupies behind a red velvet rope in a big hall where the players passed on their way from the locker room to their cars. Yuban Taylor, the star of the team and damn good-looking, stopped to talk to some people a few feet away, and when he turned to go Kay yelled that he should be a movie star. He came over, Kay made a few quips and a minute later he leaned down, dropped his voice and invited them to a party. At Rod Yardley's house a little later he took Audrey aside and told her she was the reason: "You a little dish, you know it?"

And took her upstairs and showed her a dick that made Howie's look like a midget's. It hurt, but it was worth it, imagining how Daddy would feel if he knew one of those big dumb overpaid jungle bunnies, as he would say, was hosing his little lily-white honor student.

When she showed up for her Tuesday session and Howie tried to put his arms around her, she pulled away saying it wasn't going to happen that day or ever again. "I'm not even coming here anymore. Either you tell my father I'm normal and there's no point in continuing this or else I'm going to tell him what your favorite therapy is. How 'bout that?" She was out of there two minutes later, and the next day he said Dr. Lefkowitz had called him saying she was fine, more or less a normal teenage girl with normal teenage moods—nothing he could do for her, and nothing for Dr. VanKirkman to worry about. She was carrying a 3.8 at Catlin Gabel, the ritzy private school, and keeping her room clean, and hiding her smoking from him, so there wasn't much he could say.

She told Yuban and anyone else who asked that her name was Daisy, she was a psych major down at OSU, her family had a Plunderdome suite and she came up for weekend games. She and Yuban got together six or seven times at Yardley's house, where the players partied after games, until that season ended and he went off to Hawaii, Europe and eventually his Alabama hometown.

Even then she realized it was crazy and she probably was disturbed. But by the next fall, a year ago, Daddy was being a bigger butt than ever and she made up her mind that if he was going to ruin her Friday and Saturday nights by making her go to the games, she was going to keep fucking with him. Even if she didn't dare let him know she was fucking with him, not that way, or she'd find herself in a mental ward like Mom did.

Yuban had moved on to other girls by then, but the first time she went to Yardley's house Fleet Mays was on her before she'd hung up her OSU jacket.

Daddy wouldn't have committed her, he'd have shot her.

In the suite at the next game he started yapping about jungle-bunny ballplayers who couldn't spell their own names, couldn't get an honest job if they had to but were raking in millions—and she hated him, and waited for Fleet afterward, rode out to Yardley's with him, did some cocaine and then did Fleet. *Damn, you somethin' else!* he moaned. *Where you get that mouf, girl?*

It lasted a few weeks. She had enough pride to drop him the night she and Kay showed up at Yardley's unannounced and he was coming down the stairs with a slinky black girl, no mistaking what they'd been up to.

She didn't lack for company. The word was out. Sammy Dee was next, even more excitable than Yuban or Fleet. "Yuban said you a *treat*," he told her one night, worn out, "and that ain't no lie." There was Zip Henry, briefly. Bobby Oscar one time, after the last playoff game last April, a week before she turned sixteen.

Because you're fucked up, Daddy.

But she's pretty sure, when she stops to think about it, that she is, too.

Turner's the first one to practice on Sunday, out on the floor with an earlybird ballboy feeding him, the shots going down like Turner wishes they'd go down in games.

The rest of the team gradually drifts in, the trainer, the equipment man, finally the coaches. LaPrince not here yet, or Brisbee, but everyone else.

Turner's still shooting at the far basket, with Michailovic now and Sammy Dee and a couple more, when the moon-faced PR man LaPrince calls Porky Pig waves him over. "Mr. Puckerman wants to see you for a minute, Turner. He's in the coaches' office."

About the scuffle with LaPrince in Houston? A trade? Probably not a contract extension.

Puckerman sits behind Colabello's desk with a crabby look on his face—Turner thinking, Well, it's his normal look, so maybe this won't be anything bad. The boss points him to a chair and Turner sits down and waits while he fiddles with some papers on the desk, still looking crabby.

He finally looks up. "Turner, we're letting you go."

It's no surprise, somehow. Turner waits, nodding slightly—not that he understands why he's being cut, but he understands it's a done deal.

"Remember when we talked?" Puckerman says. "When I told you we were keeping you? Remember what we talked about?"

"That I needed to work hard in practice, play hard when I get in a game, be a good guy?"

Puckerman nods—like he's saying Yeah, but that was window dressing. He says, "There was more, wasn't there?" And then gets to it. About LaPrince, he says. About Turner being a good influence, and letting him know—Puckerman—if LaPrince was going wrong. "Remember? Well, I've heard some things that convince me you haven't held up your end." Pauses. "Anything you'd like to say?"

What can he say?

The boss leans forward, elbows on the desk, fingertips making a steeple in front of his face. "I've heard about parties with marijuana and substances. I've heard about undesirables, both male and female. I've heard you've seen all this."

Turner spreads his hands, helpless. It's over, the man already said so, so why say anything? What's there to say?

"And you two aren't getting along, I hear. This scrape down in Houston, what's that about? We don't need that between teammates, any teammates."

"Well, sir, *that*," Turner begins, because *that* he can explain—

But Puckerman waves a dismissive hand as soon as he opens his mouth. "Doesn't really matter. Maybe he was out of line, maybe not, but he's a teammate."

"He started it!" This bullshit, Turner can't put up with. "We're teammates but I'm a man, too, and when he starts with cheap shots and talking that trash—"

But Puckerman raises a hand to hush him. "That's really not as important as this other—as you not coming to me about these other things like we talked about that day in my office. Not as important as the fact that you're apparently involved in the same activities, involved with the same undesirable people. Which is obviously why you didn't come to me about LaPrince."

Turner sweating a little now. What does he know exactly, and who else knows?

"I think you're basically a good kid, and maybe talented enough to get in a few years in the league if you keep all your ducks in a row. Emphasis on *if*. It won't happen here, but maybe somewhere."

Leading up to something. Turner waits, at his mercy. Wondering if he's going to try to wiggle out of the guaranteed contract.

"I tell you what, Turner. You're finished here, but instead of cutting you outright and making everyone in the league wonder why, we'll put you on injured reserve, say back spasms or something. You go home, see your family, whatever you want—but *out of town,* you understand? You don't talk to anyone about this. In a few weeks you'll have faded out of the picture, out of everyone's mind. Then you go ahead and do whatever you want, hook on with another club or overseas. You understand me? But that's *if* you keep quiet about everything here—parties, drugs, women, everything. Otherwise, you're still our property and I won't let you play ball anywhere. You understand?"

Turner waits. He's not finished.

"You do like I say and we won't say anything about the fight, since a guy like you has to be able to get along with his teammates. And we won't say anything like you're not good enough to play in this league—it's strictly back spasms or a pulled muscle or whatever I end up saying—so maybe you can hook on with someone else. Follow me?"

"Yessir." Getting screwed, but what can he do?

"But if you say anything about anything—about LaPrince Wheatley in particular—I'll make sure you never play in this league again. You're not good enough to stay at this level if people think you've got an attitude, much less a drug problem. There are a—"

"I don't have a—!"

"—a thousand nobodies out there dying to fill the last spot on any roster in this league, not a cunt-hair's difference between them and Turner Boyd. Understand me?"

Turner could strangle him, pop those icy eyes out of his head, but anything like that *will* finish Turner Boyd in the league. But he can't just take this. "Can I say something, Mr. Puckerman?"

Icy eyes. "There's really no need."

"Well, anyhow. What I have to say is, I'm not perfect, but LaPrince is gonna do what he does no matter what I say, no matter what anyone—"

The raised hand again, cutting him off. "I've heard enough. It's your decision."

Heard enough from who, since he's hardly let Turner get a word in? But don't say it, don't smart off. He'll smoke you, he don't give a rat's ass.

"I'm sorry it turned out this way. It didn't have to. I think I made myself clear in my office that day. I thought you understood me."

What can you say?

Max knew something was wrong, very wrong, after the two muscleheads showed up Wednesday evening looking for Tommy. He had no idea what the comment about blackmail meant, but he was positive that Tommy's abrupt departure on Monday wasn't about his guilt over staying too long at Max's house.

No idea how to find him. Max doesn't know any of his friends' names and hasn't had any luck reaching his wife by way of phone listings.

Thursday morning he drove down to Central Precinct and talked to homicide sergeant and old buddy Stan Kearns. No murders in town since Tuesday except for a woman, probably a hooker, baseball-batted to a pulp under the Burnside Bridge. Kearns promised to let him know if anyone approximating Tommy's description turns up dead, then called his sketch artist and told her to work with Max when he came downstairs. By noon they had likenesses of the muscleheads.

Next he went to the county License Bureau, but couldn't find a marriage license for a Thomas Mason born in the late fifties. It required a drive out to the Washington County bureau, where he found a 1992 license for Thomas Mason and Julie Rose. *Bingo.* Drove back downtown and called Jerry O'Leary at the office—ace DA investigator, steadfast friend and mentor—and they met at Starbucks across from the courthouse. After Max explained things, Jerry got on the Starbucks pay phone, called Portland General Electric and came back with the address for an account in Southwest in the name of Julie Rose. She apparently held on to her maiden name when she married Tommy.

She wasn't home Friday morning, but that evening there was a light on and a black VW in the carport and she answered the door, a slight, pale woman who would have been pretty if she weren't so tired-looking, washed-out. Max recalled Tommy saying she wasn't well, she'd been diagnosed with a degenerative illness similar to lupus the week after their wedding.

She said she hadn't seen Tommy, hadn't even heard from him in a few weeks. When Max said Tommy had told him the two of them had been talking about getting back together she shook her head, smiling faintly. "When he left this last time and then wanted to come back, I told him I couldn't let him jerk me around anymore, I needed to think, and would he please give me some time and space. He couldn't, or wouldn't—he was calling me all the time, writing me long pleading letters. I finally called him, wherever he was staying at the time, and told him he was ruining it for me, ruining any chance we might still have. He's left me alone since then, six weeks or so, and it's been so peaceful. . . . I've got some physical problems, I don't know if he told you, that get worse with stress, and I've been feeling so much better since he's been gone that I know I can't take him back. There are so many good things about him—along with the immaturity, the moods—but if being alone, even being lonely, makes life bearable for me, that's what I've got to do. I need to let him know, but it's hard." Sadness in her eyes. "It's hard, and I just haven't."

Hardly what Max expected. He said he was sorry about her health and all of it . . . But he needed to find Tommy. Could she possibly help?

She wasn't sure. "You could try the friend he stayed with after he left, Glenn Waldron. And I know a couple more of his friends, I've got their numbers. And I can give you his e-mail address."

They talked a little more, then Max took down the information and left.

Glenn Waldron, it turned out, hadn't heard from Tommy since he moved out of Waldron's place, weeks ago. Neither had Teddy Doe or Blake Nichols.

And Tommy didn't respond to Max's e-mail yesterday.

This morning it's DA touch-football in the rain and muck at Wilson High, followed by beer and bullshit at Charlie Witty's house. And it's quite a story Witty tells, even before the name Yardley rings a bell.

A few nights ago a woman named Alice Richardson called the police, hysterical. Even when they got to her a few minutes later, it took awhile to calm her down to where she could tell them what happened. What happened, she said, was that she dropped by a friend's house—friend, not boyfriend—where she was grabbed by two black guys she'd never seen before. No sign of her friend. These two take her upstairs, they're going to rape her, and she knows they'll kill her afterward. They take her into a bedroom—and there's her friend on a straight-back chair, naked, just sitting there, a couple of little turds on the carpet and some yellow spots where he's peed. She's freaking out, begging him to do something, but the guy just sits there like he's tied to the chair. He's a mess, black eyes and bruises and all, they've obviously kicked the shit out of him, and one of them takes her to the bed while his partner, this little muscular guy, stands over her friend telling him it's his choice: he can sit there like a good boy and watch the fun or he can stand up and get his ass kicked again. The guy sits there. The lady's freaking out, about to get raped. She catches his eye for a second, begs him to help, but he can't look at her.

The one guy makes her undress and suck him, and then he rapes her. Then he goes over and sits by the wimp while the other one does her.

She's sure she's going to die (Witty goes on). She's seen their faces, she's seen their tattoos—no way they'll let her walk out of there.

But she did, obviously. They told her she'd be dead if she said a word, they'd get her or make sure someone else did. They slapped this wimp around a little, this Yardley—

Yardley?

—and he sat there taking it, not even getting off the chair, telling them no, no, *he'd* never tell. They told him to stay right there, don't move, and they walked her downstairs with her clothes in her hand, still talking about killing her if she ever said a word, and threw her out.

"Trusting guys, huh?" Witty says. "If not very bright."

Max thinking, *Yardley? The prettyboy from the Swim?*

Exactly a week after the nightmare started, Yardley's watching *Sunday Night Football* again—in the living room this time—trying to comprehend his incomprehensible situation through a heavy Percodan haze.

The sound of a car out back sends him into an instant, full-blown panic. No, he didn't close the gates when he got back from the ER on Thursday, but hell, they don't keep out anyone who wants to get at him. God, are *they* back? As car doors slam he jerks upright on the couch—four broken ribs screaming, Percs or not.

They're coming through the porch. Now pounding on the lower door panel—he hears more of the shattered glass up above falling out. Yelling for him: *Yardley!* Has to be the spade—the police wouldn't pound like that, wouldn't sound so pissed. Jesus Christ.

He's got to go open up. They'll come in even if he doesn't, and they'll be more pissed because he didn't present himself.

His ribs scream with every step. And the terror, the idea that you're on your way to let them in so they can bust you up some more—he could cry.

Big bodies on the other side of the curtain, more than two. Maybe it's not them after all. Or it's them *plus*.

No choice but to open up.

Three white guys he's never laid eyes on. Thirties, probably, wearing jeans, sweatshirts, regular stuff. Not criminal types. Two of them not even pissed-looking, sort of standing by like they just came along with . . . this guy. Lord, big bruiser wearing a letterman's jacket from somewhere—blue, with a gold L over his heart with little gold footballs and basketballs attached—and a Seattle Mariners cap.

"*Yardley?*" he snarls, and Yardley backs up—but not fast enough, the guy stepping in and giving him a two-hand shove that sends him reeling across the floor and smack up against the counter.

"What the—? Who the—? You—you—"

"*Shut the hell up!*" he bellows, his eyes flaming, advancing on him as the two others hang back by the door. "So, punk, you don't do a thing, huh? You just . . . you just"—towering over him now, Yardley backed up against the sink—"you . . . you"—spluttering, enraged.

Suddenly Yardley understands. Yes, there's a resemblance to Alice. Her brother, cousin, something.

Looming over him with mad eyes, breathing hard, ready to explode. Yardley caught between him and the sink.

Terrified, he slides out of the squeeze and backs toward the doorway into the hall—all but fleeing, which would be a very bad idea. "L-listen, hey"—as the guy, six-four or -five at least, advances on him with a couple of giant strides—"look—"

"Shut the fuck up, I said!"—one massive paw jumping out again, landing flat on Yardley's chest near his right shoulder and sending him staggering back toward the table. "Shut up and sit down!"

He sits and shuts the fuck up, not sure he could speak even if he had permission, no idea what he'd say if he could.

The big letterman, Mariner or whatever, stands over him, pointing a thick, threatening finger in his face. Dark stuff under the nail, maybe he's a mechanic or something. Yardley thinks he remembers Alice having a brother, maybe more than one, but can't remember anything else.

"So you didn't do anything!"

Keep quiet.

"I'm talking to you! You didn't do a fucking thing, right?"

"You don't understand. . . ."

"I guess not. Help me if you can, goddammit."

"Wh-what could I *do?*" Hearing the whine in his voice but way past worrying about it, way off the deep end.

"What could you do?" He looks at the other two, over by the door, like he can't believe what he just heard. Now back at Yardley. "What could you do?"

"They broke my ribs, they broke my nose! Look at this!"—the swollen, discolored lips, the swollen nose packed with cotton, the swirls of black and yellow and purple around his eyes. "Four broken ribs—I could hardly move, and they would've pounded me if I did! What was I supposed to—"

"You do *something,* you punk! You don't sit there while they"—snapping Yardley's head sideways with a slap—"you don't just sit there and let her get raped!"

Yardley knows he's right. Alice's terror when they brought her up to the room, her pleading with them . . . and finally pleading with *him,* to do something. *Rod, please! Please!* The crazy one slapping her then, telling her Go on, get them clothes off, Candyass ain't doin' nothin'; the babyfaced bonebreaker standing in front of the chair with his huge arms folded and a little smile like *You wanna try?* Yardley telling himself no, he couldn't change anything, couldn't stop it, could only get busted up some more and maybe get them both killed. No sign of the gun but he'd seen it the night before, he knew they had it. . . .

But still! He and Alice might be dead now if he'd tried anything, yeah—but for him, at least, it would be as good as the fix he's in now.

"You faggot, you do *something!*" The big hand twitching, itching to whack him again. "And the police came here Friday and what? *What?* You little . . . despicable little"—can't even find the words—"despicable little godawful little creep! You tell 'em you don't have any idea who these scumbags are, why they were over here fucking you up all week! *Protecting* 'em! Wha'd they do—tell you you're meat if you say anything?"

"It was true," Yardley whimpers, "I didn't know." Praying the lie will fly.

"Like hell. Now, who were they? They didn't even steal anything, just camped out here fucking with you, and you have no idea what it's about?"

"No! I don't know." Whimpering, but he can't help it, doesn't even care. All he knows is that it all starts unraveling if he tells anyone anything. "I don't know who they were, why they stayed here and beat me up. I told the police they must be on the run, hiding from someone, and decided on my place. I told the police all I know."

Staring at the blue snaps on the front of the letterman's jacket, asking himself why he didn't just swallow all the Percs and do himself in when the burrheads left that night. They took Alice with them and he was sure they'd kill her and he'd either have to go to the police, which he couldn't do, or live with the secret and the shame for the rest of his life, which would probably drive him insane.

Feels the Mariner glowering down at him. Wonders if the meaty paw will fly out at him again. Hears Alice wailing *Rod, please!*, then pleading with the crazy spade and then screaming as he slammed away, slammed away, and finally started laughing at her, cackling, telling her *Bitch, you lucky to get some real thang if this candyass over here and his little tweeter's all you been getting.* The two of them switching then, the crazy one watching him while the little bonebreaker hurt her, either hung like a horse or just plain violent. Yardley unable to look, shell-shocked. . . .

Shell-shocked again now, staring at the snap-buttons on the Mariner's jacket, barely noticing one of his friends coming over—until the friend grabs a fistful of his hair and jerks his head straight back, leaving him staring at the ceiling with his breath caught in his stretched-out throat. "I'd like to bust you up," he growls, holding him there, Yardley gasping, the Mariner leaning over him now like a dentist and saying, "The police don't believe your shit either. Don't think they're done with you either, shithead."

"I c-can't breathe!"

"Too bad," the friend snaps, and jerks his head forward so hard Yardley nearly pitches off the chair.

Upright again, he looks at the Mariner—who looks fit to kill, and would be doing him a favor. "I'm s-sorry," he whimpers. "But I thought they'd k-kill us both."

Whack! A backhand rattles his teeth and splits his bottom lip open where the ER doctor sewed it up. Blood in his mouth.

"You *thought*. You didn't think shit about her, mister, and you're not thinking about anything but yourself now."

"No, I—really, I—is she all right?"

"Great. Excellent. You can imagine. Thirty-six hours in the hospital fixed her right up. But I for one don't think she'll ever be the same."

Meaning what? But he doesn't want to know. Wants to, but he's afraid of what it might be. And isn't sure he should open his mouth anyway.

"She's home now, you prick, and she should be more or less OK one of these days. Physically, anyway. Not that you care, or you'd have done something at the time. Tried."

What can he say?

"They did smack her around right in front of you, right? After they finished raping the hell out of her? Otherwise tell me she's a liar, because that's what she says."

"I . . . I . . . no, they did, and I sat there. I started to get up then"—he did!—"and the little musclebound one came and smashed my ribs again. They were broken already, I couldn't've done anything anyway, but I got up, I was gonna—"

"Shit. Fuck off and die, mister. You didn't do shit. You sat and watched these sonsabitches rape her and then watched 'em try to put the fear of God in her, smacking her around."

"No—"

"You heard 'em tell her she better not say a word or she'd be messing up *your* world too, under the ass-headed impression she's your girlfriend. . . ." Shaking his head in disgust.

Nothing to say.

"You haven't heard the last of this, shithead. Not from the police, not from me. The cops think you're lying and I *know* it and I'm not gonna let you have a good night's sleep until *she* does, maybe not even then—and she's not gonna sleep good for a damn long time, I can tell you that. Now get up." Grabbing the front of his shirt and pulling him up off the chair. "Now, you say your poor ribs hurt?"

"Broken, four of—"

He doesn't even finish before the guy smashes a righthand uppercut to his lower left rib cage, same spot the babyface spade hit at the bottom of the stairs a week ago, *crunch,* and his breath leaves him and he can't even scream, just doubles over sobbing and gasping. Pain like he's never experienced or imagined.

The friend straightens him up with a forearm shot to the chin as they depart, but it hardly registers against the fire in his ribs.

"We'll see you, shithead, and I suggest you give some thought to telling the truth. That or assisted living, because if you don't help 'em nail those two I'll make sure you need someone to wipe your sorry ass for the rest of your life."

I don't know what to do about my friend," Max tells O'Leary, "the guy I told you about the other day. I talked to his wife after you got the address, she says she hasn't seen him. And yeah, I believe her. Hasn't seen him and it's clear she doesn't want to. Gonna divorce him."

It's Sunday evening, the Veritable Quandary nearly deserted, Max and O'Leary in one of the back booths they favored when Max was going through his second divorce and Jerry, alone since his wife's death, helped him close the place so many times. Jerry's got his Wild Turkey, Max the Max Blaster the waiters have automatically delivered since Nick Bella, the owner, brainstormed it one night—Rumple Minze and Jagermeister on ice.

"So," O'Leary says, "still no idea what it's about? None?"

"Not really. Something to do with the Plunder, maybe? I don't know."

"The Plunder?"

"Probably not, when I stop and think about it. I just don't have a better idea. And this guy who called wanting Tommy to meet him, two days before these goons showed up, said he was from *Sports Illustrated*, so he knew Tommy writes sports. . . . Hell, I don't know, I'm groping. Anyone wanting to draw him out might say that."

O'Leary merely sips his Turkey, indicating it doesn't strike him as a hot lead either.

"But one of these goons said something about blackmail as they were walking off. 'Tell Mason blackmail's a dangerous game.' But I've got no clue. Blackmail? Tommy Mason? I can't see it."

Over another Turkey and another Blaster they speculate, speculate, which is what you do when you're clueless.

"Then there's this guy Witty told me about, guy named Yardley."

"The guy who watched a friend get raped."

"You've heard?"

"Witty got the case Friday and wants me to check the guy out. I'll start tomorrow. What about him?"

"I met him—through Mason, indirectly. After the first Plunder game, Friday night two weeks ago. Mason took Paige and me for drinks with LaPrince Wheatley, Yuban Taylor and a couple of others, and this Yardley was there too. Friend of the jocks, a realtor, sells 'em their mansions."

"And?"

"And I don't know." Shrugging. "I mean—well, nothing."

Nothing adds up, so what's to say?

He doesn't feel like going home to the dark house alone. It's only nine when they leave the VQ and O'Leary heads home, but Max is reminded of too many late nights before and after the second marriage: half-smashed, bar-smoke in his clothes, nothing but the empty house and empty bed waiting for him.

It's been almost two weeks since he's talked to Paige—since the argument in the car on the way back down Mount Hood, Veterans Day—and maybe she doesn't want to hear from him at all, but he stops at the booth in front of Sellwood Market, a few blocks before the dark house, and calls.

"Hello?"

"Hi."

A moment passes. Finally, hesitantly, "Max?" He can tell she's relieved and a little bit thrilled.

He asks how she's doing, how she's been. Fine. What she's been doing (since Donald Royer hanged himself with a sheet in the Justice Center jail the night before her big trial)? Reading, she says, relaxing, getting over. . . . Her voice trails off, and he knows she means getting over Royer's suicide and the aftermath, which Max doesn't want to think about: her standing on the Justice Center steps beside sleazy co-counsel Pennington the next day, for instance, at Pennington's hastily arranged press conference, where he not only trashed the police again for using knock-and-talks but called for an independent investigation of the suicide, as if the jail deputies might have hoisted up the 270-pound Royer and let him drop.

Leave all that alone. Pennington was senior co-counsel, she couldn't have stopped him.

"I need brains," he says.

"Oh."

"Hey, come on. That's not all I need, or want, but I would like to know what you think about . . . I don't even know exactly what. Tommy's gone, and maybe in some trouble, and I need someone smarter than me."

"Such a flatterer."

But he can see her little smile. "You saved *my* bacon," he reminds her. "Who else would I call?"

"What do you want to do?"

"See you. Talk. You're probably in for the night, but—"

"Come over if you want to, Max."

"I was hoping you'd say that."

"You've still got a toothbrush here."

She looks great in jeans and sweatshirt—and more than that, glad to see him.

Glass of wine?

He'd love one. What's she been doing? What was she up to when he called?

In bed reading.

She didn't need to get up, get dressed.

Well, all he'd said was that he wanted to talk, wanted her brain-power. She didn't take anything for granted.

"I said your brains weren't all I wanted. Depending on how you feel about me, of course."

She fills the glasses on her kitchen counter and turns to him— Paige again, the tight-jawed Miss Prescott gone. Hands him a glass, takes his free hand in hers and leads him to her little bedroom, where she sets her wine on the nightstand and props her fat pillows against the headboard. Max notes the bookmarked Faulkner on the floor, imagining her under the covers in her nightgown a half-hour ago . . . maybe wondering, as she read, if he'd ever call again, or if he was going to be another disappointment.

"So, what do you need my feeble brain for?" she asks when they're settled on the bed, on top of the royal-blue comforter.

"It's about Tommy, like I said, so you might not care."

"What's going on?"

Relieved to know she doesn't want to fight anymore, not even about Tommy, Max tells her he moved out last Monday. "Very suddenly, within hours of some guy calling the house claiming to be a recruiter for *Sports Illustrated,* an editor, wanting Tommy to come meet him. I took the call, didn't think anything of it . . . left the message, went out for a while, and when I got home he was halfway out the door. I still didn't think much of it—he said he knew he'd stayed too long and he had somewhere else to go, which was reasonable. I didn't think anything of it till Wednesday night, when two bruisers showed up looking for him."

"And you think *I* might know something?"

"Not really. I mean, obviously you wouldn't. But who better to talk something over with? You might come up with an idea. You've had 'em before."

Like back in July, after Tower had fired him and filed the complaints with the Bar and Max was moping around, hopeless: her freakish suggestion, after the voluminous research she'd undertaken, that they might locate Teddy Cunningham, the key to everything, at a certain condominium in Clearwater, Florida. Cunningham was there, sure enough, and the next day Max and O'Leary were on a plane to Florida and two weeks later Dan Tower was toppled and interim DA Mike Johns was begging Max to come back.

Looking straight ahead—the blank TV on the chest of drawers, the framed Mount Hood Jazz Festival poster on the wall—he says, "As these goons were leaving, one of 'em said something about blackmail. 'Tell Mason blackmail's a dangerous business,' something like that."

"Blackmail?"

Max looks over at the flawless profile—Paige looking straight ahead now—and says, "I love you, you know it?"

"You think I might be able to help, that's all."

"That too. But I do."

But she doesn't want to get into it. She's not much help with the Tommy issue, either. Not that he really expected her to be. He's at a loss, after all—Tommy's friend—and she barely knows the guy. When Max speculates that it might have something to do with the basketball players, she reminds him that basketball players are way outside her expertise.

Still, they look back to the night at the Swim, the four players

they met. Paige says, Tell me who they were again? LaPrince Wheatley, Max says, the one who invited them out after Tommy's fawning
story—"the one you said looked like Snoop Doggy Dogg trying to
be Harry Belafonte, or vice versa." Yuban Taylor, "the handsome
one you sliced and diced—the star, everyone's favorite." Mark
Mona, the crude white guy with the raggedy head and the stutter.
Turner Boyd, the southern boy, who only had a beer or two and
seemed like he didn't want to be there . . . who was put on the injured list today, Max heard, and sent home to get over some back
trouble. Wheatley's buddy, for what it's worth.

She sips her wine and admits she's stumped.

Max tells her about visiting Tommy's wife, which yielded nothing
except the story of their doomed marriage.

"So your best guess is that it involves the basketball jocks somehow? Maybe he's trying to blackmail one of them?"

"It's my only guess, and it's only a maybe."

He's ready to drop the whole thing, move on to what's happening
with them, but she's staring at the Jazz festival poster with the look
that says she hasn't let go quite yet—which is enough for Max to
give it a little more time, considering her track record.

Finally, absently swirling the last of her wine in the glass, she says,
"Did he do anything with them that night after we left? The realtor
kept telling me the party was moving out to his place later, but I
don't know who-all he was talking about."

"You'd have been included, I'm sure, if you hadn't stomped out
like that. You know? The host's special guest?"

"Very funny"—and a light elbow in the ribs from her. "Come
on, seriously."

"Seriously, no, I doubt he did. He'd have said something when
we got back from Hood. But speaking of your not-so-secret admirer,
have you heard . . . ?"

Always good to be back in Macon County, and especially good after what happened in Portland. Turner's back where none of that matters.

He called home Sunday afternoon, after getting the word from Puckerman, and flew out a few hours later. To Atlanta, then the puddlejumper to Asheville, where Gum and Momma met him at 3 A.M. Eastern. Then the drive he's made how many times in his life, some new highway now but mostly the same, most every bend in the road familiar: Enka, Canton (where the paper-mill stink recalls Granddaddy's story about the lady on the bus asking him if he farted), Waynesville (with the McDonald's Turner went to after so many ballgames), Sylva, Dillsboro—finally around the mountain to Franklin, home, on out to Cartoogechaye and the long way out Homer Boyd Road (Gum's granddaddy) to the old house. The familiar smell of it, everything in its place like forever.

Almost five by the time he got to sleep, but something made him drag himself out like old times when he heard Gum banging around at six, on his way to feed the pigs and put out hay for his prize steers in the pitch-dark and freezing-cold before he headed for breakfast at the Sunset and to work at the rec park. Turner wanted to be with him, that was it, and back in the house after they tended the animals Gum called Sunset and asked his cousin Myra to have two breakfasts ready instead of one at twenty-five till seven, his boy'd be with him.

His boy. Stepson, but it had never felt like that, whatever that was supposed to feel like—never felt any way but right. Turner thinking about it on the way to the café in Gum's pickup (with the 0–60 IN FIVE MILES bumpersticker), and thinking about LaPrince and all that *half*-brother mess and feeling bad for him again, somehow, even though Turner's out of the league and LaPrince is still back there collecting his millions. Not earning, but collecting.

Then Turner was thinking, Without his stupid shit I'd still be in the league myself.

It felt good at Sunset, the old boys saying howdy and Turner saying Y'all right? and them saying Fine, fine, always a fine day when you wake up and y'ain't got dirt in your face. They don't have much, most of 'em, and most of 'em have never set foot outside Macon County, but they've got everything they need and they mostly never wanted to go anywhere anyway. Turner remembered Gum's daddy Lester, eighty-something, sitting in his chair in front of the old house on a summer evening after supper, telling little Turner this is the specialest place God ever made, no reason to leave.

Gum came home at noon to check on the cow coming into heat, and found her bawling and took the afternoon off and they bred her down in the barn. Then, with a light snow swirling down around the mountain, they took Gum's truck along frozen-over Cartooge-chaye Creek down to the woods and filled her up with red oak and poplar Gum had already cut and split, drove home and stacked it out back to dry for next winter.

Turner asking himself, Why leave? Like old Lester said way back when, why ever leave? For millions of dollars, maybe, but that wasn't going to happen for Turner now. In the league today the names get millions, many millions, and the rest . . . well, it's not chicken feed, but for a guy like Turner it's one year at a time, no security, stressful. Like Puckerman said, he's not quite good enough to stick unless the situation's just right, unless someone needs a scrapper who won't cause trouble and they choose Turner out of a whole lot of guys like that. He can get more money overseas, *if* Mr. Shapiro can get him a job, but it's overseas, and it's one year at a time, and Turner's heard stories about guys in some of those leagues, even guys in Italy, signing contracts—guaranteed—and never getting paid at all.

It's how his career is shaping up. And he's not even sure Mr. Shapiro will stick with him now. So . . . get a new agent, go begging to ones even lower in the order than Shapiro.

Or stay here.

Coach at the high school. Be an assistant over at Western Carolina

U in Cullowhee, like they've asked, until the head job opens up—and they'd probably open it up before long if you're interested, the biggest name to come out of the area in a long time.

Or forget ball altogether, except for pickup, and work with Gum and the prize steers and pigs, or buy some of Gum's fine land out here, fields and forest, and raise your own stock and work the land yourself. Or buy some other property. After two years in the league, even at the minimum, and the year in the Spaghetti League at a half-million (with house and car provided, bills and even your taxes paid by the club), you've got plenty salted away, definitely more than LaPrince and most all of them with their cars and mansions and sound-systems and jewelry and kids they're supporting in every city. Plenty to buy most any piece of Macon County you want.

Forget the fast life, the sharpies with stony faces and icy eyes who tell you anything that suits 'em and then shitcan you; forget the crazy ghetto-boys with their woofing and their boogie music; forget the uncertainty every year. Go see if Marcie Ledford's still got her little weaving studio on the Georgia Road, see if she's married yet.

It sounded so good yesterday, and it still don't sound half-bad. He's had a nice run in ball, got himself set up. And when your best quality on the pro level is that you're tough as a pine knot—not your shot, not your D, not *game*—maybe that run better be enough.

He's thinking about it again when the phone rings, midafternoon. Gum at the rec park, Momma at Public Health.

"I'm looking for Turner Boyd, the basketball player," someone says. A *ferner*, as they say around here, with a *fern* accent—the kind that says they don't have no accent, you're the one got an accent.

"Thiz Turner."

"Turner, my name's Max, Max Travis—I'm out in Portland, a friend of Tommy Mason. You know who I mean? Writes for the *Rose City Review,* wrote a story about you a couple of weeks ago?"

"I 'member."

"He brought me and my girlfriend along to that club downtown, the Swim, after the first game, and we met you and LaPrince Wheatley and some others. Remember the night?"

Shit yeah, Turner remembers. The night the mess started, LaPrince firing up a fatty in the car later and pulling Mason in when he came walking along and saw them . . . asking him to score . . . driving

them all over Portland in the middle of the night to get the cash
together for three bags. . . .

"Turner?"

"Yeah, I 'member. You the guy with the woman?" He sure remembers that woman.

"At the other table, yeah. Tommy's friend. What I'm calling about
is, I think Tommy's in some kind of trouble. He was living with me
and he moved out all of a sudden and I haven't seen him, can't
reach him. I don't know what it's about, I might be way off base,
but I know Tommy thought a lot of you, not that he knew you very
well, and . . . I don't know, I thought you might know something."

. . . Mason meeting them at the nice bar the next night and following them out to the real-estate man's house with LaPrince's three
bags; the tasty-looking girl going upstairs with LaPrince, then
coming back down looking jangled and yelling for her friend and
the two of them taking off; everyone wondering what happened,
and LaPrince appearing in his shorts, fucked up on drinks and
smoke and coke and going off on Mason, whacking him . . .

"Anything you know might help," Max Travis says. "Anything
about why someone might be mad at Tommy."

"I can't think of anything, sir."

But Mason was a good guy, even if he was crazy to buy weed for
LaPrince. He was good to LaPrince with that big story about him,
and then to Turner—calling him "Colabello's Victory Cigar" without making a joke out of him, saying how other things are more
important than basketball—and though Turner doesn't know why
LaPrince went off on him that night, he does know LaPrince was
fucked up and there's a good chance Mason didn't deserve the trash-
talk and the whack.

*But . . . you ready to talk about LaPrince, maybe get him in some
trouble?*

"No idea?" Max Travis says. "Well, then, maybe you can help
me with something else. Do you remember the skinny blond guy
sitting at my table that night? His name's Yardley, he's in real estate,
sells houses to some of the players? He told us he was having a
party later that night. Do you know if there was a party, and if
Tommy went to it? Like I said, Tommy's in some kind of trouble.
I have no idea if it involves any of these people, I just don't know
where else to start."

But Turner really *doesn't* know about a party that night, even if he felt OK to talk about LaPrince. It was the *next* night that Mason met them and they went out to the fella's house and things happened.

Tell him that, then.

Turner says, "I really don't know, sir."

"Did you go over to that man's house after you left the club? I'm not trying to put you on the spot, Turner, I just want to help my friend if he's—"

"I didn't, sir. I went home that night, after. To the Residence Inn, I mean."

"All right. Did you see much of Tommy after that night? At the games, or after the games—anywhere? After his story on you came out, maybe?"

"Not really."

Quiet now, the man in Portland not knowing where to go next.

"Well then," he finally says. "Hey, Turner, sorry to bother you, and I'm sorry about your back. Hope you heal up and get back out here—nice to see a good guy in the league these days. Meanwhile, will you give me a call if you think of anything that might help? Let me give you my number."

Turner, who's supposed to have some of that old Boyd honor, sits there looking around the front room at all the old furniture and the framed pictures of Gum and granddaddy Lester and great-granddaddy Homer before him—the one Turner always liked especially, old Homer with his twirling mustache and riding britches and suit-coat, up on a big white horse, with someone's faded writing at the bottom, *The Knight of the Nantahalas.* He stares out the window at land the Boyds have owned since old George, back in 1822, bought 184 ½ acres of Cherokee Territory for $276—Gum's aunt found the original deed years ago, researching her genealogy.

What would old George Boyd do?

But Turner hears Puckerman: "If you want to play in this league again, Turner . . ."

What would Gum say? What will he say if you tell him exactly what happened out there?

Turner's torn. *You want to mess up LaPrince—your friend, some-*

times? Your compadre? *Poor dumb black boy, he'll mess himself up soon enough without you.*

But should LaPrince slide, right now? Probably he's not involved in Tommy Mason's trouble, but if he is. . . . Remember in high school when the six dropouts robbed ten homes around the valley and burned them all to the ground to cover their tracks, including the Harrises'—your friends' whole house, the family heirlooms and picture-albums and letters and all? Remember how the county manager, Sam Greenwood Jr., bailed his no-'count son out and then waited till the night before the trial to get him committed as a mental case? The trial was delayed for six months but the hospital didn't keep little Kelly, didn't buy his fake-crazy act, and he was on the loose all those months, no telling what he might do. Slicker'n owl shit, Gum said, and it only happened because Greenwood was county manager. Lots of people said any parent would do the same for their young'un if they could, but Gum made it clear to Turner: not this parent, not for any young'un'a mine, because right's right and wrong's wrong. You pull something stupid, something mean, don't expect no savin'.

M ax didn't believe the southern boy had told all he knew.
Didn't necessarily expect him to call back, either, but he did—a little after two o'clock, three hours after the first conversation, saying he didn't know much and sort of doubted that anything he did know would help, but for what it was worth. . . . Hesitating then, but finally saying he liked Tommy and wanted to help if he was in trouble; he just didn't want to get in trouble himself. Max asked if Turner had done anything he thought was seriously criminal—hurt someone, something like that—and Turner Boyd said no, nothing, and Max assured him he didn't need to worry, Max wouldn't compromise him, he only wanted information that might help Tommy and he didn't need to let anyone know where he got it.

Boyd was still hesitant, and even when he started talking he probably didn't tell all he knew. But what he told was plenty.

"You asked if we went to the real-estate man's house that night after we met you at the club—the Swim, it was called? Well, not that night, but the next night we did, and Mason went too. People were drinking and getting a little wild. I didn't even want to be there, but I was riding with LaPrince."

Hesitating again, then.

"And something happened over there?" Max coaxing. "You don't need to tell me everything people were doing, but whatever involved Tommy, whatever might have led to him getting mad at someone or someone getting mad at him—was there anything like that, Turner?"

"They got into it a little bit, Tommy and LaPrince, later on."

"Got into it?"

"LaPrince was a little messed up, drunk or whatever. . . ."

"Whatever," Max said. "Doesn't matter, Turner. Go ahead."

"Well, I didn't hear what it was about, it happened pretty fast and all, but people were in the fella's office, like a library, and Tommy and LaPrince sorta got into it about somethin' and LaPrince lost it and gave him a whomp—you know, with the back of his hand. Everything kinda stopped, you didn't quite believe it, didn't understand it . . . and then Tommy just left. Everyone kinda looked at each other. Looked at LaPrince. Not saying anything, everyone just looking at each other, and then LaPrince went out . . . back upstairs, I guess."

"Yeah?" *Go slow. He's nervous.* "Back upstairs?"

Nothing.

"Turner?"

"To—uh, get his shirt on."

"He'd been up there with a woman?"

"I guess. . . . And then we left. He dropped me off at the Residence Inn I was staying at."

"What did he say on the way? Anything about what had happened? About Tommy?"

"No sir. Not as I remember. And I didn't ask anything. I was mad because I never wanted to go to the fella's house in the first place, I just wanted to get back to the hotel and go to bed 'cause we were leaving on a trip in the mornin'."

"Did Wheatley say anything about the woman?"

"No sir."

"Do you know who she was? You saw her, I guess."

"I . . . guess I saw her, just quick . . . if she was even the one he was up there with. I'm not sure."

Enough. Don't scare him off.

"That's fine, Turner, if you're not sure. Let's get away from the party. Let me ask you a few more things, then I'll quit wasting your time."

How friendly were he and Wheatley?

Kinda friendly. Sorta. Played together a year in LA, year before last. Boyd hedging, probably afraid he'd said too much already.

Did he know about any trouble between Tommy and Wheatley before that night? Anything?

No sir. Probably the truth, because Wheatley had invited Tommy (and his friends, Max and Paige) out to the Swim the night before.

Did he know about anything else going on with Wheatley at the time, anything unusual or stressful?

Well . . . his brother was up from LA, his *half*-brother, with a friend. Been trying to get in touch but LaPrince didn't call him back, hoping they'd go away. The half-brother had been in prison, La-Prince said, and showed up looking for money or a bodyguard job or something. Finally showed up at the Plunderdome before the second game—the night they ended up at the real-estate man's party—came right down on the court during warmups, the half-brother and this friend of his, short little weightlifter-looking guy.

And were these two at the party later?

No sir. Never saw 'em again.

Names?

Titan, that was the little weightlifter. Boyd's sorry, he can't ever remember LaPrince's half-brother. La-something, same as LaPrince—LaBeemus, LaTeetus, something. But called himself Wink, LaPrince said, like you wink your eye.

Black, both of 'em?

Both.

Max didn't want to push. He thanked Boyd sincerely and promised to keep him out of it.

Called O'Leary at the office. Who got back to him a half-hour later, having contacted the California Department of Corrections, whose computer revealed "Titan" to be Marcus Milton, thirty-three, five-four and 215 pounds, did four years for first-degree assault, current address Grape Street in Compton—gangland. "Wink" was LaMetrius Jefferson, thirty-one, five-eleven and 175, did stretches for armed robbery and burglary, paroled last month, current address Wise Street in Compton.

"Jefferson," O'Leary said, "is a half-brother of LaPrince Wheatley, our dubious Plunder. You know that?"

"I did," Max said, and asked if O'Leary had time to get the address for a Rod Yardley in the Portland area, in an upscale neighborhood.

*   *   *

Called Charlie Witty, after O'Leary got back to him with the address, for details on that rape that Yardley allegedly sat and watched.

An hour later he's facing a bruised, beat-up basket case across a big round oak table in a roomy, high-ceilinged, all-white kitchen.

"Two black guys," Max says. "One average-sized, with a scar on his neck you can't miss, one short and muscular with C-R-I-P-S tattooed on the fingers of his right hand. Your friend Alice Richardson described 'em to the detectives as the two who raped her here last Wednesday night."

The guy's not half as cocky as he was at the Swim that night. Not cocky at all—but holding on, holding out. "I don't know. Maybe that was them, I don't know. If it was, I still don't know why the hell they came here. Never saw the bastards before."

Max just looks at him, lets him squirm. He's seen a lot of pathetic people, desperate people, but none any worse-off than this. Hasn't seen many worse liars, either.

Shakes his head, almost sorry for him. "Maybe I can help, you know?"

The poor sap makes a dismissive sound, "Shhh," sadly shaking *his* head. As in "shit," or "sure you can." As in, "No one can."

"Maybe I can. But you've got to help me, Yardley."

"Like how?" Looking like he might cry.

"Tell me what it's about. Why two guys you've never seen before come over here and beat the shit out of you and stay three or four days. They don't beat the shit out of you and leave, don't beat the shit out of you and rob you and leave, but just stay. Until your unfortunate friend Miss Richardson drops by and they take her upstairs and rape her in front of you—*then* they realize they'd better hightail it."

He just sits there, hangdog, across his nice oak table.

"Raped her while you just sat there," Max says.

He doesn't look up. Max can't imagine what's running through his mind. What he's into, what he's hiding.

"Although that might be understandable," Max adds. "Maybe you were in danger."

The head comes up. "I was, dammit. Aside from the fact I could barely stand up anyway. I got four broken ribs, man, and if you don't believe it you can go to Good Sam ER and find out. I can barely move now and I sure as shit couldn't've done anything with those spades last week. Plus, the one had shown me a gun one of those days before . . . which, I didn't know if it was in the room then, but I knew they had one, at least one. Even if I didn't have broken ribs, you think I should've tried to be a hero?"

"That's what I mean. There's no obligation to intervene in a crime in progress even if you wouldn't be putting yourself or the victim in danger, and the way you describe what happened here, I think anyone could understand. But what I'm asking you is why these two were here in the first place, and now that I've told you that Mr. Jefferson is Wheatley's half-brother I'm pretty sure you've got some idea, if you didn't know damn well all along. And I assure you, the DA won't think twice about slapping you with a grand-jury subpoena to talk about it under oath."

"I don't know," he peeps.

"If you do know and don't say, they can hammer you for obstructing justice when it comes out."

"I don't. . . ." Pathetic.

"Let's go over it again, then, see if it comes to you. LaPrince Wheatley's half-brother shows up here with another ex-con—this is about two weeks after he gets out of prison in California—and he's looking for a handout from Wheatley. A handout or maybe some bodyguard work, some asskicking work. We know you'd been hanging out with Wheatley, showing him some houses, since you made a point of telling my girlfriend about it the night we met you downtown, and now these two show up, break your ribs, make your face look like they used it for batting practice. And you're telling me you don't have any idea why? You're insulting my intelligence, Yardley. You've already insulted the cops."

He gives Max sad eyes and a shrug.

"How about the party? The night after we saw you downtown, the night Wheatley went after Tommy Mason?"

Another simpy shrug is all.

"Because I'm interested in my friend, is why I'm here. I'm unemployed right now, not investigating rapes or ex-cons who're probably violating their parole; I also don't give a shit what kind of dope and drugs you keep around here—I just want to help my friend. So help me out, and maybe I can help you. But if you keep sitting here simpering, bullshitting me, I'll watch the authorities flush you down the toilet. If someone doesn't finish you off with their bare hands first."

The simp finally looks up, like maybe he's about to speak, but then the eyes drop again.

Max stands up like he's had enough: Die like a dog, then, if that's the way you want it. Sometimes it wakes someone up.

But not this one, who sits there and lets him walk out the back door that's got cardboard taped over the broken panes—Max giving it a good slam, hearing a few more pieces fall out.

Bodie keeps unzipping the bag and looking at the $200,000. Touching it. Staring at it.

He still can't quite believe it.

He might have to give some up if Mason ever shows up ($25,000, say—tell him that's half), but even if he never shows, hell, this is just too damned sweet an opportunity for Bodacious Bodie to rest on his laurels, to quit at two hundred grand. He's run some beautiful scams, but nothing like this, and he'll probably never see anything like this again. Most people never get a chance, or don't have the balls to take advantage if they do.

Puckerman was right to call his bluff; Bodie knew it even as they were having the conversation in the honcho's cushy Plunderdome office on Saturday afternoon. What *would* Bodie do if the organization refused to pay? Go to the cops with a copy of the video, like he threatened? The *Oregonian*? ESPN? He wouldn't get a dime out of it, except maybe a couple hundred bucks to tell his story on *Hard Copy*—where, as Puckerman pointed out, they'll superimpose FAILED BLACKMAILER on the screen while he's telling it. The cops might say "Thanks, we'll see what Wheatley's got to say, but we're locking *you* up right now."

Puckerman knew he had him.

Up to a point. But the honcho didn't think it all the way through, either. Not right then, and Bodacious didn't leave a phone number.

Yeah, the new plan could work. He slept on it that night and it still made sense Sunday morning. He found the place on the tape where the girl was most clearly visible: her blond hair on the pillow, her chin obscured by Wheatley's shoulder but the rest of her face right there, clear, as Wheatley fucks her. Her eyes are closed all the way through and she's talking most of the time, talking dirty to him, and when Wheatley really gets going she's groaning, wincing, her face contorted—not a picture Bodie would want to show around, but afterward, with the big stud wheezing on top of her, done, she's eased up and her eyes come open—*there!*—the face clear as can be on his high-resolution Sony VCR. He freezes it, shoots it with his Polaroid, scans it on his slick new machine and runs off five 8½x11s on his laser printer.

Tuesday evening, with his beard shaved off and his ponytail tucked up inside a Chicago Bulls cap—Bodie not quite nervous enough to lop off years' worth of his pony—he's in a short line of walkups buying tickets for Portland–Denver. No problem getting in at the last minute these days, a far cry from the early-nineties glory days when season-ticket holders had every seat in the Plunderdome tied up.

The action on the court barely holds his interest. Denver's about the worst team in the league, but even at that they hang close. Wheatley, matched up against a slothlike Denver rookie, keeps trying to go one-on-one. A few moves work, but he also dribbles off his foot, whips a behind-the-back pass into the stands and misses everything with an ill-advised three-point try that gets Colabello fuming on the sideline.

What would he do if he knew the guy who took advantage of his stupidity—two hundred G's worth—was watching him from a couple hundred feet away?

Halftime is what Bodie's waiting for, and when it comes he takes an escalator to the third level, where the luxury boxes are. Hoping Mason's information is good, because otherwise he's got no idea how to locate this girl.

The suites run all the way around the Plunderdome. These doors, with the high rollers and their families and friends going in and out . . . caterers in black pants and white jackets, serving them . . . Bodie with the full-color laser copy rolled up in his hand, looking for the right person to show it to.

He starts with a young guy, college age, wearing jeans and a satin Lakers jacket and carrying three beers in a cardboard holder. "Ex-cuse me, man"—unrolling the picture, holding it at the top and bottom—"you know this girl? My cousin. I just got in from Chicago and had a message to meet her at the family suite here, but she didn't say what number."

The kid studies the picture, shakes his head. Buys the bullshit but can't help.

A girl around the same age can't either. "I'm just visiting too. I don't know anyone here except my relatives."

A pleasant-looking middle-aged lady seems suspicious. "What's your cousin's name?" Or maybe it's his imagination—but either way, she's no help.

Back to younger people, her peers. And *bingo*! A kid with a butch, a rat-tail and a ring in his eyebrow says, "Audrey, yeah. Van-something. They're three or four doors down this way, but I saw her leaving a minute ago. With a girl named Kay, long black hair, and another girl I don't know."

"Little Audrey," Bodie says, shaking his head. "Thanks, buddy."

Audrey Van-something.

"My cousin Audrey," he tells a slightly older guy, showing the picture. "Left me a message to meet her at the suite but forgot to say what number it is. Know where I can find her?"

Nope.

The next kid recognizes her immediately. "The VanKirkmans' suite? One of these right along here, I'm not sure which. Knock on a door and ask someone."

"I'll do it. You're a prince, man."

VanKirkman? Like the cheeseball on TV, stroking his goatee and trying to sound profound?

The hall's nearly empty now, people back in their places as the second half gets under way. All right, start knocking on doors.

Damn, he must be living right! He starts with 346 and *bingo, bango, bongo!* A heavyset girl in a tight black dress opens the door, lots of activity behind her, and as Bodie's asking if she knows where he can find his cousin Audrey—Van—

—and he spots her, *knows* it's her! Good-looking. Blond. Thirty feet away in a soft blue chair, wearing jeans and a white cable-knit sweater—*there's* a nice rack!—talking to a couple of kids on barstools. The suite's full of kids, a dozen or so, no grownups in sight.

"There she is, I think," Bodie says. "Could you ask her to come out here for a minute?"

And the heavyset girl, unsuspecting, turns and heads for Audrey.

Leans down to her, interrupting her conversation with a few words in her ear. Audrey looks this way, probably wondering which cousin has dropped in (if she's even got cousins). Looking bewildered when she spots him, but pushing up out of the chair and heading over.

Christ, nice walk. She fills up those jeans just right.

And what a face, up close. Features, coloring, all of it.

She's baffled, looking at him.

"Just kidding," Bodie says. "I'm looking for your parents."

It's warm and sunshiny in LA, even the day before Thanksgiving. Not very much like Thanksgiving.

Not that Max plans on being here tomorrow. With any luck he'll be back in Portland's beautiful gloom tonight and over at Witty's tomorrow, or out at Oceanside with Paige and her parents.

From LAX he takes a cab downtown, to the LA County DA's office, and locates lead investigator Hal Paxton, O'Leary's counterpart—about O'Leary's age, too, mid-fifties, a stout light-skinned black without much hair left but with a classy, almost elegant way about him. Vice President of the National Association of DA Investigators, O'Leary said, and a lot of fun at their annual conventions.

"I appreciate the help," Max says. "Jerry said you know La-Metrius Jefferson's neighborhood and're willing to take me out there."

Paxton smiles—a warm, sunny smile, big white teeth. "I'm the right shade, and I've definitely been out there plenty. Know a lot of people there, the good and not-so-good."

"Jefferson?"

"I know *of* him. A low-level banger—Crip—going way back. Not a shooter, though—no one who scared anyone much. Been mostly out of circulation the last few years, I'm sure you know, but still on our list of known associates."

Max says, "You realize I'm not with the office right now? Jerry told you?"

"Yeah, he did. Said you might not want to tell me what it is you want with Jefferson. Fine. I told him I'd get you out there and back and you can tell me whatever you want. Or nothing."

"I appreciate it. It's unofficial, that's all, at least for now. But I'm going to try not to let him know I'm unofficial. Let him think I'm here to deal, to help him out of his trouble in exchange for the information I want. Trouble he probably doesn't even think he's in."

Tough neighborhood, a lot like the gang sections of Portland where Max worked so many crime scenes over the years. Desolate streets littered with beer cans, used rubbers, broken glass. Dingy little houses with old cars (and the occasional Cadillac, indicating a dealer or pimp) pulled up in short driveways; old furniture on the stoops, some occupied by wary residents eyeballing every passing car they don't recognize. Graffiti spraypainted on walls or abandoned storefronts, Crips and Bloods stuff, vile drawings. "Always," Paxton says.

It's especially desolate under the blue sky and brilliant sun. A trash can overturned at the curb, a cat nosing around in the mess. Max wonders what Thanksgiving will be like.

Wonders if the house they're going to is the one LaPrince Wheatley grew up in. Remembers Tommy saying Wheatley (according to Wheatley) never saw his father until he was nine years old, when someone pointed out an addict nodding out on one of these front stoops.

He knows they're close when Paxton turns right on Wise Street, pulls up in front of 219, parks at the curb.

The front steps creak and give a little under their weight. The faint smell of dope on the stoop, a few dead matches in a beanbag-bottom ashtray between two Salvation Army easy chairs. A warped screen door, the splintery wood-panel door behind it standing open. Rap music playing inside, faint, as if from a back room.

LaMetrius Jefferson—must be—appears from a shadowy hallway just as Paxton raises his hand to knock. Sleeveless T-shirt, baggy knee-length jeans, high-top Jordans: the uniform. Red eyes, as he comes to the door. And yes, a long ugly scar down the left side of his neck.

"Yo." To Paxton. A suspicious eye on the white guy.

"LaMetrius Jefferson? Hal Paxton, LA County DA's office. Man here from the Portland, Oregon office would like a few words with you."

Jefferson checks them out for a few seconds, then decides to push the screen door open and let them in.

"I'll wait out here," Paxton says, "let you two talk."

Max follows Jefferson down the short hall to a little kitchen. Frosted Flakes on the counter, dirty dishes. As Jefferson swings into a chair at the Formica-top table Max can see he's nervous, trying too hard to be cool. *Portland, Oregon* means bad things.

Use it.

"So," Max says, taking the chair across the table from him, "you probably know what this is about."

"Nah."

"No?"

"Uh-uh."

"Well. . . . You *are* LaMetrius Jefferson?"

He nods . . . slowly, warily.

"On parole here in California?"

He doesn't like that. Stares back, not even a nod.

"Not supposed to leave the state without your PO's permission? That's a parole violation, right? Could put you back inside?"

He's frozen.

"I believe so," Max says. "Now, you wanna tell me what you were doing up in Portland?"

Paralyzed, except for eyes darting around as if there's help somewhere in the room.

"You and your man Milton? Titan, you call him?"

"Hey—hey, man—"

"Yeah, you and your man—tell me what you were up in Portland for." Max feeling the rush you get when you've got someone's pecker in your pocket, in LBJ's famous words.

"Man, I went to see my brother, you know? LaPrince, you know, play for the Plunder?"

"And?"

"And what?" The huffy, indignant tone, like you're disrespecting him. "You ast why I went up there for. That's why."

Max waits, watching the beads of sweat appear on his forehead. *Wink's* forehead. Can't resist. "You give yourself the nickname? 'Wink'?"

He's shaking his head like *Why you doin' me like this, man?*— looking down at the table, back at Max, out the window at his mother's shabby little backyard. Max wondering why Wheatley hasn't gotten their mother out of here, like other millionaire jocks you hear about.

"Forget it," Max says. "Not important. Let's talk about Portland. Let's talk about why you and your man Titan beat the crap out of a guy named Yardley."

Wink rolling his eyes to the ceiling now, twisting his hands on the tabletop. "Maaaaan . . ." The whine they get when they're cornered.

"Or we can talk about other things."

And now he doesn't even whine. Too scared, because he knows Max means the rape. Or maybe he thinks Max is talking about other things—things Max doesn't, in fact, know about. But that Jefferson doesn't know Max doesn't know about.

"Like my friend Tommy," Max says. "Tommy Mason, a writer—wrote a nice story about LaPrince."

"Yeah?" The fool relieved it's not about the rape, relieved to talk about anything but the rape.

"What do you know about Tommy Mason? You know who I mean? White guy about your size, brown hair . . . wrote a nice story about LaPrince in a little newspaper up there, then they got into some kind of argument at a party at a guy named Yardley's house and LaPrince pushed him around a little. You know anything about that?"

"Nah, man. . . ."

"You weren't invited to that party? All right, a few days later a couple of friends of LaPrince"—Max guessing here, but why not?—"couple of husky white guys came looking for my friend, and about that time my friend disappeared. You know anything about that, Wink? Know who those big dumb white boys are?"

"Maaaaan, why you askin' me? Nah, I don't know what you talkin' 'bout, coupla white boys."

Max stares him down, stares at the sweat beading on his forehead . . . thinking, It's too bad this guy was born into the life he was born into, yes it is, too bad anyone's born black in this fucked-up country, especially in the 'hood. Only the very few make it out of here, and usually they're six-nine and can shoot a ball, or hit a baseball or run with a football—only the minuscule few make it out on smarts and a fierce determination to get out. Max wonders about Hal Paxton.

Recalling a classy black LA detective who came to Portland to testify in Max's first murder trial, years ago. With this detective on the stand for cross-examination, the defense attorney went on and on about the mean streets of LA—about how the defendant could hardly have turned out any better than he did, isn't that true, detective?—and this guy exploding the whole sad story, the whole pity defense, saying No, that's not true, sir, because I grew up in that same neighborhood; I wanted to make something of myself, that's all.

But it's rare, and Max Travis can't be sure he wouldn't be in LaMetrius Jefferson's spot if he'd been born here instead of in upper-middle-class northeast Portland.

But he wasn't, and the speculation gets you nowhere. "Wink," he says, "I've got a bunch of people who can put you in Portland the last couple of weeks"—exaggerating the number but making the point, while keeping the rape up his sleeve—"and isn't that enough to put you back in the can for a while?"

"Man, I said I don't know who you talkin' 'bout, coupla white boys! What you want, man?"

"I also heard the word *blackmail* somewhere, Wink. You know anything about any blackmail?"

Relief crosses his face, faintly. Because someone else is doing bad things too. Because this DA might have to back off a little now, if he wants Wink's help. "I heard the word up there, yeah," he says.

"Yeah? Help me out."

"You wanna know? Yeah? Awright, your boy Mason tryin' to get money outta LaPrince, your boy and some other cat, wantin' money for some video'a LaPrince jammin' some bitch. Awright? What I heard."

Bafflement. A sex video? Blackmail, really? Tommy?

Don't let the bafflement show. "What else?"

"Tha's what I know, man. I never seen neither of 'em. I just heard some cat with a ponytail come up to LaPrince in a club one night talkin' 'bout he got this video'a LaPrince with this *bitch,* young bitch, and he want two hunnert thousand for it. LaPrince call his agent for help, agent come to town—"

"Who's that?"

"Bernie somethin', somethin' like that, I don't know. LaPrince tell him he was with this bitch at this Yardley's crib one time, only time he did her—so tha's who made the video, this Yardley. Bernie go talk to him and this Yardley tell him yeah, he made it but thas all, he didn't do nothin' else—"

"Which Bernie-something believed," Max says, "because you and Titan had your ways of persuading Yardley to talk, am I right?"

"—and he talkin' 'bout a car parked on his street the day the thing got stolen"—ignoring Max's interruption, admitting nothing— "and he figured out it was your boy stole it, this writer cat."

"And?"

"And tha's all, man."

"So . . . LaPrince paid this guy with the ponytail? Two hundred thousand dollars?"

Jefferson shrugging, helpless. "Don't know, man. I come back here."

"Why'd you come back here, Wink?"

A pained look. Max can hear him thinking *Maaan, why you wanna do me like this?*

"Things not working out for you up in Portland?"

Maaaan . . . "Man, why you doin' this?"

"Looking out for my friend, I said. Now, I wanna know everything you know, before I decide to call your PO and then maybe bring you back to Portland for beating the crap out of Mr. Yardley—that and who knows what else?" Still keeping the rape in reserve, letting the pea-brain believe that maybe, somehow, no one knows about it. "So what do you know, Wink?"

"Thas all! What you want, man?"

"What'd they say, LaPrince and Bernie-something? They're looking for my friend, wanna hurt him? Maybe send a couple guys looking for him?"

"I don't know 'bout that."

Wait. Sweat him.

"Awright, yeah, they b'lieve he in it with the ponytail cat, but I don't know if they find him or what. I come back down here."

"After you visited Yardley? After you and your pal convinced him to talk?"

Jefferson rolls his eyes. *Why you do me like this after all I told you?*

"I'm letting you off easy, Wink."

"I done told you what I know, man!"

"I don't think so. Not hardly."

But it's enough for now. Max is pretty sure it's everything Jefferson knows about Tommy, anyway. Let him sweat what you might do about the rest.

Max pushes back from the table and gets up. Looks around the sad kitchen: dirty dishes, Frosted Flakes, speckled linoleum floor curling up at the edges. "Where's your mom, Wink?"

"She workin', man. Do laundry at the hospital."

"You let her support you? Isn't it a condition of your parole that you find a job?"

"Shit, man. I told you I just got home from up there, ain't had time."

"Oh, that's right." Out of the kitchen, down the short hall to the front, Jefferson following. "And am I correct," Max asks him at the door, "you weren't supposed to be up there in the first place? Weren't supposed to leave California, weren't supposed to leave this address without your PO's permission?"

Jefferson scowls, undoubtedly wishing he could put a bullet between this motherfucker's eyes.

"And you didn't get permission, did you?"

Fuck you, man! It's in his eyes, on the tip of his tongue.

It's such a kick sometimes, fucking with these people. As long as you don't get hurt.

"Nice talking to you, Wink."

God's will is exactly what we would want if we knew everything.
Tommy read it somewhere once. And thought, It must be nice to believe that.

And who knows, maybe it's true. Maybe there's been a reason for all this. Maybe to get him back with the one he loves—but scare the hell out of him first, bring him to his senses so he doesn't blow it again.

You want to be with her again, and stay with her? Well, grow up. Quit the dope and booze, drop the writer fantasy and get a real job and take care of her—she's sick, after all, she doesn't need to fret about supporting both of you. Quit running around with idiot ballplayers and lowlifes like Bodie. "Bodacious," shit. Talk about never growing up. But then, at least he supports himself.

He sits staring at the e-mail on his laptop, the night before Thanksgiving, in the guestroom of Patty's condo.

> Tommy:
>
> I hope this message reaches you. Since I don't know where you're staying now, I couldn't call.
>
> I miss you. It's Thanksgiving, and I think back on the others we've shared and how we talked about sharing them forever, with green-bean casserole and all. Maybe we can still work things out. I'd like to talk if you would. I'll be here in the morning if you want to come over.
>
> Julie

If he wants to. She knows it's all he wants, all he's wanted since three days after he moved out, when he called and she stunned him by saying no, he couldn't come back, not right then and maybe never, she couldn't keep putting herself through it. She said she needed to be left alone, needed time to think.

But he couldn't keep from writing desperate letters nearly every night—and driving out to leave them in the box instead of mailing them, so desperate for her to get them and understand him and let him come home. She didn't respond and he wrote more, more, until she called him at Waldron's place and said the pressure was killing whatever feeling she had left. He stopped then, back in August, and has only contacted her the one time since, a few weeks ago, asking where things stood. She wrote back (he was at Shrag's place then, just before he ran into Max downtown and moved in there) saying she missed him but her symptoms were a little better, the pain was less, possibly because her stress level was down, and she didn't know if she could put herself through it again; she was still talking it over with her doctor and her therapist, and she'd let him know when she made up her mind.

But she misses him, the e-mail says. He'd known she would, eventually—prayed she would, anyway. Now the holidays are here and she's alone, and if her condition is better she's probably forgotten, somewhat, what the stress does to her. Or she's hurting, and remembering the comfort of having him there, Tommy who made himself wake up, wake up and be awake with her in the middle of the night when she couldn't sleep for the pain—the two of them lying there in the dark watching dumb reruns, holding hands at 2, 3, 4 A.M., Julie saying how grateful she was, how lucky to have found him, how she treasured him.

She must be remembering some of that now, at last. Remembering he's not *only* a schmuck.

She said she'll be there in the morning, *if* he wants to come over.

God's will? Nothing has made a believer out of him in forty-one years, but this could.

Tossing and turning all night. Gonna see her. Maybe be with her again. For the rest of his life. Forgiven one more time, and he'll never need forgiving again. No more bullshit.

Seven A.M. Way too early to go, but he's wide awake.

He stays in bed, reads awhile, dozes, wakes again and lies there staring at the ceiling until he hears Patty leaving for her parents' house. Comes out of his room, makes a stiff Bloody Mary, reads the paper, then shaves and showers and gargles and flosses and brushes and chews some gum to make sure there's no smell from the Bloody, even though vodka's not supposed to smell. Puts on the sweater she knit for his birthday way back and takes off. The first day of the rest of his life, a Hallmark card would say. Today, the line doesn't seem so cheesy.

Across the Sellwood Bridge in the fog and drizzle, up Macadam, up the Taylors Ferry slope, through the Burlingame intersection that delivers such pangs: the market, the video-rental place, his liquor store. Left on Eighth. Jesus. Butterflies. She's got the power.

What if she really only wants to talk?

So familiar, yet so alien. The mailbox at the curb, where he dropped so many pleading letters on so many semidrunken summer nights. The short driveway, the eight-foot hoop, her black Vee-Dub. The door into the rec room he painted during the Super Bowl the week they moved in, while she sponge-painted the table she was going to put her sewing-machine on.

Chills.

She won't be downstairs. He takes the outside steps up to the front door, past her pride-and-joy rock garden.

Deep breath, then he knocks on the door that replaced the one her crazy ex punched a hole in one night. Waits. *Will she come to him? Kiss him? Cry?*

Waits, with that nervous stomach, until at last the lock clicks, the knob turns, the door opens—and he's looking at *Max.*

"Come on in, buddy."

No sign of her.

"Come in, sit down," Max says. "We need to talk."

Max isn't pleased with him. Asking where the hell he's been, who the hell these goons are, who the guy with the ponytail is, what the hell's going on.

Repeats himself, when Tommy stammers. "I said, what the fuck's going on?"

"What's—where's—?"

"Forget it. I told her you're in trouble and we need to talk and she helped me out. Don't expect her. Now, what the hell are you into? Blackmail?"

Tommy's got no idea what he knows or how he knows it, no idea what's happened since he, Tommy, went underground. What he knows is that Max has seen it all and dealt with every kind of thing and is the one person who might, maybe, be able to help him. If he's inclined to, at this point.

"*Blackmail?*" Max coming over to the couch and snapping his fingers in front of Tommy's nose. "Hey? You wanna start talking? You and your friend with the ponytail and probably some others are in trouble, including myself, which I'm not happy about at all. I don't like Godzillas showing up at my house threatening to pull my fingernails out if I don't tell 'em where you are."

There's nothing to do but tell all. Shit, he probably knows most of it, one way or other. And if he finds you're not leveling he might just say fuck off, you're on your own.

Tommy tells all, feeling like the dumbest ass God ever made. Knowing it's all over between him and Max.

"I knew I blew it the second I gave the tape to Bodie, but by then it was too late."

"I'll say." Mercifully, Max seems to be looking through him, past him, working the problem. "That's the guy with the ponytail—Bodie?"

Tommy manages a wimpy nod, looking out the window.

"So Bodie tells Wheatley he wants two hundred thousand bucks for this video?"

"Tells the agent. Yeah. I guess." Staring now at the carpet they bought one Saturday, he and Julie, at the discount place down by the river. The same carpet he stared at, sitting in this same spot, the July evening he came over to plead his case and she told him no, she couldn't make it that easy for him, she needed to think.

She sure as hell wouldn't let him come back now, knowing what Max must have told her.

"What was the arrangement? Fifty-fifty split? You knew he planned to do something with the tape—you must've said something about splitting proceeds, or he must've."

Tommy would blow his own head off right now if he had a gun. It was hard enough touching on this part a few minutes ago, the whole stupid thing from the moment he saw the tape in Yardley's VCR—now Max wants the sleazy, sordid details. "Jesus . . . I swear—I never meant. . . ." Voice trailing away.

"Excuse me?" Max, peeved, not making it easy.

"I said I never meant for . . . I don't know. I showed him the tape, yeah, but I didn't mean for him to . . . I mean, I left it there and right away I knew it was a mistake. I never went back, I haven't talked to him since, I just wanted it all to go away—"

"Like it's all just gonna go away, like a bad dream?"

How fucking stupid are you?

"So you don't even know if he's gotten anything for it? He tried, I know that much, but you don't know what came of it?"

Tommy shakes his head, speechless. Why even bother?

"You don't know anything else? Nothing?"

Dumb as a fucking donkey.

"I swear." Max gets up, rightly disgusted. "Come on. You're coming to my house until we sort some of this out. If the goons show up again, I guess we just do what we can."

On the walk down Taylors Ferry to where he parked his car he says, "Did you hear me? You stay at my house. You leave, I'll bring the police into this and you can try to get yourself out from under."

39

An excellent Thanksgiving, Bodie thinks, most excellent. They started before noon at old pal Wally's place, Wally and his hotsy little girlfriend and a few others, primo smoke and hot buttered rums and NFL on the tube. Kick back and relax. Give thanks.

So much to be thankful for. Two hundred grand stashed and no sign of Mason, the sap. Wheatley's people scared him shitless, if they didn't erase him altogether. If he does show up. . . . Well, if he clearly knows you pulled it off, and for how much, you've got to split the 200 K. But then, how bad is that? If he knows you pulled it off but doesn't know the figure, you say it was fifty grand and you happily give him twenty-five. If it's clear he doesn't know squat, you say Wheatley told you to go pound sand and you didn't get anything. What's he gonna do, ask for the tape back? Give him one of the copies.

Yeah, a lot to be thankful for. Audrey's father does turn out to be the "Doctor Henry" of local radio and TV fame, who's doing very well. Well enough he might not care about soaking Wheatley. He'd want to take the high road—the upright, outraged parent just looking for justice, looking to hang Wheatley legally for defiling his teenybopper.

Either way, the videotape was the key. Doctor Henry wasn't doing anything without it. Without it, what happened at that party didn't happen.

Bodie disliked him right off, the guy opening the door half-stewed, striking Bodie as a little too well-fed, a little too pleased with himself. But hey, a potential partner, you make nice.

Bodie showed him the picture and said, "Recognize anyone here?"

He stepped out in the hallway. He recognized his girl, but there was no outrage. He barely seemed surprised—not that any shrink types Bodie ever met let their feelings show. If they *had* feelings, which wasn't a given.

It took about two minutes for Bodie to realize this cold fish not only didn't want to do anything, he was scared of the thing blowing up. "W-w-we . . . don't need this," he stammered.

Bodie—still bodacious, if he says so himself!—understood. "Let's talk again," he said.

The guy didn't think they needed to. He'd deal with his daughter.

"We need to," Bodie told him. "How 'bout in a couple days? Let you think this over. But no, two days from now is Thanksgiving, and Friday is for recovering from Thanksgiving. How's Saturday?"

Day after tomorrow.

Bodie will give him his choices. One: Go to the cops and say you want to press charges—but you'll need the videotape to prove anything, and that'll cost you. Two: Don't want the ordeal of cops, lawyers, court, publicity? Go to Puckerman, say you've got this tape and you'll press charges against the stud unless the Plunder come across with $250,000—which you split with Bodie, naturally, because without the tape you've got nothing to sell. Three: Give Bodie a hundred grand for the video, Bodie goes away, it's over, your good name isn't muddied.

Bodacious.

Meanwhile, be thankful for turkey and dressing, hot buttered rums, primo homegrown. And Tommy Mason, the sap, for showing up with that video.

It's almost midnight and he's stretched out on the couch in the upstairs TV room when someone rings the doorbell. Damn!

Could they possibly know he's here? He only stayed in Black Butte two days—a little bit of Lonnie Shank goes a long way—but he's kept the house dark since slipping back in at 3 A.M. Sunday. All curtains and blinds are drawn. The only light is from this upstairs TV, and in here he's got two dark blankets tacked up behind the curtains as an extra precaution.

Did someone see him come in two hours ago? Then why would they wait till now?

The doorbell again. They know he's here.

Could they possibly?

Ding-dong again.

Out in the hall he stands still, listening. Feels his own heart beating, hearing the blood pounding in his ears. Is this how it ends? They trap you in your own house and . . . do what?

"Bodie!" From the front porch. "Police! Open this door *now!*"

He creeps into the bedroom and pulls the .38 from under the mattress. Creeps back out into the hall as the cops (or whoever) rattle the doorknob.

"Bodie!"

Moving slowly down the stairs with the .38 leveled at the front door. Each step creaking under his weight, not that his weight's so much.

Protect yourself, but not too fast. Shoot a cop and you'll never see the light of day again.

He's at the bottom of the stairs, ten feet from the door.

"Bodie!"

Christ, they can hear him breathing.

"Open it!"

He's afraid to go up and put his eye through the peephole.

But afraid not to open up. He squeezes the pistol-grip in his right hand, steps up and slides back the deadbolt with his left, backing off again even as he does. *See anything you don't like, blow their fucking heads off.*

The door swings toward him.

Nobody there. Nothing. The porch. Streetlight shining on the wet grass.

"Richie Bodie?"

"Who's there?"—the .38 trained on the doorway.

He's no cop, he admits when they're finally face-to-face. Name's Max Travis, he says, Tommy Mason's friend. Bodie remembers Mason talking about him: brilliant guy, the one who got run out of the DA's office last summer but wound up bringing down the big man, Tower.

He says he knows all about it—Wheatley, the video, the blackmail—and wants to help everyone survive. Unarmed, see? You mind putting that gun down?

"How'd you know I was here?" Bodie asks.

"Walked around the house, saw a teeny bit of light at the edge of the upstairs window in back. Took a wild guess that you're hiding."

Bodie locks the door and nods toward the living room. "Let's sit down." Holds on to the gun even though Travis doesn't seem to be armed, doesn't look threatening.

They sit in the near-dark, nothing but a little streetlight filtering in at the edges of the curtains: Travis on the loveseat, Bodie in the armchair from his grandma's estate.

Travis says, "You got the money, Richie?"

" 'Scuse me?"

"The blackmail money. Two hundred thousand, wasn't it?"

So he does know something. But he's nuts if he thinks Bodacious Bodie's gonna fall apart and volunteer anything. Which he probably knows, because he probably ain't nuts.

"Well?"

"I got nothing. It didn't happen. It didn't come off."

"So why you hiding out, coming to the door with a strap?"

"Because they don't like someone even trying to fuck with 'em. I'm not taking chances."

"So you did. Tommy showed you the tape and you took it and tried 'em. What happened?"

"This guy, Wheatley's agent I guess, told me to fuck off. Asked me what I thought I'd gain by going public if they didn't pay. Ballsy, but when you look at it that way he's right—what's in it for me? He called my bluff, you might say."

"So you were bluffing?"

"I didn't know it till then. Never really expected them to do anything but pay, as shook up as Wheatley was the night I hit him with it downtown. But this agent or whoever, he wasn't so easy."

Travis thinks it over, Bodie wondering how much he'll buy. Finally the guy says, "So the agent didn't cave, but sent a couple of bruisers looking for Tommy anyway? And you're still hiding out, won't answer the door without a weapon? Won't come to the door at all, I'm guessing, unless you think it's the police and you're afraid they'll kick it in and ask you why you're hiding."

Mason was right, the guy's not easy.

"Help me out, Richie," he says. "Tommy's hiding, you're hiding . . ."

Give him a shrug.

". . . which tells me you're blowing smoke up my ass. They told you to fuck off, didn't give you a dime, yet you're so scared you sit here in the dark holding your heavy artillery? Doesn't make sense."

Keep quiet. Let him flap his gums in a vacuum.

"No explanation?"

I don't have to explain, mister. I don't even know you.

He says, "I think this says it all, the fact you've got nothing to say. This bullshit you're feeding me doesn't make sense to either of us, you can't make it make sense, so you sit there like a stooge. But listen: I don't care two cents about you, and shouldn't care what happens to Tommy, the ridiculous position he's gotten himself in. But this girl on the tape looks like the innocent victim, if you can call anyone who fucks LaPrince Wheatley innocent. Ignorant victim, more like it. Either way, I can't help thinking they'd want to find her even more than they'd want you two dumbshits. They probably think she's part of the scam, and even if not . . . once they find out she's jailbait, they know she can hurt Wheatley. So, you gonna leave her out there? I mean, assuming they haven't found her already."

"Hey, she wasn't in on it. There's no *it* anyway, no setup, just an X-rated video Mason ripped off from some sickie. I don't even know who the girl is, other than a kid getting her kicks. I can't help you."

"Mmmm."

Does he know better, or not? Unless Smooth went to the cops—which he wouldn't have, obviously—or unless Travis somehow located him, he doesn't know shit. Mason could have sent him to Wheatley, but even that fool's not fool enough to tell on himself. *What video?* he'd say. *What girl? What party?*

Sure, Audrey knows she's a little messed up—maybe more than a little—but who wouldn't be, growing up around *him*? *He's* messed up.

Maybe she can go live with Mom.

Be there to drive her to Providence when she checks into the mental ward again.

Thanks to *him*. He says she was always nutty, lazy, tranq'ed out, but that's not how Audrey remembers it. Not what Granddad says, either. He says she was a happy kid, a happy young woman, fine until she married him. The weirdness came later.

The bastard. He came in after the game Tuesday night drunk and pissed off. *LaPrince Wheatley?* Glaring, and she was thinking, *Oh shit.* And yet . . . fuck him. Didn't she always know, didn't she secretly hope it would come out sooner or later, somehow or other? Wasn't that the idea? She would never tell him, but whenever he found out, fine. Fuck him. Throw it in his face, rattle his comfy little cage—that *was* the idea. Make him go get himself some help.

Like he made Mom go, when she started lying around all the time. Audrey was in third or fourth grade and she'd come home and Mom was always there, not working at the library anymore or doing much of anything. She remembers the two of them arguing when he came home at night, but mostly she remembers Mom wanting to be left alone and just letting him carry on when he started up, sometimes just sitting there covering her ears until he stopped. Just like Audrey let him carry on (afraid to cover her ears but tuning him out all the same) when he'd tell her Mommy was letting them both down.

* * *

"*LaPrince Wheatley?*" Like he might smack her, bloodshot eyes popping out of his head. "*You . . . fucked . . . LaPrince . . . Wheatley?*"

Scary, ready to beat her—the moment she always knew would come.

"Huh? Say something! This fucking braindead basketball player? I couldn't believe what I was hearing! You sucked his black cock?"

Audrey flinching then, sensing a slap coming, but he just threw up his hands and raved on.

"You sucked this nigger's dick? Did I hear it right? And you're using *cocaine* . . . ?"

"So?" She remembers saying it, kind of squeaking it—not so much scared by then as thrilled, something like thrilled, the racist bastard face to face with the fact that his little Catlin Gabel girl took big black cock. His trophy girl, with her private-school straight-*A*s and 1400 PSAT, prim and proper in her Catlin uniform, pretty and smart and surely a virgin, smart enough to save the prize for someone worthy a few years down the road, someone respectable, say a psychologist. . . .

Like Mom did, right?

She remembers Mom's depression, the way she lay around with the sad look, and him giving her a hard time at night. Not always—she remembers him coming down to the TV room once saying Mommy had a problem and they needed to help her out—but mostly he chewed her out, telling her she had a family and responsibilities and she needed to shape up and clean the house, cook dinner, do the things an adult had to do. Finally he put her in Providence (warning little Audrey not to tell her friends, not to tell anyone) and afterward she was better for a while, more like she used to be. But she slipped back again, and he yelled at her that it took more than tranquilizers and antidepressants, she needed to get off her dead ass and make an effort, do something, buck up!

She went back to Providence. Audrey remembers visiting, nine or ten years old: the creepiness of it, the smell, old people in wheelchairs, skinny girls who (he said) didn't eat because they thought they were fat.

At home the little girl watched TV and read books, always behind a closed door.

"*So?*" he kept raging the other night. "That's all you've got to say, *So?* About using cocaine and fucking this jig? And I want to know, where did this take place? And how long has it been going on?" Towering over her, the trophy daughter he doesn't care about any more than he cares about Mom or anyone else. The daughter who was suddenly anything but a trophy.

He was surely thinking it couldn't have been going on very long, Wheatley had just joined the team. Should she tell him? Blow the whole thing open? *That was the only time with Wheatley, Daddy dear, but there was . . . let's see. Yuban, of course. Sammy Dee. Remember the thing Sammy Dee started doing with his tongue at the foul line—you wanna know about that? Fleet Mays. Zip Henry. Bobby Oscar helping me celebrate Sweet Sixteen.*

Mom went away again when she was in eighth grade, not to the mental ward but to spend some time with her parents over in Antelope, and when she finally came back she only stayed long enough to pack. She took Audrey to lunch downtown and seemed much different, much better, but said she had to get out of that house, away from *him,* or she'd slip back. Rose's Deli & Bakery, not long before it closed, a summer afternoon Audrey will never forget. *No, Mom, please!* I'm so sorry, Mom said, tears in her eyes, but there's no way you can understand.

Of course, by then she did understand. She'd seen enough of her father.

Mom said she couldn't take her with her. Maybe sometime, but he wasn't giving her any money and she didn't know how long until her lawyer could get her some. She had a one-bedroom apartment on Shattuck Road, close enough so Audrey could visit anytime but not big enough for her to come live. *I'll sleep on the couch, Mom. On the floor if I have to.* Maybe later, she said, but she didn't trust herself enough right then, didn't know if the improvement would last—maybe he was right and she was just a nutcase. Stay there, she said, and be good, and we'll see—

"I *said,* how long have you been fucking this jig?"

She wanted to blurt out everything. *Just the one time, Daddy, but there were a few others. All niggers, as you like to say, with big black dicks that tasted so good I can't even tell you. And it only started after I got tired of your scrawny, hairy friend Howie telling me how womanly I was—"preternatural"—and porking me in his office every week after you decided I was fucked up and needed to see him. Fucked up because I smoked and skinnydipped and what would happen if people found out the warm-and-fuzzy "media shrink" had a delinquent kid?* Let him suck on that.

But he would have gone nuttier than he was already. She said, "Once. We only did it once."

Still . . . if looks could kill, she'd have been vaporized. "Once," he muttered. She watched him, still not sure he wasn't going to snap.

Almost wanting him to, somehow. Hit her, do something. Lose it. "What about it?" she said, the little smartass tone that always gets to him.

But he only glared. Said he needed a drink, and went to his living-room liquor cabinet.

She said she was going to bed.

He whirled. "You sit!"

She sat. Glad he was having a drink, though he'd had plenty at the game.

He took a glass of Chivas to his big chair, the king's throne. Glared. "You liked it, huh? Got your kicks fucking a goddamn jig?"

"You know what they say about black men. And a big basketball player, you wouldn't believe—"

He was up off his throne then, slopping his drink before he thought to set it down, stalking across and looming over her, almost frothing at the mouth. She braced for the blow, almost wanting it.

He slapped her hard, stumbling with the effort and the drunkenness, then righting himself and ready to do it again as she held the sneer on her face, asking for it.

It didn't come. He stood over her, breathing heavy through clenched teeth, but suddenly she knew he wouldn't hit her again.

"Go to bed, you sorry little cunt."

She pushed up out of the chair and past him, went to her room and locked the door and fell on her bed and lay in the dark cussing him until she burst into tears.

She didn't see him Wednesday. He went to his office and then Channel 2; she went to school, came home to change clothes afterward and then went to Kay's. He was still up when she came in at midnight, on his throne with Chivas and a book—didn't look up, thank God, and she walked on by and went to bed.

She stayed in her room until noon on Thanksgiving, listening for him, debating what to do: they were supposed to go to some couple's house for dinner, friends of his, but she wasn't about to. Finally she heard him taking a shower, and a few minutes later there was the incredible relief when she heard the door and then his Porsche starting in the driveway.

She went to Rita Holt's, where she's always welcome and where he would never know to call. Rita's parents invited her to stay for dinner, probably seeing she was a mess, and a little later she called home and left a message saying she was staying overnight with a friend, be home tomorrow. If he didn't like it, fuck him. What could he do, put her in Providence? Take a chance on people finding out his girl had fucked a big black ballplayer?

It's 1 A.M. when Paige gets back from Thanksgiving at her folks' place out in Oceanside. Max is just back from visiting Bodie. Tommy's upstairs, feeling like a schmo in general and steering clear of Paige in particular, and out in the hot-tub Max tells her the story Tommy told him that morning: how he bought dope for Wheatley, got into it with him at Yardley's house, went back to Yardley's the next day and ended up stealing the videotape. Paige making the same weary face at every revelation: *Imagine my surprise. Didn't I tell you so?*

In bed afterward he tells about staking out Bodie's house that afternoon. Bodie never appearing, and Max going back tonight, just a couple hours ago. Snooping around outside like a cat burglar, seeing a crack of light at the edge of the upstairs window, suckering Bodie out. Bodie with a .38 in his hand.

"Why?" she wants to know. "You risk your life over this?"

"I wasn't gonna send Tommy to the door, the one person this guy knows can dime him up now or next month or next year. And I know how to sound like a cop—and Donald Royer notwithstanding, most people won't blow away a cop at their front door."

"Maxie, Maxie," she sighs, snuggling up to him. And a moment later, "You miss it, don't you?"

Work, he assumes.

"You've been sitting around here three months now, more bored every day. Relaxing, you say, but you don't have hobbies or anything to absorb you so you're sort of anxious all the time, sitting here watching sports and doing crossword puzzles but mostly wondering—correct me if I'm wrong—mostly wondering what's going on out in real life, who's getting the good cases, what-all you could

185

be doing. You're a lot more relaxed when you're busy, doing what
you do. Cops and robbers."

"You think so?" Instead of *You're probably right, as usual.*

"I think so."

He can't argue. Can't deny he misses the camaraderie, the stimula-
tion, the significance of it all, the edge. Even before he got caught up
in all this, which brought the fact home to him, it was a rare day when
he didn't talk to someone in the VCU—Witty, Racy, Kuykendall—
picturing them up in their little corner of the eighth floor of the
courthouse, in and out of each other's offices talking trial strategy,
sharing all the amazing stuff they see and hear every day, making
their sick jokes about it all. Kuyk, the Elvis fanatic, gets a rape
suspect by the name of Elvis Aaron Presley Hair. Racy gets this
strange Yardley thing. Witty, who replaced Max as the DA on the
county's Major Crimes Team, gets a tip and rides out to the Colum-
bia River Gorge with the detectives, where they find a decomposed,
decapitated corpse in a shallow grave—deposited there years ago,
according to the tipster, by associates of Sandro Morelli, capo of
what passes for an organized-crime family in Portland. Max's case,
except that he's busy wasting his time.

Was, until today.

"But now you've got this to sink your teeth into, right?" she says
as if she's reading his mind. "You're all over this, and probably not
only because of some misplaced loyalty to this old buddy—who
turns out to be pretty much what I've said ever since I met him, I
might add."

"You're a genius. But what's your interest all of a sudden, considering your feelings about him?"

"The girl. Plus it's fun to be on the investigation side of something
for a change"—defense attorneys only getting a case after an investigation leads to an arrest. "Plus it's fun to work on something with
you. Wasn't last summer the first time we ever got to tolerate each
other? It's fun, isn't it?"

"Fun. Having a sociopath point a .38 at me on Thanksgiving
night."

"But now we're lying here together and we're gonna have some
fun and then fall asleep together, and eventually we'll sort this out
and feel selfless and virtuous like public servants and officers of the
court are supposed to feel." Laying a soft, lingering kiss on his neck.
"Now, we agree this girl could be in trouble, whoever she is?"

"I'd say."

"And your buddy is, of course. Not to mention you, if these big guys come back and Mike Johns isn't here to protect you."

"Funny. Except we don't know if these people are even looking for anyone anymore. If the agent told Bodie to fuck off like Bodie claims, if there was no payoff, they might've left it at that."

"Or not."

"Or not. Maybe they tell him to fuck off, then try to make sure he doesn't do what he threatened to do. And that's why he's hiding, not because he's got Wheatley's two hundred thousand. As for the girl . . . if they had any way of identifying her, she might be taken care of already. If not—well, we sure don't know who she is."

She snuggles closer, aroused—Max knowing he's in for a ride before long, recalling the wild nights last summer when they were closing in on Tower.

"But we've got ways," she says. "Don't we? Sources, even if they're unwilling? Witty said Yardley didn't tell the detectives a fraction of what he knows . . . so can't you squeeze him now, with what you found out in LA?"

"I could try. Not that he'll say any more until he's in front of a grand jury, and probably not even then."

"So you won't bother?"

"Hey, I'm thinking about it. I'm also thinking about saying forget it and dropping it all on Johns and letting him do what he wants."

"Huh. And let your buddy sink?"

"Maybe. I'm tired of it all—everyone lying, trying to get over. Tommy, too. I gotta admit: how stupid is he, to get caught up in this?"

But they both know he's not about to drop it. Not only is Tommy a friend, but cops-and-robbers is what Max Travis does.

She leaves in the morning: to her office for a while, then to a meeting of Portland's senior public defenders.

Curious about Bodie, Max calls Ticor Title Company and finds out the house on Pettygrove was purchased back in 1988 by a Rebecca Wallace. No surprise it's not in Bodie's name, considering what Tommy said.

O'Leary's not in the office but Max reaches Greg "Ace" Macy, another world-class investigator, and gets him to call PGE. The news, a few minutes later, is that Miss Wallace also pays the electric bill for 2326 NW Pettygrove. Macy calls DMV and finds out that a Richard Bodie who would be forty-two years old now—which must be this Richard Bodie, since the only others in the Portland area are twenty-two and fifty-eight—hasn't renewed his driver's license in nine years. As Tommy said, the guy almost doesn't exist.

A Rebecca Wallace, thirty-nine, has a valid license with an address over in Northeast.

Lacking anything more productive to do, Max drives over there with Tommy. It's a nice garden-apartment complex on well-tended, tree-plenty grounds between 70th and 74th, between Halsey and Tillamook. Miss Wallace is in an upper-level unit of 72nd—or would be, if she were home. Not that she'd necessarily have any idea what Bodie's into. Not that she'd admit it if she did.

Dead-ended, essentially.

He knows what he wants to do. Back in August he swore he'd never break-and-enter again, after the gods allowed him to get away with going into Teddy Cunningham's condo in Florida, but what else can he do?

Maybe it grows on you, the thrill of it.

No. It's terror, not a thrill.

Yeah? Then why not go dump it all in Johns's lap? He gets a warrant to search Bodie's place, legal, and you're out of it.

But that means telling all, and you're not quite ready to do that to Tommy, even though he wouldn't get charged with much in the end. No one's even dead.

So, do what?

He finds himself hitting the Banfield and sailing back across town with Tommy, back over to NW Pettygrove, and parking along the curb where they sat staking out Bodie's place last night.

After a half-hour with no activity he walks down the block and up to the porch, pushes the button, hears the *ding-dong* inside. Nothing. *Ding-dong.* Nothing. Maybe he's in there, laying low like last night, or maybe after last night he's staying away.

Walks down to 23rd and gets espresso at Coffee People. Then they sit in the car for another hour, watching the house and going over everything again, Max wondering if he can trust Tommy even now. People in trouble rarely tell you everything. Or people who stand to lose a pile of money—say, half of two hundred thousand bucks.

*   *   *

Unlawful entry is a bad habit, but at three-thirty he flips his cellular open and calls O'Leary up at Mount Hood. "Hate to ruin your four-day weekend, pal, but can you maybe help me out a little later?"

With his great friend, of course, it's all he needs to say.

Waiting in the long narrow hallway on the seventh floor of the courthouse, Yardley prays for some sympathy. They've got to see he's been through hell, and understand he couldn't have done anything for Alice.

A nice-looking brunette, saying she was an investigator with the DA's office, delivered the subpoena Wednesday afternoon—more bad news at the back door. *You're being asked to testify to a grand jury about an alleged rape here at your home.*

Now, a few minutes after three on Friday, a guy with a manila folder in his hand comes around the corner, asks if he's Rodney Yardley and introduces himself as Deputy DA Charles Witty. He's got freckles and a cowlick, glasses, not very impressive, but he's all business. No sympathy here.

Tell your story and then deny, deny, deny everything else. What can they do?

A few minutes later he's in a tight conference-type room with Witty and seven dopey-looking citizens, the grand jury. Young guy in a plaid shirt, looks like a carpet-installer. Chubby girl, community-college dropout, reads romance novels with pastel covers. Rickety old man. It must be true, what you hear: juries are made up of dopes because anyone with a decent job or even a tea-spoon of sense can get out of jury duty.

He prays the other thing you hear isn't true: that a grand jury is always on the State's side, that people assume the DA wouldn't be grilling you without a damn good reason.

He's in the chair at the head of the U-shaped table arrangement, the dopes seated down the sides, Witty on his feet behind them.

"Mr. Yardley," Witty begins in a high-pitched voice, scanning his papers, "you understand that you haven't been charged with a crime, correct? You're here to tell this grand jury, under oath, what you know about an incident that allegedly took place at your home at—uh, 465 Southwest Felton Drive on Wednesday, November twentieth, nine days ago. The grand jury has already heard testimony from others in this case, and they're interested in your account of events. You understand?"

Others in the case? Huh? Did they find the spades? Jesus, what do they know?

"I'll ask you some questions," Witty says, "and later the jurors will have the opportunity to ask you anything else they might want to know, anything I might neglect."

Deny, deny, deny.

He doesn't need to lie for a while. He's pretty sure he's believable as he describes two black men he'd never seen before showing up the Sunday night before the incident, lobbing rocks from the flower-beds up onto the deck where he was hot-tubbing ("Two detectives came out last week and saw the damage"), then coming in the house and beating him up ("You can see my face, and I've got four broken ribs").

"Never saw these men before?"

"Never." Looking at the jurors: *You can trust me.*

"Any idea who they were?"

"No idea."

"Or why they came to your home and broke in and beat you up?"

"No idea."

Charles Witty repeats it: "No idea?"

Jesus. What does he know? "No, sir."

"But they seemed to know who you were?"

"I don't think so, no." Wondering if Witty knows better. Suspecting he does and adding, "They asked me later and I told them, but I'm pretty sure they didn't know when they showed up. I was pretty sure it was two guys looking for, you know, money and valuables, and thought my house looked as good as any."

"Just like that?"

"That's what I thought."

"And you continued to believe that, Mr. Yardley?"

A trap?

Who knows? But there's nothing to gain by conceding. "To be

quite honest, sir, I don't remember thinking much of anything after they beat me up the first time. That's when my nose and four ribs were broken. I also blacked out for a while, I know that, and afterward I couldn't think of anything but the pain."

Witty studies his papers. Looking at the testimony he's gotten from "others," or just fucking with him?

It goes on for more than an hour. Occasional questions from Witty, long explanations from Yardley—about being forced to sit on the chair in the guest-room under the threat of more violence, about them laughing at him and slapping him around when they came in every so often, about being so scared to disobey that he "urinated" and "defecated" on the carpet instead of using the bathroom ten feet away. (They've got to be sympathetic!) And finally, the last night—absolutely truthful—about a car pulling up out back and the black men coming upstairs a few minutes later with Alice Richardson, an acquaintance who dropped by every so often; the short powerful one threatening to bust him up while the crazy one raped her on the bed, then the powerful one raping her while the crazy one taunted him, dared him to do something. ("I could hardly move, with my ribs, and I knew they had a gun somewhere.")

Believable, he knows, because every word is true.

Then again, he's seen enough *Court TV* to know Witty will tell these people, If you find the witness has lied in one part of his testimony, you may choose not to believe any of his testimony.

"And then they left, pretty soon after. They told me I'd be sorry if I didn't stay where I was, and they took her downstairs. I was afraid what might happen, they might kill her, but I knew they might kill us both if I tried to do anything, which I couldn't've anyway. I heard the car drive off, Alice's, but I wasn't sure one of them wasn't still downstairs. I didn't dare move. I was still in the room the next morning when the detectives came over."

It goes pretty well, he thinks. Maybe even some sympathy in the eyes of some of the dopes.

Except it's not exactly what Charles Witty wants to know. He goes back to who these two men were and why they might have come to Yardley's house—"assuming for a moment that it wasn't a random thing as you've suggested."

"I can't tell you, sir. I spent four days in that room wondering, and I'm still wondering. All I could think of at the time, after I realized they weren't there just to rob me, was that they were on the run or something, hiding out, and they needed a place to stay. I don't have a better explanation today."

"I'm sure that's possible," Witty says. "You told the detectives they didn't take much? Broke a few things, but didn't take much?"

"That's right."

Witty skims his papers for the hundredth time. "You're absolutely sure you never saw these men before they showed up that previous Sunday night while you were in your hot-tub on the upper level?"

"Positive."

"And there's absolutely no reason you can think of why someone else might have sent them? Nothing they said to indicate anything like that?"

"Nothing, sir."

Pray they believe it.

Witty's stumped, even though he's asked every possible question.

The jurors sit there shaking their dopey heads when he asks them if they've got questions.

Finally Witty thanks him and lets him go. "We'll get in touch, Mr. Yardley, if we need you again."

Yardley's pretty sure he'll be hearing from him, unfortunately. For all he knows, someone else identified the spades and Witty's had them in and knows plenty and just wanted to see how long Yardley would lie to him. *Let me remind you you're under oath here*, he'd said at the beginning, *and that perjury is a felony.*

Of course, people lie under oath every day and nothing happens. If they nail him, they nail him, but no point in making it easy for them.

The good news was that Witty didn't ask a single question about Wheatley, the party, the videotape, the blackmail . . . meaning he probably hasn't had the spades in, and if he has, they kept it all quiet.

And if all he's got on Yardley is that he witnessed a rape, shit, that's no crime. So fuck Witty and the white horse he rode in on.

Max misses their morning coffee the most, O'Leary dropping by the VCU and the two of them walking over to Starbucks or Seattle's Best or one of the dozen other spots within two blocks of the courthouse, having a leisurely cup and talking cases, sometimes, but more often fishing or sports or whatever arcane subject was on Jerry's mind, voodoo or emus or rare stamps, Max constantly amazed by his fund of knowledge and amused by the twinkle in his eye and the raspy, rapidfire delivery.

A wiry, gray-haired guy in his fifties, worth his weight in gold to the office. After years as a police detective he quit to care for his cancer-ridden wife, and sometime after she died, about seven years ago, joined the DA as an investigator. He was lead investigator before long, a whiz, and they worked numerous murders together. The working relationship was great, and the friendship developed during Max's second divorce when Jerry kept him company at the Quandary so many nights. The last few years they worked together constantly, and fished, and worked on Jerry's vacation place on Mount Hood.

A lot of history. But when Jerry shows up Friday evening, all the way down from the mountain on request, it's those trips for coffee every morning that Max remembers. Maybe he misses the office more than he's admitting.

Paige is glad to see Jerry too, hasn't seen him since the morning Tower was arraigned back in August, but she doesn't like this scheme at all. She's been saying it since she got here an hour ago: "An officer of the court breaking and entering?"

"I'm not an officer of the court, remember? I'm unemployed."

"Which is how you'll stay if this doesn't work out. And for what?" Meaning, for this so-called friend of yours?

"Must be the cops-and-robbers thing," he kept telling her, and she'd give him the disgusted look and drop it—for about five minutes, and then start in again. It was a relief when Jerry showed up.

Max calls Tommy down from where he's hiding from Paige, introduces Jerry, and they all walk out to Jerry's vintage Park Avenue. Max riding shotgun, Paige in back with Tommy—Paige not happy about it, but too bad. She doesn't like what Max has in mind, either, but too bad. Like it or lick it.

They ride across town in silence, Max asking himself, Why are you doing this? Picturing Bodie in his front hall last night—Bodie's .38, actually, pointed right at him.

So why? Sentimental about your freshman-year roommate, a guy you used to get high with twenty-some years ago? (Who still hasn't outgrown it? Who, as his soon-to-be-ex-wife said, needs dope and drink to cope with a life he screwed up with dope and drink?) Whom you've hardly seen all these years?

That must be it: sentimental.

Huh? You, a prosecutor, sentimental? Paige would howl at that.

Jerry parks in front of Coffee People on 23rd, a block from Bodie's house. "Wait for us in here," Max tells the odd couple in the backseat, and hands Paige his cell phone. "I'll call you if we get hauled in."

No light in any windows, not even a sliver. No reply to repeated dingdongs at the front door.

It hits him now, what he's doing—him, the prosecutor's prosecutor, trained to do things by the book straight down the line. It's wrong. But hey, he's no prosecutor now.

In the darkness they slip around back, alert for prying eyes in the windows next door. They're going to try the basement door. Max saw the X-Pert Security sticker on the front window last night and called them this afternoon, posing as an insurance adjuster looking at Rebecca Wallace's homeowner insurance. *Does Miss Wallace in fact have an alarm system at 2326 NW Pettygrove? What kind, and which floors are covered?*

Miss Wallace has a laser system, the lady said, on the ground floor and upstairs. The box is in the basement.

So that's where they want to go.

The door is solid oak, with two and maybe three locks on it—no chance of getting in there. But Jerry's prepared, as always: pulls on some latex gloves, slides down into one of the window-wells, duct-tapes one of the six-inch-square panes, punches it out with scarcely a sound, reaches in, turns the sash-lock, raises the bottom window and scuttles inside. Max follows.

In the musty basement, with his penlight, Jerry finds the alarm box attached to a post. Bodie obviously never expected anyone to come looking for it: the key's on top, and when Jerry opens the box the manual is inside. Max holds the light while he skims it, and two minutes later they've bypassed the system.

Crooks, in the service of justice.

The thin ray from the penlight shows boxes stacked everywhere, skis and water-skis and snowboards leaning against one wall, golf clubs, stacks of magazines, washer and dryer and deep-sink, an old laundry basket full of rags, beat-up furniture. Two smaller rooms are crammed with more junk, including three halide dope-growing lights in a carton.

The main floor doesn't yield anything much more interesting, not that they can do a thorough search with a penlight and a time crunch: kitchen; bathroom; a room intended as a den, probably, with a pricey sound system and shelves of CDs over shelves of cassettes over a shelf of albums running the length of one wall. Back around to the front room, with big-screen TV and VCR, where Max and Bodie talked last night.

Upstairs: no money, no videotape. Max doesn't even know what else he's looking for.

But he knows it when he sees it.

It's got to be the girl. Four full-page laser prints in a manila envelope in Bodie's office, on a long table between his PC and his printer. She's blond, like the girl Tommy described, and could be as young as sixteen. Could be older—you'd probably take her for older if you didn't know—but she could definitely be sixteen.

Max replaces three copies in the envelope, puts the envelope back where it was, and then they're hustling back down through the house to the basement. Jerry reactivates the X-Pert system, then Max gives him a leg up and out the window, hoists himself up and out, and a moment later they're back around front, hitting the sidewalk and heading down Pettygrove to meet up with the odd couple at Coffee People.

Just when Yardley imagined the worst was over. Sure, there's still the little matter of $200,000 that Wheatley and his people aren't about to forget, but after the grand jury yesterday he'd almost started believing he might squeeze out of the rest of it.

Now, fifteen minutes after he rolls out of bed Saturday morning, groggy from too much booze last night—five minutes after bringing himself to life with a nice long line—here's this fucking Max Travis at the back door again.

"Yardley," he says, and walks right in—with an all-business look on his face, which must have something to do with the folded sheet of paper in his hand. Now what?

He sits down at the table, unfolds the paper and holds it up: a grainy closeup picture of Little Bang, her face filling the page. Eyes wide, not quite looking at the camera—some kind of candid shot. Her chin not visible, something in the way.

"Know her, Yardley?"

Deny, deny, deny. Except that he knows you know her, or he wouldn't be here.

"What I mean," Travis says, "is you do know her. I'm pretty sure this picture came off the infamous videotape. And you know what videotape I'm talking about."

Yardley tries to look baffled.

Travis looks like he's about to burst out laughing. "Come on. We both know what I'm talking about. You made a secret videotape, right?"

"V-videotape?"

Now Travis does smile, as he smooths out the picture on the tabletop. "Sit down here, Yardley, and let's talk. I think you've got a lot to tell me. Everything you didn't tell me the first time I came by."

Yardley sits. What's his choice?

"You didn't tell me shit that time," Travis says. "About the party here, the cocaine, this girl, LaPrince Wheatley, your video setup, any of it. Someone getting their hands on your prize tape and black-mailing Wheatley, or trying to, which I figure is why the half-brother and his homeboy came over here and made you look like you look." Staring at him, at the discolored face and packed nose. "Correct me if I'm wrong."

"You're telling the story." All he can manage, something he heard in some cheesy movie.

"OK, I'm telling it, but we both know the story. We both know, also, that you lied to the grand jury yesterday, which is never a good idea and is an especially bad idea when Mr. Witty's on a case. He might not seem brilliant, I know, but that's his act. He's always the smartest person in the room, no matter what room he's in. And surprise, surprise, Opie gets mad when he finds out someone's jerking him around."

"Hey, I told 'em—" But stops. What, now you're going to try to bullshit this one too?

"You told 'em shit, mister. I talked to Mr. Witty an hour ago. Asked him what happened with a case he told me about last weekend, a couple days before I came over here—a case where a woman named Alice Richardson claimed two African-American men raped her at a guy named Yardley's house while this guy Yardley sat there letting it happen. Mr. Witty said he brought this Yardley in yesterday on a grand-jury subpoena and the man sat there insisting he had no idea who those two were or why they came to his house and whipped his ass and sat around for three or four days." Max not quite smirking at him, but close. "Didn't Mr. Witty tell you lying under oath is a felony?"

"I've heard." Meekly, ridiculously.

"Yeah, I'll bet you've looked into those statutes. But you went ahead and lied anyway."

What's he supposed to say?

The prick just waits, lets him squirm.

"What do you want me to say?"

"Well, I'll talk some more, then. I think you lied your ass off because you're afraid of the whole can of worms opening up—parties, girls, drugs, videotapes, who-knows-what."

Remain silent, on the grounds that responding might tend to incriminate you.

"Talk to me, Yardley."

"You talk." *Since I'm coming unglued.*

"If you insist. OK, I guess you understand I've found out a few things since we talked the other day. Things even Mr. Witty doesn't know. At this point he only knows about the rape, but I've been looking into the other stuff on my own, the whole tangled thing, because my friend Mason's caught up in it. And I wish I could tell you it might all work itself out, Yardley, but I don't see how. This Miss Richardson was pretty brutally raped, and the police and the DA's office take that very seriously. As far as the man who got his hands on your video and tried to blackmail Wheatley—"

Got it from your friend, Yardley almost blurts, *who broke into my fucking house,* but thinks better of it.

"—I don't know what's gonna happen with all that. All I can tell you is that I'm concerned about my friend. And the other person who might be in danger here, who might not have any idea she's in danger at all." Tapping a fingertip on the picture of Little Bang on the table.

"Her?"

"Well," Travis says, "does she know? Was she in on it? Some little scam you worked up together, except someone else got their hands on the tape before you could cash in?"

"Hell, no." Weak. He can hear himself, weak.

"No? So she's something like an innocent bystander, except that Wheatley's people might not see it that way. To them she's dangerous, as soon as they find out she's underage. She might say something anytime, now or next month. You see what I'm saying?"

Yardley sees. Nods. Thinking about someone . . . killing her? Jesus. Even if he'll never get anywhere with her, he doesn't want her dead.

"So what I want to know," Travis says, "is who she is and how to—"

"I don't know. I'd tell you if I knew but I don't, I swear."

"Don't lie. I don't see any way under the sun you're getting out of all this clean, but I promise it'll be one hell of a lot harder on you if someone dies."

Yardley swears he doesn't know who she is. Admits she came to the house a few times before that night, last season, but swears he never knew who she was or how old; she claimed her name was Daisy, and that she went to OSU, and that her family had a skybox at the Plunderdome and she came up from Corvallis for weekend games. He never believed her name was Daisy, but maybe it is, who knows? She did wear an oversized OSU letterman's jacket sometimes and looked old enough for college, and always talked about the Plunder games like she'd just come from there, but that's all he knows!

"That's all? How about what Wheatley says to her on the tape, something about going downstairs and doing some more coke to loosen up?"

"I don't know about that." Shit. Knowing the desperate honesty's gone from his voice and Travis notices.

"Did she drink, then, when she came over? Smoke dope?"

"Man, I don't know. I don't." Telling the truth about that night, although he knows Travis doesn't mean that night only.

But Travis lets it go. "Daisy, huh? What she said her name was?"

"That's what she said, and that's all I know."

"And said she goes to Oregon State?"

"That's right. And she looked old enough."

Travis gives him an unsympathetic eye. "You might get out from under one charge when this blows up, contributing to the delinquency of a minor. But there's always the perjury, and some felony drug charges, and the criminal invasion of privacy for taping sex acts for sale or distribution without the—"

"What? It wasn't for—"

"—without the participants' knowledge or consent. No one knows what you intended the tape for, but it sure got out there and someone tried to sell it for two hundred grand, and you're sure as hell gonna have to explain your way out of it. And who knows what else'll be piled up on you when all's said and done?"

Almost laughing at him, the smartass fucker.

"Now, you sure you can't tell me anything more?"

When Max gets back from Yardley's house with nothing more than the improbable name "Daisy," Paige believes there's nothing to do but take the girl's picture to the Plunder offices on Monday and find out who might know her. Two days from now.

They're in Max's living room talking about it, she and Max and Jerry O'Leary, when Mason comes downstairs and finally contributes something.

He avoids her eyes, as usual, goes to Max on the couch and hands him a soft-cover book with a basketball action photo on the front. "I don't know if this'll help, but . . ." He stands by, uncomfortable, as Max glances at what she realizes is the Portland Plunder media guide. "Up front, where it's got all the employees' pictures. Lapinsky-Davis."

Paige moves over to the couch and looks. Several pages of employee photos, yearbook-style, with names and titles underneath the photos.

Sheryl Lapinsky-Davis, a round-faced woman around thirty with an unfortunate haircut and too much makeup, is Director of Preferred Seating and Luxury Suites. Max says, "I guess she's the one we need to see on Monday."

Paige thinking, Monday? On her feet, on her way to the kitchen for the phone book.

S. Lapinsky-Davis is there (no address), and up front there's an M. Davis-Lapinsky with the same number. Hubby.

O'Leary makes the call.

"Mrs. Lapinsky-Davis, with the Plunder? My name is O'Leary, I'm an investigator in the Multnomah County District Attorney's office, and I need to see you as soon as possible about one of your customers . . . Yes, very important . . . Noon would be fine. Your office at the Plunderdome?"

He's back before one.

Her name is Audrey VanKirkman. The daughter of Dr. Henry VanKirkman, the psychologist on KXL and Channel 2. An outstanding student at Catlin Gabel, Mrs. Lapinsky-Davis said—a junior, she thought, possibly a senior. A very striking girl, Mrs. Lapinsky-Davis said, much more so than in the picture.

The address is on Skyview Terrace, one of the narrow twisting streets up in the southwest hills where rich people live in classic old houses on tiny lots. Paige remembers being inside one once, visiting someone back in high school. Remembers the feeling that you could reach out a side window and into the neighbor's kitchen.

She says she's going up there, and goes.

"Striking girl" is an understatement. She answers the door in faded navy-blue sweats—not made up, maybe not even showered yet today, but she's striking at the very least. Sky-blue eyes, silvery-blond hair casually knotted in back, perfect features and the creamy skin you only have when you're young, if you're lucky enough to have it even then.

She's young, yes, but she could certainly pass for eighteen, legal. Five-three only, maybe five-four, but even in the loose sweats it's clear she's developed.

"Audrey?"

"Yes?"

"I'm Paige Prescott, an attorney with Metropolitan Public Defenders downtown . . . although I'm not here as a Metro attorney, not here in any official capacity actually. I'm concerned about you, though, and I think we need to talk. The two of us, and then your parents too, probably."

Paige hardly knows what to say.

They're sitting in the VanKirkman living room an hour later, the two of them, her father still out somewhere. Vaulted ceiling, expensive modern furniture, a wall of windows looking out at the river and the east side and snowy Mount Hood in the distance. Paige thinking it must be nice to be privileged . . . unless you end up with the look this girl's got in her eyes.

Her parents have been divorced for five years, and she's always wished she could live with her mother but apparently there's no way. And what a story she's just told about life with father. Father who found out at the Plunder game last Tuesday that she'd slept with LaPrince Wheatley, and went ballistic when he got home.

"He'd probably be *glad* if they killed me!"

"No, Audrey"—Paige on the sofa now, arm around her, trying to comfort.

"He would be!" She's sobbing, shaking. "I'm disgusting! Fucked a nigger! 'Sorry little cunt' is what he called me."

What can you say? What can you do besides hold her?

What a story.

But then, what do you believe of it? She's convincing, but what's her father's version? A lot of defendants are convincing, too, when you meet them privately in the jail, but trial comes and you feel like a fool when a half-dozen perfectly credible prosecution witnesses blow the story into a million pieces.

"He's afraid of how it'll look! Sure! Afraid of how *he'll* look, as if everyone hates 'em like he does!"

M ax loves her, he's pretty sure, but come on.
Paige Prescott, true believer. Champion of the downtrod-
den and oppressed, even if she has to expand the definition to in-
clude a trampy teenager from a ritzy neighborhood whose father
must be worth a million dollars. Paige has to save her.

Not that she's wrong. It's the attitude, which reminds him of all
the times she's been wrong over the years, manipulated by sociopathic murderers, rapists, armed robbers, various scumbags who
recognized a bleeding-heart a mile away.

"What did she expect," he can't help asking, "when she gets involved with people like Yardley and LaPrince Wheatley?"

The offended look, a Prescott classic. "Aren't we a little beyond
that now?" The tone. "Isn't that beside the point? She did get involved, and this creep makes a videotape, and your buddy steals it
and his sleazy friend gets big ideas and a sixteen-year-old girl is in
way over her head—"

"So," he asks when she stops to catch her breath, "what do you
want to do?"

"I want to advise her father of all this, first. I gave Audrey my
cellular number and the number here and told her to have him call
me when he gets home. But I think you need to talk to the police,
Max, even if it means Tommy has to be accountable for what he's
done."

Somehow he's not surprised.

"Or," she says, "would you rather wait till these people find her?"

"You're assuming they're looking for her."

"You're assuming they're not?" she snaps. The old Miss Prescott,
adamant, and Max is pretty sure she'll give up their love affair be-

fore she'll back off her position. "You'll be comfortable with yourself if we do nothing and something does happen to her?"

"Of course not, but I want to keep Tommy out of it if I can."

Her mouth drops open like she can't believe what she's hearing, another maddening Prescott affectation. "Based on what? The fact that all he did was buy some dope for this Plunder guy, walk into a man's house uninvited, steal a videotape and instigate blackmail? Or on friendship?" she adds tartly.

"Friendship." Twitting her. Irritated by the emergence of the old Miss Prescott, even if she's right.

She mutters something, shaking her head. "Not concerned about Audrey, huh?"

First-name familiar already. He can still hear her saying "Michael" this, "Michael" that, talking about the murdering Mikey Parker last spring. And the other scuzzbuckets, "Willie" and "Lewis" and "David" . . .

All right, this girl is no murderer, just a kid with problems, but the true believer in Paige drives him crazy.

"I'm concerned about her," he concedes, "even though I'm not sure I need to be."

"So?"

"So, I can't stop you from doing what you're gonna do, but I'd prefer to hold off and see what her father wants to do. He's supposed to call you? How 'bout we wait? Hot-tub." He doesn't like thinking they're utterly different despite all the good stuff, and that the whole thing could blow up and be over.

Because there's a lot to like. And after they do it in the tub and she's sitting on his lap with her head on his shoulder, he knows she feels the same way. And that she's probably got the same fear.

She's still a mystery. He was sorry to miss Thanksgiving out in Oceanside because he's wanted to meet her parents, try to get some clues about her. Her dad's out in Alzheimerland, but maybe he could talk to her mom. Or just watch, listen.

All those years, he assumed she was rich—private schools, cotillion, summers in Europe. She seemed a little hoity-toity, full of herself for all the wrong reasons. It wasn't until last summer, lying in her bed one of those first nights, that he found out Dad had been a taxi driver most of his life, lucky enough to hook on with Tri-Met when the bus system started, and that she went to Grant High and might not have gone to college at all except for a partial academic scholarship to UO and some additional money she was awarded: the Horatio Alger–Randall Gardner Enriching America Award for Outstanding Community Service, for spending three years of after-schools at a youth center over in Albina, the 'hood, tutoring black kids who'd decided to make an effort.

So he understood a little about how she'd become what she became, and had to consider that maybe he was the middle-class kid who didn't understand so well.

She'd made the most of her opportunity at UO, a young lady so smart and focused that by the time she sailed through that middling law school she had the appearance and manner of the upper crust. A young lady who knew big words and a lot more—who knew how to dress, how to move, who had the bearing of someone who knew what she was about.

And what she believed, more or less (Max remembers her early months in the courthouse, the impression she made), was that life is easy for the well-off and not so easy for the rest, and that she was one of the fortunate few among the rest who had the ability to do something for people like the ones she'd seen in Albina all those afternoons after school a few years back. Do something not only for them, the ones who made an effort, but for the ones who refused to, who murdered and strongarmed and dealt drugs instead. They were the saddest ones, she believed, too misguided or hopeless to even try. Desperate.

Yes, you could tell her, *but the desperation makes them cold, makes them brutal, and innocent people's lives are destroyed.*

And she'd tell you, *Yes, but there's a bigger picture. Don't you see?*

She'd drive you to drink if you didn't tune her out, so that's what most people tried to do. Including Max, all those years.

Tommy's stretched out upstairs watching Steelers–Dolphins when he hears Max come in from his Sunday-morning DA touch-football game. Tommy feeling pretty good, having gone out back for a blast a few minutes ago.

Max calls from the bottom of the stairs. Tommy calls back "Yo!" instead of going down, afraid his eyes will give him away despite the Visine.

Max calls, "You sticking around awhile?"

"No plans."

"I'm gonna take a shower. . . . Paige'll be showing up. I've got news you both need to hear."

Yardley killed himself, is the news.

"Witty said Stan Kearns called him last night, the homicide sergeant. Yardley had called a lady friend around six, smashed, and rambled awhile and then hung up on her. The lady thought he sounded weird and she finally drove over, found him passed out, called the EMTs. They pumped his stomach at the med school ER, but too late. He had a blood-alcohol of point-two-three, must've been drinking for hours, and ate about twenty Percodans on top of it. One hell of a cocktail."

Prescott says, "Probably drank all day after you went over there. Saw things falling apart."

"Whatever. I laid out his situation for him, that's all. Offered to help if I could, if he'd wise up and tell me what he knew. The dumbshit just kept jerking me around."

Prescott studies him. Is she blaming him somehow?

Max wonders, too. "Look, this isn't on me. He got himself into the situation. And if he'd kill himself after our conversation—well, if he hadn't done it then, he sure as hell would've done it later. Witty would've come down on him with spiked shoes when he found out everything."

"Any note? Anything?"

"The detectives didn't find anything last night. I'm sure they'll look a little more."

Prescott looks at him, looks at Tommy, then back at Max—Tommy a waste of her time, of course. "So," she says. "Why?"

"No idea. Probably saw things falling apart, like you say. Maybe he heard from Wheatley or the agent or the two Neanderthals who came over here—maybe they told him they wanted their two hundred thousand back or they'd take it out of his hide, and he decided it was time. Who knows? I don't really care. I'm glad he slept soundly, that's all."

His honeybun looks at him hard, disapproving. She probably doesn't care much either, but it wouldn't be right to say so. So proper, so correct.

"So what now?" she says. "You go tell Witty everything, right? I take it you didn't level with him this morning."

Max looks at Tommy—Tommy's legs suddenly unsteady, a hot prickly sensation in his face. Tell Witty everything?

Prescott snapping, "Max?" Like, You go tell everything.

Max ignoring her, bless him, looking at Tommy with something like concern. Concern, sympathy, loyalty, something.

Tommy can only wait.

"I do have to tell what I know," Max says at last, looking from one to the other, "now that there's a dead body. I'm going to get grief anyway for not going to Witty as soon as I got back from LA . . . for not calling him after I saw Yardley yesterday, when I knew he lied to the grand jury Friday . . . for not saying anything this morning."

"Call him now," she says. "You've got to. The man is dead, and you said yourself these people might have driven him to it. They might have force-fed him the Percodan. If that's it"—she turns to Tommy—"I'm sure they haven't forgotten about you either. Or your friend, who I guess has their money."

They're both looking at him, as if he could possibly have anything to say.

It's all he can do to make it to the soft chair on his rubbery legs. He makes it, and sits, and wipes his overheated brow, and when he looks up they're still eyeballing him. "So?" he says. His voice is hollow.

Max says, "So, I can talk to Charlie Witty about the rape, ID Wheatley's brother and his homey, which will lead back to the video and open the whole thing up, and—now wait, just wait"—raising a hand as Tommy's blood turns cold and (he's positive) all color drains from his face. "Just listen. It's going to come out eventually, and if we talk to Witty now—"

"You have to, Max." The bitch.

"—if we talk to him now he goes to Johns, and the cops come in and talk to Wheatley and the agent, whoever, and sort the thing out and maybe save your ass. Locate Bodie and the money and maybe get it back to Wheatley, which might be the only way you can ever live in this town again without looking over your shoulder every second. I don't know, I haven't thought it through—"

"Max!" His honey demanding his attention. "You haven't thought what through? Whether or not to come forward with information you should have provided already? Are you serious?"

Tommy's cringing. He must have known it would come to this, yet it all seemed so unreal, it seemed so inconceivable that he'd end up facing cops and prosecutors, answering questions about—God, he can't bear to think about it all. Inconceivable, yet it's about to happen.

"You'll be OK," Max says. "You're worried about charges, right? Listen, you'll be helping them out with the information you provide, so they won't be looking to bust on you. Even if they were, look: Yardley's not around to claim you walked into his house, so there's no illegal entry. You gave Bodie the video, so you're not in possession of stolen property. Bodie'll never admit to any blackmail scam, so there's nothing to implicate you in." To his honey: "Am I right?"

She sits there on the couch with her arms folded in front of her, stony.

"Believe me," Max says, back to Tommy. "Hell, Johns would probably give you immunity to get what you know. Oh yeah, the dope. Well, you think Wheatley's gonna bring it up? Tell people he had you score three ounces for him? I don't think so."

They're quiet—a few seconds, a minute. Tommy staring at the carpet, fantasizing about bolting out the front door and throwing himself in front of the next passing car. Picturing Prescott over on the couch with her look.

"Think about it," Max says.

"Ma-ax." The bitch up off the couch now, over to Max, standing there glaring at him.

Now turning the look on Tommy. *You cowardly, loathesome—* she doesn't need to say it out loud.

Turning it back on Max. Finally hissing "I can't believe this," actually reaching out and giving her lover-man a shove, then whirling away and stomping out of the living room.

And on out the front door, with a slam.

At home, still furious, Paige changes into sweats and goes for a run, trying to blow off steam. Light rain in her face, her breath forming in the wintry air.

She can't believe Max can be so loyal to someone like Mason, can be so plain stupid, can ignore his duty as an officer of the court or even consider ignoring it.

She wonders why Audrey's father never called her yesterday. Now more than ever they need to talk.

But back home, going to the phone, she checks her messages first and hears Audrey, shaken: "Paige, I'm scared! I did a home pregnancy test"—sobbing, losing it—"and when he started yelling at me I told him—told him I won't give it up. I-I—don't know—I don't know! I'm in my room now and he's out there and I'm scared! Can you come? Can you call?"

She picks up the phone and calls, but no answer. Just the recording, finally, in a chilly, measured voice: *This is Dr. Van-Kirkman. . . .*

There was never any question they had to go to Witty and the detectives, even before Paige stormed out. Max wanted to ease Tommy into it, that's all.

Five minutes after she leaves, with Tommy paralyzed and nearly speechless in the chair, he calls Witty. Witty listens to a short version, says he's going to call Detectives Houser and Franks, and calls back five minutes later telling Max to bring Tommy and meet them at Central Precinct.

Max tries more reassurance. "You'll be fine. You'd be in trouble if there was a felony-stupidity law, for getting into this in the first place, but these charges you're worried about will go away."

It doesn't help much. "Do I need a lawyer?"

"Hey, I'm a lawyer."

"Not defense."

"No, you don't need a lawyer. We're going in for a conversation, that's all, with two detectives and a senior deputy DA—all friends of mine. And we're going in to help them. You'll be fine, trust me. Just tell what you know. Maybe leave out the dope thing, like I said before, but tell everything else. All right?"

A pathetic look is the only response.

"You ready, then?"

"Need a shower," Tommy peeps. Max says OK and he trudges up the stairs, Max wondering if he's got any sharp objects up there.

It's one of the longest showers anyone's ever taken.

*　　*　　*

But downtown Tommy's good. Nervous, but once he gets started he seems almost relieved to be coming clean, getting it out there so the pros might start resolving things.

Witty shoots Max the occasional look saying *This is a friend of yours?* but he's glad to be getting the story.

Witty's pissed, of course, that Max withheld the information he got from LaMetrius Jefferson on Wednesday and from Yardley yesterday morning. But too bad. And if Johns doesn't want Max back in the office when the word gets to him, fine.

They're almost finished when Witty leaves the room to answer a page from Stormin' Bob Norman, who moved up to first assistant when Johns moved up to boss. A murder, probably, about the only reason the FA would call the head of Violent Crimes (Witty, since Max's fall) on a Sunday.

Five minutes later Witty's back, a strange look on his mug. Looks at Max, looks at Tommy. "This Bodie you've been telling us about—a longhair, you said?"

Max understands. "Where'd they find him?"

"Up in McLeay Park, a couple of hours ago. With an extra hole in his head, small-caliber. Young couple out for a romantic Sunday walk in the woods see a leg sticking out of some bushes."

"Who's on it?"

"Kearns and Gonzalez for homicide, Heyworth for us."

"They know anything yet?"

"They're pretty sure it happened yesterday. Somewhere else—the park's just a place to dump a body. Beyond that . . . shit, it took 'em this long to identify him. No ID on the body, which is consistent with what you've said. Gonzalez had the John Doe search going when they lucked out with an AFIS hit on him from eleven years ago, when he was manufacturing psilocybin." An old fingerprint and the almighty computer. "Richard Thomas Bodie, B-O-D-I-E, forty-two years old, long brown hair going gray—sound like your friend?" he asks Tommy.

Tommy barely nods, the dread back in his eyes.

"Well, it looks like these people found him."

"Now what?" Max says as Tommy stares out the window like a condemned man.

"I'll see if Heyworth and the detectives have anything yet. If not, I guess we go to Wheatley and his agent, go from there."

"How 'bout *him*?" Meaning Tommy.

"It's up to you, Mr. Mason, if you're afraid these people might still be after you. Which they might be. We can offer you protective custody in the Justice Center jail for a few days, or you can leave town or go wherever you think you'll be safe. It doesn't sound like Max's house is that place, if they've already come looking for you there. It's up to you."

Weakly, Tommy says he'll find a place to go. Not jail.

They talk about the girl, Audrey VanKirkman, who might be in danger too. (Paige probably right again.) Witty says he'll talk to Heyworth and the detectives, see what's going on, and get together with the girl and her father.

A few minutes later they're on their way out, Witty telling Tommy to let Max know where he is. Telling Max—with a look, still pissed—to be available.

"Let's drop by Paige's place," Max says. "Let her know we did the right thing, and tell her the latest."

Tommy, staring out the window on his side, doesn't care. Or more likely, can't speak. Max heads for Northeast 27th, off Halsey.

Her car's not in the driveway. Maybe in the garage, though. She left his house mad and might have figured he'd come over to apologize, or at least continue the fight, and she wouldn't want to see him, wouldn't want him to know she's here.

But she doesn't come to the door.

Maybe lying in bed reading or watching TV, thinking *Fuck you, Max Travis*. He's got his key, he goes inside. Down the short hall toward the bedroom, calling "Miss Prescott? Anyone ever tell you you're beautiful when you're mad? More beautiful than usual, I mean?"

She's not here.

The little red light on the phone is blinking, a message. What the hell.

What a message! *Paige, I'm scared! I did a pregnancy test. . . .*

It's the girl, gotta be. This machine doesn't give the time of the call, but it had to be sometime since Paige stormed out of his house a couple of hours ago.

He hits the redial button. Four rings and then a flat voice on the recorded message: *This is Dr. VanKirkman. Neither I nor my daughter is available at the moment, but if you care to leave your name, number and a brief message—*

Max recalls the skyview Terrace address that O'Leary brought back from the Plunder Office yesterday.

As fast as she can get there: across the Morrison Bridge, through town and up the narrow, twisting West Hills streets to Skyview Terrace.

Like yesterday, there's no car on the short driveway. Paige pulls in.

No one answers the door. Drapes are pulled over the front windows.

Where are they?

What to do? Come back in a little while?

She heads back to the driveway, walks around her car and is about to get in when she sees the side door of the house standing open, with serious splintering along the edge where the deadbolt slides into the frame.

Approaches. Listens.

Nothing.

Calls out, "Audrey?" Nothing. "Dr. VanKirkman?"

Steps hesitantly into a kitchen with a black-and-white parquet floor, a few glasses on the counter by the sink, a box of Ritz crackers, a corked half-bottle of red wine. Some mail and a couple of magazines on the table at the other end. Silence.

Through the doorway beyond the table she sees a hallway and part of the opening into the living room. Slowly, listening for any sound, she crosses the checkerboard floor.

Into the hallway, which heads off to the right. Several doors down there. This way, it opens into the big, high-ceilinged living room: wide fireplace on the right with a heavy mantel over it, a big mirror in a gold-leaf frame over the mantel, huge windows along the far wall looking way, way out. . . .

Audrey lying on the floor behind a black velvet-covered couch, a huge bloodstain on the white carpet at the back of her head.

Paige gagging—clenching her teeth, running back to the kitchen to vomit in the sink. She's seen thousands of murder-scene photos, still gets queasy over some of them, but she's never been at a scene, surely never discovered a body.

Thinking, *They found her.*

She runs water in the sink to wash it out, splashes her face, finally straightens up. Still hot, queasy, her breath coming in short gasps. She doesn't know if she can bear to look again. She can call it in on this wall phone and wait right here—

Maybe she's not dead.

Even knowing Audrey *is* dead, she forces herself back into the hallway, back around the corner; forces herself to look, and then stands there staring at the beautiful girl crumpled on the carpet, on her right side—barefoot, wearing jeans and a burgundy T-shirt with script on the front that Paige can't make out from here. Eyes open, staring blankly, mouth slightly open, that lovely creamy skin now a ghastly yellowish. . . .

Dead.

Drawers pulled out of the desk in front of the windows, papers on the floor. Books and small framed photos pulled out of the built-in shelves on the north end, on either side of the opening into what looks like the dining room.

Trembling, she forces herself to approach the body. Leans down and tries to locate a carotid pulse. Nothing. *She's dead.* Just yesterday they were talking, right here. . . . Feels at the left wrist, knowing there will be nothing. There's nothing.

They found her.

But what were they looking for in the desk, on the shelves?

It's a hunch, merely a hunch, and she thinks of all the times she's cross-examined homicide cops about their so-called hunches, giving them as hard a time as she could. But she's got to play it. Maybe it will seem like craziness later—she can't claim she's thinking straight right now—but it all seemed to fit for a few seconds there in the living room. The racist Audrey described who couldn't bear the thought of his daughter in bed with LaPrince Wheatley and would be mortified by the thought of anyone else finding out. Audrey, who despised him, finding out she was pregnant and letting him know, then twisting the knife by saying she was going to see it through, keep the baby. Wheatley's baby.

Who knows? Only a hunch, and no time to think it through. If she's right, she needs to surprise him while he's still out of his mind.

He should be at KXL from 3 to 4 P.M. on a Sunday. It's three-fifteen. Back in her car, heading downtown, she flicks on the radio, spins to 980-AM, and when the commercial ends, sure enough, the producer or whoever says "It's Sunday afternoon in the Rose City and you're listening to *Dr. Henry Says* on KXL. The doctor is in, folks, and the call-in lines are open, so if you've got questions about relationships, children, jobs . . . if you're upset, distressed, worried about almost anything at all, our esteemed Dr. Henry VanKirkman is here for you."

Not wanting her call to be traced, she finds her way to Durgin's, the upscale supermarket she knew was up here somewhere, and gets out and calls 911 from the pay phone out front. "I want to report an emergency, a death, at 2733 Southwest Skyview Terrace. A murder"—trembling again as she says the word, as she pictures Audrey lying there with her eyes open, mouth slightly open, the blood on the carpet.

The lady asks who's calling.

"A . . . murder," Paige repeats, "at 2733 Skyview," and hangs up.

Gliding down and around the curves, down and around, heading downtown, she plans what to say. That is, she alternately plans what to say and wonders if she's crazy even to think about doing this.

But there's a dead girl up there, and Paige has information no one else has, and she's got to surprise him with it before the police and a DA get to him and he gets his attorney and has time to think about how to cover it up—a clever, diabolical man, no doubt.

Finally down from the hills, downtown, she pulls into a curb space on 18th, alongside Civic Stadium. Tries to collect herself. Wonders if she's nuts.

Then pictures Audrey again, the blood in the blond hair—thinks of her yesterday, the lovely face pinched as she cried, the sad story, the messed-up girl with the messed-up father—and flips open her cell phone, punches in the number the KXL voice kept giving.

"KXL, *Dr. Henry Says*. What would you like to ask Dr. Henry about?" A woman's voice.

"A problem." She's doing it, crazy or not! "A pregnant teenager, still in high school, trying to figure out what to do."

"Are we talking about you, ma'am? You sound too—Is this your child, your daughter?"

"A—uh, friend." *Audrey lying on the floor, the white carpet stained at the back of her head.* "She's a friend."

"All right. Will you hold? It'll be a minute or two."

"I'll wait."

The woman clicks off and leaves Paige listening to the program, Dr. Henry talking to a man whose wife walked in last week and said she'd had a lover for two years and was leaving the marriage to be with him. The doctor perfectly composed. *Is she all wrong?*

But she's going through with it.

A moment later the woman comes back on the line and tells her she's up second after the commercial break, then clicks off again.

Can she do it? Should she?

She listens to the commercials, Blockbuster and Olive Garden and Fred Meyer One-Stop Shopping Center, and then the doctor's back, advising a woman whose mother is going crazy with an "absolute pathological dread" of Alzheimer's. Paige thinking of her folks out on the coast, Dad already far gone with it, not even recognizing her most times; they need to move back to town—

And suddenly she's on the air. "Dr. Henry here. How can I help?"

She hesitates a second or two—but only a second or two, and then just says it: "You can tell me why you killed your daughter, doctor."

A hesitation on that end, then he clicks her off. Quiet. But a few seconds later the program's back, the doctor going to another commercial, and she knows he didn't hang up on her. A sign. Maybe.

She knows she didn't get on the air. There's an eight-second delay, and he cut her off almost the instant she'd gotten the words out.

A click, and his voice on a live line. "What the hell is this? What the hell do you mean, lady, whoever you are?"

"Don't you know?"

"Don't I know what? Listen, I'm doing a program here, I don't have time for sick jokes."

No time? Let him hang up, then.

He doesn't hang up.

"What the hell do you want, lady? What kind of sick joke is this?"

"You think I'm joking?"

A pause, and she knows. He'd have hung up, otherwise. But he tries to be cool. "You're joking or something," he says, "and I've got to get back on the air." But too late.

Or is she just crazy? Hearing what she wants to hear?

Push him. "Get back on the air, then, doctor. But you need to explain to me. I saw Audrey yesterday to let her know she might be in danger, I asked her to have you call me so I could discuss it with you, and when you never called I was pretty sure she'd told me the truth—that you really don't care about her. Didn't care."

"Listen here," he blusters—but stops, not knowing where to go with it.

Paige knows where to take it. "I know about the pregnancy, doctor. And I know you know, and that you weren't happy about it."

Nothing from him.

"Care to comment?"

"You're mad, lady, and this is a mad, sick joke. My daughter's at home. I left her there not an hour ago—maybe an hour ago. Now, I've got a program to do."

"I know you left her there, doctor. But we both know how you left her. You go ahead and finish your program. I'm going over to Starbucks at Pioneer Square for a coffee . . . and unless you meet me there to explain yourself by, say, four-thirty—you're off the air at four?—I'm going to the police."

She waits a moment, and when there's no response she hangs up.

Coming around yet another curve on Skyview Terrace, Max sees yellow crime-scene tape blocking off a yard up ahead. Somehow he knows it's the VanKirkman yard.

An ambulance in the driveway, two black-and-whites behind it. Two tan four-door detectives' Chevrolets at the curb. A couple of neighbors or passersby on the sidewalk, curious, and a few others across the street.

No sign of Paige.

He pulls up across the street. Two young uniform cops in the front yard give him the eye. Max recognizes a kid named Sands, one of dozens he's had in classes at the police academy.

He gets out of the car. Tommy stays.

The familiar cop, Sands, recognizes him and comes over to the tape. "Mr. Travis. What's up?"

"I was gonna ask you."

"A girl." Meaning, dead. "Apparently the daughter of the Dr. VanKirkman on TV. Possibly started as a robbery, the detectives were saying."

"What else are they saying?"

"A small-caliber bullet in the back of the head. The side door was broken, someone went through things inside—"

"Who's in there?"

"Detectives? Ralston and Bowler. You want to speak to one of 'em?"

"No, no need."

Now Sands looks at him more closely, as if he's just started wondering what Max is doing here. "You know someone here, Mr. Travis? You know what might've happened?"

"No. Me and my friend've been watching football with a buddy up the hill. Just heading back down and saw the scene, thought I'd stop."

Wishing, for the first time since he left the office, that he was carrying a cellular.

Downtown he parks outside McMenamin's on 10th, goes inside and tries Paige's cell number from the pay phone on the wall. She answers on the third ring: "Paige Prescott."

"Where are you?"

"Downtown. Going for coffee. And do I have a story for you!"

"Tell me. Christ, we've been looking for you."

"We?"

"Tommy and I. We went and met with Witty and the detectives at Central after you left, and while we're there Witty gets a homicide call from Norman. This *Bodie's* the victim. So these people are probably still after Tommy too, and maybe the girl—you're probably right again. We went by your house to fill you in, this is a half-hour ago, and you're not there, obviously, but I had my key and went in, excuse me, and happened to check the last phone message to see where you might be. I hear this girl going off the deep end—the VanKirkman girl, I assume—and I hit the redial and get the doctor's message. Did you go up there? I figured you must've. That's where we went."

"And? Where are you now?"

"McMenamin's on Tenth. Just got here. So, were you up at that house? Do you know—?"

"I know. I found her. The side door was broken in and I went inside and found her."

"Shot in the head with a small-caliber. Like Bodie."

"I guess. I didn't know about Bodie and obviously didn't know what kind of bullet got Audrey. I just called it in and—"

"I'm sure it'll be a match. Anyway, they found Bodie and the girl so they're probably after Tommy now—erase the last one who can hurt 'em."

"Max, I don't—"

"What did you tell the detectives up there? Any of it? All of—"

"Max!"

He stops.

"I didn't talk to the detectives. I left and called it in from the pay phone at Durgin's. Because it wasn't those people. It was him!"

"Him who?"

"Her fucking father killed her, and if the bullets are a match he killed Bodie too!"

Huh?

But pieces of the puzzle—possibilities, anyway—start coming together. *Bodie the blackmailer. . . . Maybe . . . Paige's talk with the girl yesterday, Paige so upset about the girl being so upset by her father, who was so upset about her fucking a Plunder, a black. . . .*

"Where are you?"

"I'm meeting him, Max, and you can't come. I called him—"

"You're meeting him? Are you nuts?"

"Forget it. I called him at KXL—he went on the air like it was any other day—I told him I knew what he did, and the way he reacted I *did* know. I told him to meet me at Pioneer Square Starbucks when his show's over or I'm going straight to the police. I'm almost there now, and he's off the air in two minutes so he should be there in ten or fifteen. And I know he'll come. He'll have some lie ready, he'll tell me I'm crazy, maybe try to buy me or something—but he'll be there, because he did it."

"I'll meet you there. Five minutes, we're there."

"No. Max, no. If he sees anyone with me, if he thinks he's dealing with anyone other than one wacko lady with a wacko idea, he'll shut up and call an attorney, you know it."

"I won't approach. I'll just be around."

"No. I'll never speak to you again. I've got to get him talking now, right now while he's out of his mind, and if he sees you he'll know something's up."

"He doesn't know me."

"Max, recognize *him* from TV, and he hasn't had the air time you've had the last few years. A lot of people would know they've seen you before, and who knows this guy wouldn't remember where? Big DA, always on TV talking about murders. He'll freak and get an attorney and all the bullshit will start. Please stay away."

"Hey!" Get this girl's attention. "Are you out of your mind? You're a little carried away with this cops-and-robbers. You don't know what this guy will do, if you're right about all this. If he's already killed two people, what's three?"

"Not in Starbucks, not at Pioneer Square on Sunday afternoon with this Italian festival going on, hundreds of people around, police—"

"Are you kidding?" She's defended every kind of lunatic killer—she knows better!

"I'll be fine, and it's the only way to get him off-guard. Right now. He's freaking right now and I've got to get with him. You stay away. Stay where you are—McMenamin's? I'll come up there afterward and you can come to the precinct with me, or wherever." And she hangs up.

Lord. Miss Prescott on the case, bound and determined—who, in other circumstances, would bust her ass trying to get this guy off.

She's sitting in one of the back corners with a cappuccino when Mason appears. Dammit, not ten minutes after she told Max no! When he spots her, all she can do is give him a look saying *Stay away!* and hope her eyes are as expressive as Max says.

And goes back to her cappuccino, turning in her chair to look out at the action in drizzly Pioneer Square: the annual Italian festival, with music and dancing and food and more, hundreds of people; people in and out of the Powells Books branch at the 6th Avenue end; the usual kids on the surrounding sidewalks playing chess, hanging out. . . .

She glances back around just in time to see the killer walking in. No doubt about it, the man you see on Channel 2, looking put-together with his dark blow-dried hair and manicured Freudian whiskers and spendy overcoat . . . not even looking overly distressed, considering he's blown away two people in the last twenty-four hours, including his own daughter, and is here to meet the one person who knows it. Of course, these psychological types specialize in coming off flat, revealing nothing.

He's looking around, not knowing who he's meeting, and when his searching look swings around this way she raises her hand and he comes weaving between the tables, past oblivious java-happy Portlanders—Paige noting the lump in his overcoat, pocket-level on his right, wondering whether it's gloves, a scarf or a small-caliber pistol.

Two feet away now, looking down at her. "Miss Prescott?"
"Doctor." She nods politely. "Let's talk. Have a seat."
He sits there, waiting to see what she's got.
She studies him in turn.

Finally he says, "I don't appreciate your tasteless joke, particularly not when I'm on the air."

"Sorry, but I don't believe a killer is in any position to object."

He sits there, giving her the blank face.

"Meaning you, doctor. A killer."

He actually smiles a little. "Who are you, miss? Why are you doing this?"

"A citizen. An acquaintance of your late daughter." *Lying there in all the blood, eyes open but unseeing.* He's impassive, and she says, "You don't really seem surprised to hear she's dead. You weren't surprised when I called. Weren't shocked, hysterical, anything."

"I knew it was a joke. A sick joke. I get all sorts of calls."

"You knew she was dead."

"I know you need help, miss."

She lets it go. "You didn't call me yesterday, doctor. Didn't Audrey tell you I'd been over? That I said she might very well be in danger, and asked you to call me? Didn't you care? Or were you too shook up after you killed Richie Bodie?"

The little smile is gone, but still he shows nothing. "There was a message when I got home, yes, but it was late. Too late to call, I thought, and in any case Audrey had left a note saying she was sleeping over at a friend's house—no one could have found her, harmed her."

"I didn't hear from you this morning, either."

The faint smile, almost a smirk. *So what?*

Paige says, "I did hear from Audrey this afternoon, a message on my recorder. She was hysterical. She said she told you she was pregnant and wanted to have the baby—probably to spite you, doctor, from what I gathered yesterday—and I don't know what you said or did to her but she was terrified, asking me to come. I went up there about an hour ago, but you'd already done what you did and come on downtown to do the radio thing."

Something in his eyes now, at last. He knows she knows.

"Am I right, doctor?"

"You need help, miss."

"Isn't it true? You kicked in the side door and pulled out a few drawers in the living room to make it look like a robbery, then came on downtown? Tell me where I'm wrong."

"I'll tell you you're delusional, Miss Prescott. You're—"

"I found her stone-dead, doctor, a bullet in her head. I threw up in your kitchen sink. I was there."

"No police have contacted me. No one. You could be—"

"No, I'm not making this up. The police wouldn't necessarily know how to reach you right away, would they? I don't know how many of them listen to Dr. Henry."

He's shaking his head dismissively, faking the smile again, pushing back from the table and standing up. "This is the end of our conversation, Miss Prescott. I don't know if you're delusional or what—but if you're not out of your mind, if this isn't a delusion or a hallucination or a diseased mind's idea of a joke, then it's harassment and you'll hear from my attorneys."

He's spinning away and heading back toward the door as she says, "You'd better call an attorney soon, because the police will be coming for you. They're up at your house right now."

Henry VanKirkman, hitting the sidewalk and crossing Broadway on Morrison, knows he's got to settle this and settle it quick, before she goes to the police.

He glances back, hoping she'll be coming after him, but doesn't see her.

He needs to get her out of Starbucks.

What can he do? Stand on the opposite corner and watch for her? Maybe she's already left, through those back doors that take you out to Pioneer Square. She might already be looking for one of the police cars that cruise the square and the bus mall, up and down 5th and 6th.

He's on the sidewalk on the other side of Broadway, in front of Nordstrom, frantic.

Can't just stand here!

Nordstrom occupies the entire block behind him. The northeast-corner doors are a few feet away, at an angle from the Broadway-Morrison junction. He could go inside and look out, and with the glare from the silvery sky on the glass doors you couldn't see him from outside.

He follows a cluster of people in.

Cosmetics counter to the left, tuxedoed piano man beyond. Women's clothes on the right. He steps behind a mannequin and looks out through the glass doors.

She's coming. She's at the opposite corner in the Levi's and cinnamon-colored suede jacket, waiting for the light to change with a dozen others. Following him in here? Or simply crossing the street on the way to her car (to drive to the nearest police station)?

She crosses, hits the sidewalk on this side. Coming toward the doors—yes—following him.

But *he* needs to be following *her*. He bolts out of Ladies' Wear a moment before she comes in, past Cosmetics and the carefree piano-man, speedwalking across the Broadway end of the store, looking desperately for a safe vantage.

Up the steps at the southeast corner and out onto the sidewalk at Broadway and Yamhill. Think!

Can't afford to lose her.

Needs to get her outside. Into the car on Park Street, on the back side of the store.

Breathing heavily, perspiring through his shirt—*now or never, this is it*—he hurries across Broadway, back to the northeast entrance. Behind her. Get back inside and up on that landing where the purses and accessories are, where you can see across most of the first floor.

Now he's inside and up there, and he can see. The ladies at the glass-topped cosmetics counter, the oblivious piano-man playing another soothing tune. People, people. . . . Where's the cinnamon jacket?

There. On the far side of the escalators, in Men's Clothing near the southwest-corner doors, looking around.

This is as good as it's likely to get. Get her out the doors on Park, his car only a half-block up.

Where the hell is Max? Dropping Tommy in front of Starbucks ten minutes ago he said he'd be right back. "Get in there and keep an eye on things if the guy shows up before I make it. I'm gonna find a district car and get a couple of uniforms in there."

So? The doctor's come and gone, Prescott's gone, and who knows what the hell is going on? VanKirkman crossed the street and went into Nordstrom through the doors on Morrison; Prescott followed a minute or two later, throwing Tommy a fierce *Don't you dare interfere* look; then Tommy sees VanKirkman coming out at the Yamhill end, but hurrying right back across to the Morrison doors he went in the first time.

"Be careful," Max had said. "He might've dumped the gun, but he might still have it on him."

What do you do?

Max said wait here, he'd meet you here.

But VanKirkman might have a gun, and that's Max's honeybun, and none of this would have happened if not for you.

She thinks you're a joke, and you've given her every reason.

Are you?

But he might have a gun!

Where the hell is Max?

He's got to do something.

Inside the store he doesn't see either of them, doesn't know which way to go, what to do.

Decides to take the long aisle on his left, past the long cosmetics counter with wealthy Nordstrom ladies being shown the latest, past racks of coats and sweaters and blouses—searching, still not spotting either of them. Now back the way he came, past Ladies' Wear and Cosmetics and going the other way at the corner, past Purses and Women's Shoes, a glimpse of the guy in the tux playing the piano . . . looking, looking . . . into Men's Clothing, looking, scared and exhilarated both, doing the right thing or at least trying to.

And spots them both, as he turns left in front of the doors at the northwest corner: at the end of this long aisle, straight ahead, VanKirkman in his overcoat right up behind Max's honey, sort of bumping her up the short flight of steps to the southwest doors and out. With the gun, or at least the threat of it, or it wouldn't look the way it looks.

Where the fuck is Max?

Tommy can't wait for him. Breaking into a trot he makes it down the long aisle in seconds, up the half-dozen steps, out through the heavy glass doors to the sidewalk at Park and Yamhill. Looks to the right and doesn't spot them. Looks left and there they go, across Yamhill and moving up the block, VanKirkman hurrying her along. Jesus, what do you do? He's got a gun. He's already killed people, he's out of his mind, nothing to lose by killing a couple more.

Man or mouse? None of this would have happened, no one would be dead, and Max's honey wouldn't be in this fix. . . .

They're getting into a low-slung red sports car parked along the curb halfway up the next block. VanKirkman's got her in front of him, jammed between himself and the passenger side, as he reaches down to unlock the door. Opening it with his right hand, gripping her arm with his left, he shoves her inside, leans down and seems to be shoving her over into the driver's seat—Tommy unable to quite see, the view obscured by a gray van parked in front of the sports car.

Max hasn't found a cop yet?

But even if he shows, he won't know where the action's gone.

The red sports car pulls out from the curb.

He's got the gun out now, in the car.

"Pull out," he's saying. "Easy. Don't fuck up, lady. Don't try anything." In her peripheral vision she sees him looking behind them, looking around.

She lets a white Saab pass on the narrow one-way street, then takes a deep breath and eases away from the curb, trying to get a feel for the high-powered Porsche, afraid of popping the clutch and freaking him.

Out into the single lane, between cars parked on both sides. Easing up behind the Saab idling at the stop sign at Yamhill.

"Straight," he says, waggling the gun in front of her. "Down to the next corner and take a left."

Out of downtown, is what he's probably thinking. He wants to get her away.

"You didn't have to step in," he says. "You hear me? It's none of your business."

She can't speak. Or maybe she can, but she's terrified that anything she says might set him off.

It's over. She dies. He can't let her go, knowing what she knows.

Panicky thoughts flash through her head. Her eyes are flicking around looking for Max, police, some kind of help when she spots Mason. She's not sure it's a good thing, but maybe he understands she's in trouble and maybe it means Max isn't far away.

He must have come through Nordstrom, or maybe up Yamhill, and now he's crossed to the west side of Park, standing on the sidewalk between the deli and the Virginia Café. Looking this way. She's positive he sees her, pretty sure he knows something's wrong, but what can he do?

"Go on," Dr. VanKirkman says, waving the gun that undoubtedly killed his daughter and probably the blackmailing Bodie too. "Up to the corner, then left."

She's edging out past the stop sign when a blue Toyota full of teenagers comes hurtling down Yamhill, slowing just in time to turn left on Park, in front of her. Now, with a break in the traffic, she eases the Porsche across Yamhill. Everything slo-mo, surreal: the gun waggling in front of her ("Come on, damn you!"), the teenagers up ahead, oblivious shoppers coming out of Nordstrom, Mason in front of the Virginia Café watching her but looking helpless.

Now an old burgundy beater with rust spots on the roof and trunk pulls out in front of the Toyota full of teenagers up ahead—and stalls, apparently, because the Toyota stops. And Paige has to stop.

Make a run for it?

Get shot in the back trying to make a run for it? Die in the middle of Park Street on a Sunday afternoon?

"Dammitall!" he hisses, beside her.

Suddenly, with horns honking and teenagers popping out of the Toyota to find out what's holding them up, here's *Mason!* wheeling a big green Dumpster from the side of the Virginia Café across the sidewalk, bumping it down the curb and out into the street and turning it over in front of the stalled beater. Trash everywhere, broken glass, bottles and cans rolling across the pavement, people on the sidewalks gawking, the Dumpster settling upside-down in the middle of the street and Mason staring right at her like *What can I do? How can I help?*

In front of her a seedy kid in a sweatshirt, the Toyota's driver, reaches back inside the car to lean on the horn—seemingly having a great time, while his buddies don't seem to know if what's happening is funny, scary, what. A fat man in a dirty white apron comes running out of the deli to see what's happening. People are coming out of the café.

VanKirkman reaches over with his free hand and gives the horn a blast. "Dammit! Back out of here, get the hell out!" But looking over his shoulder he sees what Paige sees in the rearview: an SUV pulling up close behind them, hemming them in.

Run?

And get shot in the back, or the back of the head, before she's even out of the car?

"We're getting out," he snaps. "Get out!"—grabbing her arm and pushing her toward her door, throwing his leg over the stick-shift and sliding over to follow her out.

But she's not moving.

"Open that door! Get out!"

She just looks at him. Maybe stupid, maybe she dies right here, but something tells her it'll be worse out there, more dangerous for more people: a lunatic with a gun and nothing to lose, possibly a hostage-shield situation if police show up, who knows?

"I said out, bitch!" He jerks her arm hard and he's got the gun up in her face now. "I'll shoot you right here! One more—shit, just makes a better insanity defense!"

She's frozen in the seat, wondering if she'll be alive in ten seconds. No longer seeing the bedlam outside, not hearing a sound.

Not a goddam district car anywhere around Pioneer Square or the transit mall. Max circling, circling, and nothing.

He finally spotted a horseback patrol a few blocks over, at the edge of the Park Blocks, two young uniforms chatting with some street kids from up on their four-legged rides. He stopped at the curb and honked like a madman until they looked over, then waved like a madman until one dismounted and ambled over. Rolled down the passenger window and told him to get in, get his partner and get in, he's Max Travis from the DA's office and they've got to get over to Starbucks, a guy's killed two people already and might not be finished. Get in the car!—the guy looking at him like he's insane, looking back at his quizzical partner, Max bellowing *Get in!* and the partner finally swinging down from his horse, handing the reins to a baffled street kid, the two of them getting in the car and Max shooting down Taylor, screeching around the corner at Broadway and jolting to a stop in the no-parking zone in front of Starbucks.

They found no Paige inside, no VanKirkman, no Tommy, just Sunday-afternoon Starbucks.

The two young cops looking at him again like he's a lunatic, and Max with nothing for them but a shrug.

Back outside one said, "You say you're in the DA's office, mister?"

Then they heard the horns and the shouting from the west. Not far. And Max was moving, telling them to come on, come on! and when they looked at each other and then looked at him like he was a street-crazy he screamed *Come on, damn you!* and they looked at each other again, confused, but then one started moving and the other decided he didn't want to be left.

The three of them sprinting across the intersection toward the noise, up Morrison toward Park, the noise getting louder.

It's a snarl in the tight little block behind Nordstrom, a line of cars stopped from the middle of the block back to Yamhill, the one in front blocked by an overturned Dumpster in the street. Garbage everywhere, horns blowing, people out in the street, spectators on the sidewalks—

Tommy. Coming this way, maybe spotting the uniforms and now Max: gesturing, gesticulating, pointing, screaming something Max can't make out in the din. The two young cops wondering what's going on, what to do, looking to Max—

"He's got her!" Tommy's saying, hitting the sidewalk on this side now. "In the red car!"—pointing back at a red Porsche in the line of stopped cars. Two indistinct figures inside but now *yes*, the short haircut, it's Paige behind the wheel, the other person leaning toward her talking, probably yelling—

He's got her. She walked into it and he's got her.

"He's got a gun," he tells the cops. "The man's got a woman in that car and he's got a gun!"

The young cops looking at each other—

The passenger door flies open and the man's out of the Porsche—dark hair, beard, dark overcoat, gun in hand. Did he just shoot her? The man, VanKirkman, looking every which way, clearly panicked—gonna run? shoot someone? shoot himself?

"Goddammit!" Max screams at the cops as the onlookers scramble for cover—

They pull their weapons a split-second before Max reaches for one of them himself. The guy in back jumps out into the street and moves toward VanKirkman with his gun raised in both hands, shouting "Throw it away! Throw it away *now!*"

VanKirkman looking every which way, then back at the cop who's got a load pointed at him—dropping the gun—

The cops rushing him, and Max racing to the Porsche.

Unbelievable, that he lives to tell the tale.

VanKirkman jumping out of the car waving the gun, maybe twenty feet away; Tommy sure he's about to die in the street, in the garbage he just dumped. VanKirkman glancing over but seeming not to register him, the wild eyes turning across the street toward Max and two cops with their guns pulled, screaming "Throw it down! Throw it down!" VanKirkman's wild eyes flashing this way, that way, every which way; then the gun dropping and the hands shooting straight up like *Don't shoot me! Don't shoot!* The cops rushing in. Max's honey still in the car, Tommy flashing on the possibility that VanKirkman shot her before springing out—but no, she was there behind the wheel, wide-eyed. Getting out then, as the cops slammed VanKirkman up against the passenger side, pulled his hands behind him and slapped cuffs on him. Max running over, picking up the gun, coming around the car to his honey. The two of them clutching as Tommy hovered by, Paige facing Tommy over Max's shoulder though her eyes were closed. . . .

Paige somehow, not "Prescott" or "the bitch" or even "Max's honey." Who's been bitchy to him at times, yes, but maybe she just saw him clearly and reacted naturally. Who's been pushy with Max a few times in Tommy's presence, yes, like yesterday when she wanted him to be more concerned about the girl—but hey, she was right. Not that she'd identified the father as the danger, but maybe if Max had gone up to that house with her yesterday, talked to the girl with her, he'd have pressed to locate VanKirkman last night. But he didn't, so this morning Paige gave him the shove and slammed out of the house and took it upon herself.

And it came down to these mind-boggling moments on a rainy

Sunday afternoon: Tommy not knowing what she was doing when she left Starbucks or what he could do for her, only knowing he had to do something; he *wasn't* the loser she thought he was.

And now she's in the street clutching Max, making whimpery sounds Tommy can hear even in the confusion all around, gasping sounds like her heart's in her throat and she can't catch her breath; and suddenly her eyes open, and she spots him and lets go of Max and comes running to him, and stands in front of him with tears in her eyes. Like she's wondering what to do, how she feels about him now, the loser who stepped up when the killer might have taken her who-knows-where and . . . well, not much doubt what he would have done to her, the person who'd figured things out.

She throws her arms around him: one around his back nearly squeezing the breath out of him, one hard around his neck, thanking him *Thank you, how can I thank you, thank you thank you thank you.* Squeezing him and thanking him and sobbing. Finally easing up and letting go, backing up just enough to look at him—her faint blue eyeliner smudged—looking at him with wet, sparkly eyes. A smile coming into the eyes before it comes to her mouth, then taking over her face all at once, bursting out, and for the first time he has an inkling of what Max sees in her, how he feels about her—even before she starts laughing, and grabs him again, and laughs and cries and squeezes. . . .

Tommy squeezes back.

Max remembers the steamy morning, September fourth, when three-term Multnomah County DA and longtime friend Dan Tower—former friend—was arraigned here in the Justice Center's courtroom B, hours after Max and O'Leary and the Attorney General made their midnight visit to Tower's office and found the papers that destroyed him and vindicated Max. Witty got him and Paige in, past the clamoring reporters and TV crews out in the hall, and they sat here holding hands as the deputies brought the bedraggled Tower out to stand behind the Plexiglass with his high-powered attorney and hear the charges.

December second now, and here they are again: the rows behind them packed like last time, the earliest media arrivals along the wall in back. Judge Amiton presiding, Stacy Heyworth for the State, oily Bob Lobo representing VanKirkman. Shameless Lobo, who once put on a rubber pig-snout during a closing argument and told the jury "It's as plain as the nose on my face that there's nothing to these charges against my client."

Paige holding his hand like before, not mad at him anymore over Tommy.

Tommy underground again, off at some friend's house trying to decide what to do. Feeling like dirt, even though he rose to the occasion yesterday—three people dead and VanKirkman facing capital punishment, all because Tommy stole a videotape and showed it to a certain dirtbag acquaintance. He's already quit the *Review* because he can't afford to show his face around the Plunderdome. He can't really risk being seen in Portland at all. The detectives found nearly $196,000 last night under the floorboards behind a false wall panel in Bodie's basement, but even if Wheatley gets it back there's no guarantee that he and his people won't be thinking revenge. It's Tommy's call, but the only prudent choice would seem to be relocation.

VanKirkman, when the deputies bring him out in his jail blues and handcuffs, doesn't look any better than Tower did. Maybe worse. And he doesn't have the chutzpah to look around the courtroom like the arrogant DA did, look people in the eye.

"Miss Heyworth," Judge Amiton says, and VanKirkman straightens up in the cage as the excellent Stacy reads the case.

"Your Honor, the State of Oregon versus Henry Joseph Van-Kirkman. I've got a copy of the indictment for the defendant, and one for his attorney. . . ."

Amiton says, "Are you truly and accurately named in this indictment, Mr. VanKirkman?"—VanKirkman not even "Doctor" now, just one more defendant.

The detectives found a button under the Porsche's passenger seat last night, the missing button from the shirt Richie Bodie was wearing when they found him in McLeay Park.

The killing happened Saturday afternoon or evening, the ME said. It fits with what VanKirkman told Paige at Starbucks yesterday: he hadn't returned her call Saturday because he'd been out, hadn't gotten home to get the message until late.

The bullet that killed Bodie, a .22 long, matched the one that killed Audrey VanKirkman.

Two first-degree murder charges. Also, first-degree kidnapping with a firearm, for grabbing Paige yesterday. Attempted aggravated murder, for threatening her with the gun after she told him she knew everything.

Max feels Paige shudder as those last charges are read.

Walking up Taylor Street in the fog and drizzle afterward, on their way to a late breakfast somewhere, he remembers walking her up to Metro Public Defenders after Tower's arraignment, in the sweet September sunshine. Holding hands for all the world to see, even his DA pals who'd made cracks all those years just like Max had—who had no idea what she was really like, just as he'd never had a clue. He remembers hugging on the sidewalk in front of Metro, the prosecutor's prosecutor and the PD's PD—an odd couple, no doubt, but undoubtedly the happiest, most hopeful couple in Portland that day.

Some skirmishes since, but also San Francisco, the San Juan Islands, a couple of weekends at O'Leary's cabin on Hood, nights in
Max's hot-tub gazing, laughing, screwing. Always stimulating and
often surpassing.

"Now what?" he asks.

"Breakfast, I thought." Looking up with the sparkly, shiny blue
eyes. The face that still amazes him, that's amazed him since he
really saw it, finally, last summer.

"No. I mean"—but he stops, pointing across the street at the
fountain at the edge of the Park Blocks, and says, "That's where I
finally found those cops yesterday, talking to the homeless kids."
Thinking that at this time yesterday he was playing football out at
Wilson High; Witty hadn't yet told him Yardley was dead, and no
one knew Bodie was dead, and Audrey VanKirkman was fine.

He says, "I mean, now what for us? We go back to fighting? You
go back to defending dirtbags—"

"And you go back to Testosterone City?" Her name for the DA's
office.

"I'm thinking about it," he admits. She's said it herself, he's a
prosecutor, and she understands it and even accepts it just as he
understands the system needs defense attorneys, even true believers.
"I'm thinking about it. I'd like to clean up the loose ends in this
mess, for one thing."

"The rapists?"

"Them." LaMetrius Jefferson and his homeboy, down in LA.
With Alice Richardson's testimony and the DNA evidence, sending
them away would be a snap.

And it's all about sending dirtbags away. He misses the esprit in
the office, the cops, the great detectives, the crime-scene work, the
trials, the drinking after a good verdict, all of it . . . but what he
misses most is the power to hammer people who do terrible things
to others.

"What about LaPrince?" she asks as they go into the Heathman.

Ah, LaPrince. Where it all started. "Strangely enough, I can't see
anything happening to him. The detectives reached him last night
and told him they need to talk to him, but nothing will come of it.
You mean what happened between him and the girl, right? Well,
she obviously can't tell the story, and unless a videotape turns up
there's no way to prove it even happened. Even if there was . . . there
might be a contributing-to-the-delinquency charge. Rape Three,

maybe"—a misdemeanor—"if Johns decided to charge it at all. Which he wouldn't, considering she was willing and LaPrince is a famous Plunder and Johns is a wimp. LaPrince'll be fine. These guys are the nearest thing to untouchable. They do what they do, it causes trouble all around 'em, but they sail on. Like my Aunt Helen, the old crone—almost ninety years old, can't see ten feet, but she's out there driving, telling us she's never had an accident so why not? She's causing accidents all around her, but she doesn't have any idea and wouldn't care if she did."

They take a booth in the Heathman and order coffee to start.

"So," she says, "you're going back?"

"Maybe."

"Sexiest job in the DA's office, right? Head of Violent Crimes?"

"It's not that." And it's not. He's been on TV more than he ever wanted, seen his name in the paper more than he's cared to—it's not about that. "It's the kick of beating people who're trying to let dirtbags stay on the streets. The challenge of trying to beat lawyers I can't always beat, people who're smarter than me, like a certain blue-eyes. Sometimes I even *do* beat 'em."

She's smiling. "Come on back. Try."

"You gonna try to get the rapists off?"

"Not them," she says. "But someone you'll want to put away."

By noon the next day Tommy's packing. By one he's schlepped his two suitcases to the Tri-Met stop a few blocks from Max's house. By two he's sitting in the Greyhound station downtown with a ticket to the Big Town in his jacket—his life changed forever, with any luck.

He was up before six this morning, easing around upstairs so he wouldn't wake Max and Paige down below. He'd had a hard time falling asleep again after the flash in the middle of the night—such an idea, and only he could write it!—and he was just as excited when he woke up. Six A.M. in Portland, nine in New York, he got his agent on the phone and spent twenty minutes telling it, Hilliard enthralled 3000 miles away.

"Great story," Hilliard said when he was finished. "Now, you're going to fictionalize it, novelize it?"

"Why should I? It's all true!"

"A nonfiction book?"

"Yes! True-crime! Before Ann Rule gets her mitts on it! What do you think?"

Hilliard said he'd think it over, maybe talk to a couple of people, and call him back. He called back in less than half an hour, nearly as excited as Tommy. He'd talked to people at two major publishers and was seeing dollar signs. "Can you make a trip back here? Let's talk about this a little more, then go talk to these people and some others—see who wants it the most. *Ching-ching!*"

"Huh?"

"That's a cash register. But forget it. Look, can you fly back here?"

It was happening fast, but nothing wrong with that. "I can't afford to fly, but I'll come, you bet." He could stay with his old friend Bo, Bo living just outside the city and getting fat doing some kind of PR. "The bus'll take awhile, but I can leave today."

"Then leave today. And from what I heard in the last few minutes, you can believe this: you might be taking Greyhound here, but you'll be flying home. Probably first-class."

Tommy's been floating ever since. Even in a dirty seat in the bus station, facing a ninety-one-hour trip, he's floating.

Pulling out of Portland a little later, on his way to the Big Apple and a new life, he feels like Joe Buck on his way from Texas in *Midnight Cowboy*. All he needs is a cowboy hat and a transistor radio.

But he doesn't even need that. All he needs is this story, and he's got it.

Y ou got more'a this? Or can score some?" LaPrince asking about the chronic Naz and Jujube brought, that's lifting the top of his head off. "You can, I'll leave you some tickets for the game, then we hook up after."

The Plunder in LA to rumble with Shaq-dog tomorrow night. Naz and Jujube waiting in the Hilton lobby when they came in, both wearing muscle shirts and baggies, Naz with his dreadlocks and Jujube with his shiny shave. People looking when LaPrince walked over there, but fuck 'em. These are his boys. You sign a contract to play ball, don't mean you give up your boys.

A few minutes later they're in Jujul e'r Beamer, keeping the fatty low out of sight until they're out of the rich midtown section. Damn, he needs some funk-doctor of his own, since he'll never know what happened to the three oh-zees he left with that Yardley. The muhfucker dead.

Detective called him last night, wanted to meet him before the team left today, talk about three dead people he might know something about. Dead? A pretty young girl for one, the man said. And they wanted to know about Bernie Herman, did LaPrince know how they could reach him?

He called Bernie himself right after, found him at his crib in Cleveland. Bernie said be cool, get out of talking to 'em if he could and then get out of town with the team. But at nine this morning they were knocking at the door, detective named Peterson and a Chinese-looking one, and drove him downtown.

You're not a suspect, Mr. Wheatley, we only want to ask you some questions. We have information that you had a sexual en-

counter with a young lady at a Mr. Yardley's residence, which Mr.
Yardley videotaped without your knowledge.

An hour and a half he was there, in a little room on the sixteenth
floor of the police station looking out at the waterfront and the river,
nice scenery . . . admitting he was with her, OK, but she told him
she went to college and he knew she'd been with some other players
before so he thought it was cool. Yeah, he found out later Yardley
taped it with some secret camera.

You found that out when you became a blackmail target?

Well, yeah. (Since they knew anyway.) Shit, he paid 200 Gs.

How about a Tommy Mason? You know him?

Ain't seen him. (Thinking, Gonna break him in two if I do.)

Lights blurring past now as they sail out of midtown in Jujube's
new ride, his pride-and-joy. Dude bangin' all these years for nothing,
risking his ass, getting shot, doing time, now finally doing all right.

"Got more'a this boo?" LaPrince asks again, having lost track of the
conversation before. "Got a nice fade on. Like to get me some'a this."

"Not a problem," Naz says from the back. "You want, we go get
some right now."

"Nah, not now. Tomorra be cool. Before the game, though, not
after—we flyin' out right after. How 'bout a oh-zee? Two, maybe—
set me up?"

"What you want, man."

"Whatever. Two. Keep me flush awhile."

"Two. Done."

He knows he shouldn't be out here with 'em—people talking at
the hotel, for sure, probably already called Puckerface—but it feels
good. Just be careful, keep the fatty down and keep moving. Stupid
as hell to pull over that night last spring up in the hills, stop on the
side of the road in a rich section passing the can around till somebody called in and the cops came—Little Cuz dizzy, too fucked up
to drive, but somebody else could've, should've, instead of sitting
there like fools laughing and carrying on with the windows down
to let the smoke out. Cops pulling everybody out, writing citations—
nobody ending up in the paper, of course, except LaPrince Wheatley,
the name, who made the papers and ESPN and all the TV stations.
He knew that was the end for him in LA.

Shouldn't be out with the homeys now, but if they keep
moving. . . .

"Where you wanna go, big man?"

"Don't matter." Just feels good, smokin' up and chillin' with his partners.

Naz asking about Portland.

The whole thing may be a mistake, signin' up there, he's been thinking lately. "Muhfuckers been in my shit since the first day. I miss a little nothin' exhibition game out in the sticks, they go off. Bump a peckerhead TV dude, they go off—punk gettin' in the way, askin' for it, but they make a big damn deal out of it. This fat-ass fat-boy column-writer, Dwight, in my shit about shot selection, 'bout not puttin' out on D, all this shit. Some *bullshit*. People talkin' 'bout some fight with Turner Boyd in practice that wasn't shit, that they didn't know nothin' about noway since none of 'em get into practice."

Turner-man. Gone. LaPrince has been wondering, thinking about calling him back there in the hills in North Carolina, if he's there. At least calling to see where he's at.

"Then this Puckerman, the boss. Puckerface. Always comin' around askin' whassup, all this shit, talkin' how I'm his big *investment,* big risk, I gotta make him look good. Sheeeit."

"But you gettin' paid," Naz grunts from the back, sucking on the fatty. "Yeah? Getting' that good paycheck? What counts, nigga."

"Sheeit. I be gettin' that good money, yeah, but I'm thinkin' the muhfuckers best cut me loose they ain't happy with me. They still gotta pay me this year and two more guaranteed, so cool with me."

Even Yuban and Sammy Dee sat him down finally, asking whassup, saying they need him to play like he can play. Nine games so far, fuckin' *nine,* and everybody jumpy. Sheeit. Fifteen points and nine boards average—not All-Pro, but third on the team in scoring and second in boards. They don't like his shooting percentage—but shit, everybody go through slumps. Shit gonna start droppin'.

Some *bullshit*. Hey, you don't like LaPrince, don't like his game, then cut him loose. Give him his money and go get somebody you like better. Fuck it. Ain't the end of the world.

"What we doin'?" he asks Jujube. The fatty gone now, lights flashing by. Back in LA, back home. . . .

"What you want, big man? You the man tonight, we just glad to see you. You lookin' for a party? You want a bitch make your hair fall out?"

"How old? Gotta know how old."

"Twenny-three. Shit, almost wore out. But for now, man, ain't nobody like her. You know who I mean, Nazbo?"

"I hear you. Big man," Naz says, "you know what you call a bitch can suck a golf ball through fifty yards'a garden hose?"

Lights, lights, as far as you can see. . . . LA. Home. With his homeys.

"Call her *darlin'!*"—Naz finishing his joke, laughing like a crazy man. "What we call her, *darlin'!*"

"Where she at?" LaPrince says, and Jujube says he'll take him there.